Even with the recove[illegible] to grasp the truth. Someh[illegible]aire Norton who lived in this time, and the Alice Ramsay who had lived and died as an accused witch in Scotland four hundred years ago. And she had been other people as well. Leo had spoken to her once in the void between her lives, telling her that she had lived before.

Before Alice Ramsay . . .

Once again she pored over her memories of her previous life—memories only recently recalled, yet vivid as though she had lived them yesterday. And before them, at the very beginning, there lay another . . . She grasped at it, no longer frightened but eager, sensing that this new recollection held the key to her present predicament. Light . . . Strong sunlight, blazing out of a sky the hue of bleached bone. Human figures, dark as if carved out of ebony, walking slowly across a dry, dusty plain. And there came to her suddenly an image of a lion—no stone statue like the ones on Glenlyon's gates, but a real living beast with a shaggy russet mane, gazing at her with its great amber eyes.

The image faded. It was gone: that fleeting fragment of another, still earlier time. Try as she might, she could not recall it.

—from *The Warding of Willowmere*

PENGUIN CANADA

THE WARDING OF WILLOWMERE

Alison Baird is the author of *The Witches of Willowmere,* which was chosen as a "Best of 2002" by Resource Links, a Canadian reference guide for classrooms and libraries; *The Wolves of Woden; The Hidden World; The Dragon's Egg,* which was nominated for the Ontario Library Association Silver Birch Award and designated a regional winner by the participating children; and *White As the Waves,* which was shortlisted for the IODE Violet Downey Book Award. She lives in Oakville, Ontario.

Also by Alison Baird

White As the Waves

The Dragon's Egg

The Hidden World

The Wolves of Woden

WILLOWMERE CHRONICLES:

The Witches of Willowmere

The Warding of Willowmere

Alison Baird

Penguin Canada

PENGUIN CANADA
Penguin Group (Canada), a division of Pearson Penguin Canada Inc.,
10 Alcorn Avenue, Toronto, Ontario M4V 3B2

Penguin Group (U.K.), 80 Strand, London WC2R 0RL, England
Penguin Group (U.S.), 375 Hudson Street, New York, New York 10014, U.S.A.
Penguin Group (Australia) Inc., 250 Camberwell Road, Camberwell, Victoria 3124, Australia
Penguin Group (Ireland), 25 St. Stephen's Green, Dublin 2, Ireland
Penguin Books India (P) Ltd, 11, Community Centre, Panchsheel Park,
New Delhi – 110 017, India
Penguin Group (New Zealand), cnr Rosedale and Airborne Roads, Albany, Auckland 1310,
New Zealand
Penguin Books (South Africa) (Pty) Ltd, 24 Sturdee Avenue, Rosebank 2196, South Africa

Penguin Group, Registered Offices: 80 Strand, London WC2R 0RL, England

First published 2004

(WEB) 10 9 8 7 6 5 4 3 2 1

Editor: Cynthia Good

Manufactured in Canada.

NATIONAL LIBRARY OF CANADA CATALOGUING IN PUBLICATION

Baird, Alison, 1963–
The warding of Willowmere / Alison Baird.

(Willowmere chronicles)
ISBN 0-14-301529-X

I. Title. II. Series: Baird, Alison, 1963– . Willowmere chronicles.

PS8553.A367W44 2003 jC813'.54 C2003-905021-1

Visit the Penguin Group (Canada) website at **www.penguin.ca**

In memory of

Ann Walford

1929–2001

the daimons of Plato
entities free of space & time
see through our eyes
hear with our ears
our world is a game they play
our dreams are their reality

The Warding of Willowmere

Prologue

Africa, 100,000 B.C.

"THE DROUGHT GROWS WORSE. We will starve if it goes on any longer."

"See how few animals are left. When they are gone, we too will die."

The girl sat by herself, several paces away from the family group, listening to their talk. The ground beneath her was dust-dry and crumbled at her touch. In the blanched sky above her the noon sun blazed, its heat slamming down onto the parched plain, while in the distance heat-mirages offered further torment with their illusion of rippling water. A real watering hole lay not far away from where the girl and the rest of the tribe huddled in the sparse shelter of some dying thorn bushes, but it had shrunk to a shallow bed of black mud. Birds and animals thronged around it, predator and prey mingling together, their natural enmity forgotten in the desperate need to quench their thirst. A few small puddles of dirty water lingered in places, but they were fast disappearing.

As the girl sat there she saw a young lion come padding across the plain, his feet raising little puffs of dust, and approach the bed of mud. His ribs showed through his tawny hide and his half-grown mane was draggled with dirt; where once they would have fled, the antelopes gathered at the puddles now barely glanced at him. Neither did he show any interest in them. Perhaps he was too weak now to hunt, the girl thought as she gazed at him in pity. She knew this lion well. She had seen him grow from a cub, the brightest and boldest of three litters, surviving when all his siblings died of hunger or were killed by other predators. Life was cruel to lion cubs, and very few survived into adulthood. She had begun to look for him whenever his pride passed through the vicinity; he was easy to spot due to a distinctive scar on his forehead, testament to a skirmish with a marauding hyena from which, despite his size disadvantage, he had unexpectedly emerged victorious. The girl always felt something like joy stir in her when she saw that he lived still. Now that he was grown, the lionesses of his pride had turned him out to fend for himself in the wild. Bewildered at this rejection, alone and lean with hunger, nevertheless he lived on. She watched as he sniffed and pawed at the mud, trying to lap up its moisture with his tongue, and once more pity moved her. Had he survived all the perils of infancy merely to die at last of the heat?

There had been a drought like this, she was told, the year that she was born. The tribe had come across her mother, dead of thirst upon the plain, her crying infant still sprawled upon her breast. It was not usual to take in a stray girl-child—another mouth to feed and forage for, another female to bring forth unwanted children when she matured—but they had been impressed by her resilience, by the fact that she had outlived her mother in such terrible conditions. She might breed strength into their family, they thought; or perhaps the spirits that had apparently favoured her with their protection would transfer their magical guardianship to the whole tribe. And it was true that after taking her in the family had flourished for many years. Until this second and worse drought fell.

The girl's foster mother spoke behind her. "No more talk of dying. We will not die as long as we obey the sorcerer." The woman made a small, timid gesture towards the dark figure hunched by the edge of the watering hole: an old man wearing a necklace of warthog teeth, clutching a bone staff tipped with a mongoose skull. He was withered, emaciated, like something already dead and shrivelled by the drought. Only his eyes, small and black in their sunken sockets, spoke of the life lurking within. "The rain will come. He will make it come, if we do as we are told. If we do not, he will continue to punish us."

The young girl turned at that and spoke to her mother in a voice still clear and strong. "I do not believe it. Mamba is only an old man. The drought is not magic. Weather comes from the sky, from the sun and the clouds—not from him."

"Hush, Flower-in-a-drought! The sorcerer will hear you!"

"He is too far to hear."

"Child, he has ears you do not see. Spirits serve him, beasts and birds spy for him. He will send a poisonous snake to kill you. Mamba is a sorcerer—do you not understand?"

The girl fell silent, but remained unconvinced. The old man crouched and eyed the group with malevolent intensity. They had given him all the food they had, had let him have first access to any water available. But what had Mamba really given in return? Nothing that Flower-in-a-drought could see. He could not, as he claimed, make the rain fall, or he surely would have done so to quench his own thirst. Despite the extra food, he was thinner than any of them. No, had he really possessed such a power he would have used it long before now, if only to save himself. *Liar,* she thought, and looked away. It filled her with sorrow to think that her adopted family's hope was vain. That the drought might persist, and they might yet end like all the lifeless animals they had passed upon the plain. Flower-in-a-drought felt her own gnawing hunger, the searing dryness of her mouth, but she set them aside as she gazed at the lion by the watering hole. She rejoiced to see him find one tiny puddle and lap it up with an eager tongue. She forgot her own burning thirst as she watched him satisfy his. She loved him, loved his tenacity, took delight in his stubborn survival.

You are like me, she thought as he rose at last from the puddle and went to lie down in the cool, soothing mud. For a moment his dulled amber eyes, empty of expression, seemed to look full into hers, and she sent her thought towards him across the heat-shimmering plain. *You live on, even when all the world wants you to die. And you are stronger than I am, for you have no fear and you are full of hope, always. You must live! For I know, somehow, that I too will survive if you do. You are my spirit . . .*

CHAPTER I

SOMEONE WAS KNOCKING at the door.

The girl started as she sat in her chair by the window, cradling a dagger in her hands. For a moment she wondered if the sound had really been the door knocker. The house was both very large and very old, and full of unsettling sounds: creaking floorboards and clanking radiators, and the soft footfalls of its owner's cats as they roamed the hallways. The girl sat for a moment motionless, her heart thumping against her rib cage. Downstairs, a dog began to bark furiously. Angus MacTavish, the collie. She'd confined him to the kitchen; he must have gotten out during the break-in—

The knock came again, three sharp raps, firmer and louder this time, eliciting more angry barks from Angus. She could picture in her mind the old brass door knocker with its stern-looking lion's head—but what unknown hand was raising and rapping the brass ring in its mouth, out there on the darkened porch? She rose and, standing close to the wall so as not to be visible to anyone outside, peered around the window frame. The neighbourhood was darker than it should be, even at this hour; a power failure had blacked out every house and the street lamps as well. The grounds of the estate were steeped in shadow, and the night was utterly still.

The girl's hand tightened on the dagger. It was an old Gurkha blade, taken from a collection of antique weapons belonging to the house's previous owner. She doubted she could ever really use it on anyone, but holding it made her feel less helpless. Had her attackers come back? Were they trying to trick her into opening the door and letting them in? They surely couldn't think she would be that naive, after what had happened this evening . . . Then suddenly it occurred to her that the owl in the maple tree had given no warning hoot, even though the wild bird's keen eyes must have seen the intruder go up to the house. She glanced out the window again and saw that the owl was still sitting on its branch, a small stationary shape dark against the sky. Slowly she put down her weapon and took up the candle on the nightstand instead. After fumbling with the matches for a few moments—her hands were far from steady—she succeeded in lighting it and headed for the stairs. As she descended them the knocker rapped again, twice. There was a sound of shuffling feet on the porch.

"Who's there?" she shouted. Angus, standing in the hall with his muzzle towards the door, growled deep in his throat.

From the other side of the door came the last voice she expected—a woman's. "Don't be alarmed, dear!" it exclaimed. "I've just come to check up on you. I couldn't get through by phone."

She went to the door and opened it a crack. There on the porch stood a nun, clad in a dark-blue raincoat over a blue-and-grey habit. There was a flashlight in her right hand and some large dark object in her left. Her eyes peered anxiously from behind wire-rimmed glasses. "You're Dr. Moore's house-sitter, aren't you?" she asked. "Claire Norton?"

The girl was silent for a moment. *Claire Norton*. It was her name, but she had another, a name she could not share; and now the old everyday name sounded strange to her own ears . . . "Yes," she forced herself to say. "Yes, I am."

"I don't know if you remember me. I'm Sister Helena, from St. Mary's Convent down the road. I just had a call from Sharon."

"Who?"

"Sharon—Sharon Brodie."

The girl stared. "You mean Silverhawk? *Silverhawk* phoned you?" There was no end to the strangeness of this night, she thought. For Silverhawk, as she liked to be called, was a Wiccan, or practising witch. Why would a witch be phoning a nun? She opened the door wide, and Angus moved forward to examine the figure on the porch. He was no longer growling.

"Yes, we know each other quite well," Sister Helena said, answering the unspoken question. "It was Dr. Moore who introduced us. Sharon said she'd been talking to you on the phone earlier this evening. She said you were upset about something, but you hung up, and when she tried to phone back later she couldn't get through. She was quite worried and asked me if I'd mind checking on you and phoning her back. I tried to call you, too, but I couldn't get through either."

"The phone line is down."

"That's rather odd, isn't it? It can't have anything to do with this power failure. The phone lines are separate." The nun held out the dark object: it was a backpack. "I found this lying in the middle of the driveway. Do you know who owns it?"

"It's okay, it's mine," Claire replied. "I just—dropped it out front and forgot about it. Thanks." She took the pack, aware of the older woman's intent gaze.

"Sharon said you were all alone."

"Yes, Mrs. Hodge—the housekeeper—was staying over too, but she had to go visit a sick relative." This was all perfectly true, though not the whole truth. Claire had to work to keep her voice even.

"Are you quite sure everything's all right?" Sister Helena persisted. "Sharon said something about some people pestering you. I was beginning to wonder if I should call the police."

"No, it's all right, really." Claire reflected that there was little the police could do about this situation; it seemed pointless to involve them. "It was just this girl I know from school, Josie Sloan, and her boyfriend. Josie's been picking on me, and this time she really crossed the line. She came here, trespassed on Dr. Moore's property and broke into the house. I'm going to have to talk to the school guidance counsellor about her." Again this was all true, and yet she was concealing more than she told.

The nun's gaze was thoughtful. "You've been having problems for a while, haven't you? The first time I met you, if I remember correctly, you had ducked into our convent to avoid some nasty boy who was following you."

She nodded. "Nick van Buren—Josie's boyfriend. The two of them have been giving me a hard time, but I'm going to put a stop to it, believe me."

"Well—if you're sure," Sister Helena said, her tone still doubtful. "I was going to tell you we have plenty of spare bedrooms at the convent, for overnight guests and for people who come to our weekend retreats. We'd be more than happy to put you up for the night, dear, if you're at all uneasy about being on your own."

"That's really kind of you." For a moment Claire yearned to accept the offer. But she had just impressed her enemies with a strong show of resistance; to flee the house now would seem like an admission of fear, of weakness. And they had threatened to harm anyone who helped her . . . "I'll be fine here," she made herself say. "And I promised Myra—Dr. Moore—I'd look after her house and her pets."

"Oh dear, I do hate the thought of you being all alone in this great big place with no phone and no neighbours near at hand," the nun said. "And I don't think Myra would like it either. Here, I'll lend you this." She reached into her pocket and pulled out a cellphone. "I brought it along with me in case there was any kind of trouble. Keep it with you overnight, or until your phone line is repaired. You can drop it off at the convent later. I'll call the phone company tomorrow for you, if you like."

"Thanks," Claire said gratefully, forcing a smile as she took the phone. She grasped the dog's collar and pulled him back inside; he was grinning now and waving his plumy tail.

"I'll be off then. You can call me if you have any problems, any time. Myra's got my number written down next to her kitchen phone." Sister Helena turned and headed back down the drive, guided by her flashlight.

Claire closed the door and set the phone down on the hall table. She was amazed at how normal she'd been able to sound. It was a revelation, and a comfort too. Her voice was Claire Norton's voice still, as her body was still Claire Norton's body; her mind might be a welter of confusion, her identity permanently changed, but outwardly at least she was still the same person. It was a soothing thought in the midst of her fear and uncertainty. She would be able, then, to put up a front, as she would need to do in the days to come. For she could not tell anyone about what had happened tonight, here in Myra Moore's house: not Sister Helena, not the school counsellor, not even her own father. No one would believe her. Until tonight she herself would not have believed such a tale from anyone else. Her mother, perhaps, might have accepted it, so strong had the bond once been between them. She could see Mom's face now, her smooth blond hair pulled back in its usual tidy ponytail, her fine-chiselled features calm as she listened—not judging, not analyzing, just listening. But it was no use thinking of Mom; she had left three years ago, without even leaving a forwarding address. She was gone, moved, untraceable.

Claire felt again the sharpness of that loss.

Kneeling, she put her arms around the collie's neck and buried her face in his thick white ruff. *And what could I say anyway, even to Mom? One of my classmates is a witch, or thinks she is. She's taken up with some kind of weird coven in the house down the road, a coven that's given her powers, made her able to cast illusions and control animals and make people sick. And she's tried twice to use those powers on me, with the help of her warlock friends . . . And that's not even the strangest part of it. I also think I'm . . .*

She shivered and stood up again. Leaving Angus, she went into the drawing room and stood staring up at the old portrait above the fireplace: a painting of a young girl in Renaissance dress, holding a white cat in her arms. Memories filled her mind as she gazed at it: memories not of her current life, but of another, lived in a distant place and time. She remembered another body, not as tall as this one she now possessed, but slender with small delicate hands and a pale oval face—exactly like the girl in the picture. Mistress Alice Ramsay. She looked down from the painting at herself, her body clothed in jeans and sweater and track shoes, her long-fingered hands clasping and unclasping. She raised her hands to run them over her face, as if seeking to reassure herself that it was still as it had been—squarish and firm of feature, with its strong chin and cheekbones and the straight-bridged nose on which her thick-framed glasses perched. Yes, she was Claire Norton still.

Or was she? Would she ever *really* be the same again, now that she knew she had lived before? Her whole idea of self was altered. Until tonight it had always been tied to this body, to this face that she saw in the mirror every day. But now that was no longer true.

She had been Alice Ramsay.

She closed her eyes and tried to sort through the memories. They came to her in a rush, as if the unknown force that had formerly suppressed them had now given way. Images, sounds, and other sensory impressions from Alice's brief life in seventeenth-century Scotland burst upon the darkness behind her eyelids . . . The old manor house of Glenlyon, its stone walls rising to haughty crenellated turrets . . . Women in gowns with huge hooped skirts, men in velvet and lace . . . The little village in the valley beside the winding burn . . . Hills purple with heather . . . the smiling face of William Macfarlane. But the memory of him hurt her, especially that last sight of his anguished face as she sank beneath the water of the burn while the village people gathered on the bank cried, "Witch, witch!" . . . Her mind flinched from that scene and swept on to other times and images: her favourite gown . . . her white cat . . . her old nurse . . . On the memories rushed, back to early infancy, to faint blurred impressions of safety and warmth.

She opened her eyes again and glanced out of the window towards the trees at the western end of the property—the border between this estate and the neighbouring one where her enemies lived. The warlocks—Klaus van Buren and his nephew, Nick—who presided over the Dark Circle coven. There was no sign of anyone lurking there, but Claire was not reassured. Though her enemies had retreated for now, they could easily post sentries to take their place—sentries that it would be nearly impossible to see.

In one of the tall maples the small dark shape of the owl still perched. He was a *daimon,* a spirit in an animal's body—but not one of theirs. This spirit was her ally, watching over her as protector, not spy. Her familiar. She was filled with memory and longing.

Leo . . . Leo, talk to me again. Please don't shut me out. I need to talk to you . . .

There was no answer within her mind. He had not spoken to her since coming to her aid hours ago, helping her defeat the young witch sent to intimidate her. Josie Sloan had fled, running away through the grounds to rejoin her warlock mentors. Like a repulsed army they had withdrawn to the house beyond the trees, though she had no real hope that they would not return. And Leo had left her too, flying in his owl's form back to the maple tree without communicating anything but that one, brief touch of comfort.

She tried again. "Leo, listen to me, please. I'm alone, I'm scared, I want to talk to someone. You always used to be there for me, remember—" She fell silent in mid-sentence as another thought struck her. "Leo—you don't blame yourself for what happened back in Scotland, do you? I'm all right now. I've come back." Fear and puzzlement gave way all at once to pity as she gazed at the small shape in the tree. "Leo—it wasn't your fault I died."

Out there in the night the owl stirred and opened its wings, as if to fly away. But then it closed them again and perched motionless as before. No voice spoke within her mind.

That must be what was troubling him, though. Alice Ramsay had been accused of witchcraft partly because of the testimony of her maid, who had seen wild birds and animals come at her mistress's call, as if by magic. The maid and the villagers were not to know that it was Leo, her spirit guide, who caused the animals to obey, and not Alice herself. Nor would it have made any difference if they had known. To them, Leo—immortal, incorporeal, able to exert an influence on living things—would be nothing more than an evil demon. She could never have hoped to convince them that he was benevolent, that he helped the animals whose bodies he briefly inhabited. He had brought the stray cat to Alice's home, where it was given shelter and food: the white cat that had served as his primary host. She looked up at the portrait again. The cat the villagers had later identified as her familiar. Yes, Leo would blame himself for all these things; the spirit would feel he had revealed too much of himself and his power to Alice, and so paved the way for her destruction. But the worst of it she had brought on herself, unthinking: when her young neighbour Helen Macfarlane was carried off by a bolting horse, Alice had ridden her own mare after it, all the while pleading with Leo to take control of the terrified animal and save the girl. Pleading out loud, at the top of her voice, forgetful of the villagers gathered in the vicinity: "Go into him, Leo!" She must have been mad. Leo had saved Helen by stopping the horse—but this apparent act of witchcraft on her part had caused the village folk to turn on Alice in fear and anger.

Her maid had later confirmed that Alice also addressed her cat as "Leo," proving that the name did not belong to her pet but to a being that possessed it and other living creatures.

"Leo, listen. It was all my doing. I got careless and fouled everything up, even after you warned me. You said they'd think it was black magic, and you were right. Please don't blame yourself for what happened! I'm back, and there are no witch hunters in this day and age. It's safe for you to be my friend now."

Still there was no response. Leo had communicated with her once already, speaking mind to mind, so this could only mean that he chose not to do so now. He had evidently decided to watch over her in this life, and to save her from harm whenever possible, but he was not going any further than that. She gave up for the moment and turned back towards the portrait. Even with the recovered memories it was still hard to grasp the truth. Somehow, she was two people—the Claire Norton who lived in this time and the Alice Ramsay who had lived and died as an accused witch in Scotland four hundred years ago. And she had been other people as well. Leo had spoken to her once in the void between her lives, telling her that she had lived before.

Before Alice Ramsay . . .

Once again she pored over her memories of her previous life—memories only recently recalled, yet vivid as though she had lived them yesterday. And before them, at the very beginning, there lay another . . . She grasped at it, no longer frightened but eager, sensing that this new recollection held the key to her present predicament. Light . . . Strong sunlight, blazing out of a sky the hue of bleached bone. Human figures, dark as if carved out of ebony, walking slowly across a dry, dusty plain. And there came to her suddenly an image of a lion—no stone statue like the ones on Glenlyon's gates, but a real living beast with a shaggy russet mane, gazing at her with its great amber eyes.

The image faded. It was gone: that fleeting fragment of another, still-earlier time. Try as she might, she could not recall it.

Frustrated, she began to pace up and down the room, watched by the painted eyes of her portrait, thinking hard. *What should I do now? The warlocks know about me and my familiar now, thanks to Josie. That must have been why they sent her over here—to suss me out, see what powers I have and what I can do.* This was a frightening thought, and she threw an anxious glance out the window. Josie Sloan had been cowed for the moment, her malice subdued, but who knew how long it would last? When Josie recovered from her defeat she would be resentful, eager for payback. And she would have the help of her warlock allies, who were far more experienced than she at the art of wreaking havoc on innocent people's lives. *How much have they found out? Do they know I was Alice in my former life? What will they do next?*

And is there anyone else I can tell about this? Anyone at all? There was Mrs. Brodie, alias Silverhawk—she was a white witch, so she would surely be more open-minded than most people. But Claire doubted she and her coven members could do much against the organized conspiracy that was the Dark Circle. To draw them into this affair would only endanger them. And then there was Myra Moore. What was it the young warlock, Nick van Buren, had said about Myra? *"She's getting too close."* The warlocks were somehow aware of the older woman's research into magic and the spirit realm, and would no doubt be turning their attention to her before very long. Myra's family connection to Alice Ramsay—she was descended from

Alice's half-brother—would make them suspicious too. They might come to believe that she intended to follow in the footsteps of her fabled ancestor and become a witch herself. What would they do to her then?

Claire felt a stab of anxiety. Myra must be protected—from the Dark Circle, from the perils of her own curiosity. For, Claire suddenly realized, she had grown fond of the woman—the first real friend she'd had in years. She thought of Myra's amiable good nature, her childlike enthusiasm and interest in everything around her, and was appalled at the thought of any harm coming to her. Especially if it came as a direct consequence of Claire's entrance into her life.

She felt something nudge her hand and looked down to see Angus gazing up at her with anxious brown eyes. He whined softly. She bent down to caress his ears, soothing the dog and herself. "I won't tell Myra about any of this," she said out loud. "She'd believe me all right, but I won't tell. If she finds out, she finds out—but it won't be through me. I've told her way too much already: about Josie and Nick, and the Dark Circle. She can't get involved with any of them. They obviously don't like anyone challenging their power."

Going over to the window, she stared out across the grounds. They lay empty and silent, the smooth expanse of the lawns showing a dull grey except where trees and shrubberies spread their pools of black shadow. She could see the pagoda-roofed summer house from here, and the meandering stream at the west end of the property with its little Oriental bridges, and the long curving drive that wound away towards the gates with their watchful stone lions. She felt her apprehension give way to a new feeling, strong and overwhelming as a sea wave striking her and carrying her away with it: a great surge of love for this place, this beautiful old house and estate of Willowmere. For all who had lived here over the years, blood kin to the person she had once been: the family of Alice Ramsay. This place was *home,* as surely as that other house where Claire lived with her father. It was no longer a matter of coveting the estate as she had once done, of gazing at it in longing whenever she passed by and secretly pretending it was hers. Willowmere belonged to her and she to it. For decades her painted image had hung here in the drawing room, watching over generations of Ramsays like a silent guardian. Now she was here in the flesh, able at last to defend Willowmere from harm.

Claire felt a sudden fierce protectiveness. Whatever might happen in the days to come, of one thing she was now utterly certain: it was her responsibility to ensure that the warlocks never again came near Myra, her home, her pets, or her property. If they thought they could do as they wished, she would show them otherwise.

Chapter 2

SHE AWOKE THE NEXT MORNING to sunlight flowing through the spare-room window and the sounds of normal activity: traffic rushing along the street in front of the estate, loud thuds and hammering noises from a new house being constructed a block away. Two of Myra's cats were asleep on her bed: Socrates, the big marmalade, lay curled at her feet, and the tortoiseshell Hypatia was nestled in the crook of her arm.

Claire lay still for a moment, recalling the events of the previous night. It was like looking back on a strange and disturbing dream. She reached for the lamp on the nightstand, dislodging the yawning Hypatia, and switched it on. The power had been restored—or had it never been off? Perhaps she really had dreamed it all. She picked up the receiver of the bedside phone and put it to her ear. No dial tone. So the wires *had* been cut. And there by the phone lay the Gurkha dagger. It had all happened. She collapsed back in bed, letting the knowledge sink in. It must, she thought with some surprise, be Friday. An eternity seemed to lie between her and yesterday morning, when she had awakened, disturbed by the latest in a series of unsettling dreams but still thinking that an ordinary day lay ahead of her—an ordinary life. Other teenagers were getting up now and preparing for school and looking forward to the weekend. Claire reflected on this for a moment, filled with self-pity; then out of the welter of emotion she felt a decision take shape. She was not going to stay all day in this house waiting for another attack. Quite apart from her fears for herself, her presence here would draw the warlocks to Willowmere again, and she could not allow that. She must draw them off, but without making it appear that she was afraid and fleeing from them: go someplace else, a place with plenty of other people to offer safety in numbers, and the logical choice was school. They surely wouldn't dare attack her there, with so many witnesses around, and it would look as though she were merely returning to her regular daily routine.

The guidance counsellor might be back in her office, too. Mrs. Robertson had taken time off to visit her sick mother, who Claire suspected was not really ill at all but a victim of the warlocks' mind tricks. Josie Sloan had hinted at a plot to remove all the people who offered support and security to Claire, to make her feel more vulnerable. Hopefully Mrs. Robertson's mother had recovered by now. But even if the counsellor hadn't returned to school, it would still be reassuring to be with other people and to go through the motions of a normal life: classes, study, homework. It would help to make her feel like Claire Norton again.

She got up, glancing out the window as she crossed the room. The lake sparkled under the rising sun, and the grounds were brightly lit and empty of menace. Claire dressed and washed and pulled her unruly ash-blond hair into a ponytail, then went downstairs, followed by the two cats. A third cat, the black-and-white male named Aristotle, sauntered out of the linen closet where he had been sleeping and joined the procession.

Angus was lying at the foot of the stairs. When he saw her he thumped his tail on the floor in greeting, then rose and followed her and the cats into the kitchen. Here there was another unwelcome reminder of last night's frightening events: the windowpane on the back door was smashed, and the floor beneath strewn with shattered glass. Josie had forced her entry by breaking the window and reaching down to undo the chain lock. Claire pressed her lips tightly together as she swept up the broken glass. If Josie thought she was going to get away with this, then she could think again. The police would probably have to be involved, after all. She could hear Josie's sneering voice: "What are you gonna do, call the cops?" But she'd said that back when she was still confident she could intimidate Claire. Before last night's confrontation on the widow's walk atop the roof of the house, where Claire had emerged the victor.

Well, attacks on Claire were one thing; damage to Myra Moore's property was another matter. And breaking-and-entering was a serious offence, not to mention cutting phone wires—though Claire doubted she could ever prove Josie was responsible for that as well, even if she did do it. But she had probably left plenty of fingerprints in here. *Let her try her little bag of tricks on the police,* Claire thought with grim anticipation.

The other two cats, Plato and Hildegard, had shown up and joined the mewing chorus at her feet. She gave them their morning meal and tossed a few dog treats to Angus, who ate only at suppertime but always looked forlorn and reproachful when the other animals were fed. Then she had her own breakfast and loaded up her backpack. Into it, along with her books and bag lunch, she slipped a large sheaf of scribbled notes: the writings of Al Ramsay, Myra's late uncle. The old man had died only recently, leaving Myra the house and his numerous pets, including Angus. And he had left more than these behind. His notes detailed his discovery of the spirit beings he called *daimons,* some of which were good and some evil, and his relationship with his own personal daimon, or familiar. He also wrote of his fascination with his ancestor Alice Ramsay, giving details he had learned from his familiar about her life, her love for William Macfarlane, and her tragic death. And he included an account of her present-day reincarnation. Claire dared not leave those pages behind; the risk that they might fall into enemy hands was too great. The warlocks probably wouldn't attempt a daylight break-in, but she couldn't be sure of that. They must not learn who she was. According to Al Ramsay's journals, the reborn Alice would have enemies—"dark shamans"—who would try to destroy her. She felt certain this referred to the warlocks.

Claire taped a piece of cardboard over the smashed window, locked the house up, and headed off to the bus stop. She was taking the 12B bus that passed by Willowville High, which meant she must walk by the warlocks' house to get to the stop. Crossing to the other side of the street would look too much like the avoidance it was, and she had to convince them she was unafraid. But she walked very quickly, stealing only one surreptitious side glance at the huge grey stone mansion where Nick and his uncle Klaus van Buren lived. To her relief she saw no signs of life there, though the wolf-dogs were barking in their kennels at the back. The sound made her tremble. The van Burens bred the animals to sell as watchdogs, or so they claimed, but last night a dozen of them had surrounded and attacked the house at Willowmere with an evil intelligence and coordination no mere animals could show.

She walked on a little way past the bus stop to the convent of St. Mary's, an enormous brick edifice that looked like a Victorian manor house. Here she dropped off Sister Helena's cellphone, leaving it with the nun at the reception desk. Then she turned back and went to stand by the stop. As she waited, shivering in the chill morning air, she glanced nervously up the street towards the grey house, fearing to see one of the van Burens or their daimon-possessed dogs come out the front gate. For they were surely watching her since the events of last night. There would probably be continuous surveillance of some kind, and a daimon could enter the mind of any animal or bird. She glanced around her. A grey squirrel undulated along a telephone wire that spanned one of the side streets, but it seemed intent on its own business. There were no other animals about. That she could see, Claire corrected herself.

The bus arrived, wheezing to a halt in front of her, and she climbed on board feeling grateful and settled into a window seat on the right-hand side. As the bus rumbled eastwards she saw the houses slip by again: the ugly new housing development, the sinister grey mansion. She went rigid as she caught a sudden glimpse of Nick van Buren walking across the lawn, his eyes invisible as usual behind their dark glasses, his longish dark hair blowing back in the breeze. The biggest wolf-dog, the one with the ink-black coat, was trotting at his heels. Then the bus moved on and there was Willowmere, lying behind its sheltering stone walls. It was hard to believe that she had once found the place so remote and mysterious; already she felt a twinge on passing it, a pull on her heart even stronger than the one she felt for her own home on Maple Street. But the place was not hers, she reminded herself with an effort. Her stay there was only temporary, and she could never be more than a guest. However she might feel, she must go on living the life of Claire Norton, and that meant returning to her own home and family. Her father would be back from his business trip on Monday and Myra would return this weekend from her book tour; and life would return to its old familiar pattern, on the surface at least.

School reinforced this reality, when at last the bus deposited her there. None of the students hanging around the front doorway gave her more than a cursory glance, though she half expected them to notice a change in her. Because they saw only her outward self, she could go on being the same person for them, and this, she realized, would make the whole process of renormalization easier.

There was only one moment when she came close to losing her grasp on the present. A boy and girl walked past her down the hall, arms twined around each other, his chin with its wispy beard resting against her cheek; a few days ago Claire would have ignored the couple, or perhaps felt slightly amused or even wistful. Now she thought with a pang of William Macfarlane, and a memory four centuries old: a memory of blue sky over slopes of purple heather, a fresh wind, a river glittering under the sun—and William. Tall, broad-shouldered, with his curly chestnut hair and soft fringe of beard, his eyes clear and blue as the sky above him. His hand, stroking the hair at her temple. His voice, both deep and soft, gentle as his touch.

"It's settled then. We'll run away, you and I. We'll ride away into the countryside. We'll take a ship and cross the sea—"

And her own voice, Alice's voice, protesting even as she relaxed against his firm supporting arm: "Your uncle will be angry, Will. He so wanted me to marry his son. He will talk to your father—they will not let you manage the estate in Virginia, after all."

"No matter. In the New World anyone can make a life for himself, start over again from nothing. It will be an adventure for us both."

The image and the voices faded, falling back into the past. A tear slipped down Claire's cheek, and she hastened to wipe it away. *I made it to the New World after all; but four hundred years late, and without my William* . . . She had to blink hard to prevent more tears from falling.

But that was her only lapse. It was, in fact, amazing how easily she found herself slipping back into normality. Even dialling the combination on her locker's padlock helped: the familiar click as it opened, the squeak of the metal door, the thump of her backpack landing inside restored her at once to her old routine existence. So, too, did the voices of the students in the hallway.

"No way. Josh is better-looking than Corey. I totally swoon for him. And anyway he's the lead singer. Corey's just the drummer."

"But Corey's so cute! I always wanna run my hands through his hair, I just love long curly hair . . ."

Those were the voices of Mimi Taylor and her friend, whom she called Chel. (She had two friends named Chelsea, and using this nickname for one of them avoided confusion.) Ordinarily Claire would have found their chattering voices annoying. Mimi and the Chelseas bought into every fad going: movies, music, books, clothes, even the snack food they ate had to be trendy before they would touch it. But today their talk was a comfort to her, a reminder that the whole world had not changed forever even if she had. As she stood there listening a third voice chimed in.

"So are you all coming this afternoon? The guys are counting on your support." The speaker was Megan Holmes, a popular cheerleader and one of the dominant personalities at Willowville High. "We want a really good turnout for this game, okay?"

"What game?" growled another voice. That was Donna Reese, the short stocky girl who had the locker to the right of Claire's.

"Us against Maplewood, today at five. And it's right here on our own field, so it's real easy to get to and you've got no excuse to miss it! Come on out and support the team." Megan turned her fresh, pink-cheeked face towards Claire.

Her reply, and the tone in which she uttered it, came to her automatically. "Team, what team?" asked Claire, putting on an innocent look.

Megan stared, then laughed. "Our football team, of course!"

"We have a football team?" Claire looked at Donna.

"Looks like it," she grunted.

"Sorry," Claire told Megan, "but I can't make it. I have to house-sit for somebody."

"Well, *you* come then," said Megan to Donna. "Show some school spirit!"

"Haven't got any." Donna slammed her locker door shut and turned away.

Megan gave up on them and hailed Mimi's other friend Chelsea, who was just arriving at her locker. "Chelsea! *You're* coming to the game, anyway! To see Dave play."

"No, I'm not!" The blond girl whirled and presented an angry face to Megan. "I hate Dave and the whole stupid football team and I hope they lose, okay?" She threw her pack in her locker, closed it up and stalked away down the hall, leaving everyone to stare after her.

"Well," said Claire after a moment's uncomfortable pause, "that was a little unexpected."

Megan's mouth hung open in dismay. "What's the matter? What'd I say?"

"It's nothing to do with you, Megan," Chel reassured her. "Dave broke up with Chelsea and she's pretty upset about it. She won't be going to watch him play for a while—if ever."

"He found out she did this little love-charm thing on him," Mimi explained. "And he, like, totally lost it and blew up at her. Said he didn't believe in any of that witchcraft stuff, but it bugged him that she would even try to control him, and he wouldn't put up with it. The thing is she didn't really believe in the spell either, at least not any more, and she tried to explain that to him but he wouldn't listen. It's all so *stupid*." She shrugged and rolled her eyes.

At that moment Claire saw Josie Sloan walking down the hall towards them. The girl looked as if she had dressed with less care than usual: she wore no jewellery, only a long-sleeved black top over torn jeans, and her dyed black hair was unkempt. She was very pale, but her pallor for once did not come from her usual pasty-white foundation: she wore no makeup at all, and there were heavy shadows under her green-grey eyes. *Talk about Dark Circles* . . . There was no sign of Josie's familiar, a pet white rat that served as the host for a malevolent daimon. She had used it to spy on Mimi and the other girls who joined the Circle, lending the possessed rodent to them whenever they performed their "magickal rituals" so that she could see and hear everything they did. They had been thoroughly disconcerted when she quoted their own words to them later. Even Claire had almost been convinced that Josie possessed extrasensory powers; now she knew that Josie had simply linked her mind to the rat-daimon's.

At the sight of Claire, Josie turned paler still and her eyes went as wide and wary as a cat's when it sees a dog cross its yard. *She didn't expect me to be here this morning,* Claire realized.

"Oh, Josie, hi," said Mimi. "You heard about Chelsea and Dave? Is there anything you can do to, like, fix it? 'Cause she's really bummed about it."

Claire's eyes had not left Josie's. "Yeah, it seems that love spell you gave her had an expiry date."

The greenish eyes narrowed. "Why're you pretending?" Josie burst out. "Acting like you don't believe in witches when you *are* one!"

"Don't know what you're talking about," said Claire. The other girls were looking from her to Josie in bewilderment.

"You've been learning the Craft on your own," Josie hissed. "Trying to one-up me. You acted like you didn't believe just so you could throw me off. Well, you better watch it. I'm learning, too. I'll be more powerful than you soon, and then we'll see . . ." Josie turned a wild gaze on the other girls. "She's a liar! She's been lying to us the whole time!"

It was clear from the looks on the other girls' faces that they thought Josie had come completely unhinged. Claire addressed her next words to them. "It's Josie who's been lying to you. She had you all believing she was magic, didn't she? That she could read your minds. Well, it was just a trick. Josie got . . . someone . . . to spy on you, put you under surveillance and listen in on your conversations. She learned everything she knows from him—" She glanced towards Josie again and saw that she was staring, not at Claire but at someone or something behind her. Claire turned. There was no one there, but in a tree just outside the window at the end of the hall a familiar shape perched. A small barred owl, sitting on a lower branch with its face towards the window. Leo's bird-host. He must have made it fly here to the school grounds so that he could continue to watch over Claire.

She tore her eyes away from the window and looked at the girls again. "It's not really magic at all. Isn't that right, Josie? Tell them it's not magic!" Claire took a step towards her, putting on what she hoped was a threatening expression. *C'mon, Josie, 'fess up. Don't make me call my owl . . .*

Josie recoiled, her face blanching still paler; no doubt she was recalling last night's confrontation on the roof of Myra's house. Leo had made his owl-host swoop down on Josie's rat and carry it away, and had Leo allowed his host to kill it, Josie too would have died, for her mind had been bound to the daimon's. Of course Leo had not done so; but there was raw fear in Josie's eyes as she backed away. Claire stood still, suddenly disturbed. Hate and anger she could deal with, but she had no desire to have another human being look at her like that.

"Spy?" Chel repeated. "Is that true? Is it, Josie?"

Josie's face twisted and worked with emotion. Her eyes met Claire's, but could not hold her gaze and dropped again. At last in a low rasping voice she said, "Yeah."

"Well, I don't—of all the . . ." Chel didn't seem to know what to say. Mimi just stared with her large violet-blue eyes. Josie didn't look either of them in the face. She slunk off down the hall, a living image of defeat. But Claire looked after her with suspicion. She had seen the venomous look in the other girl's eyes just before she turned away. Josie wouldn't rest until she avenged herself for this humiliation.

With an effort Claire said, "See? It was all a hoax. Josie's got no power over you at all. You don't have to be afraid of her any more." She glanced towards the window again. The owl had gone.

"Thanks for clearing that up, Claire," Chel said. "You know, it was fun at first, but it really was starting to get kind of creepy."

Mimi yawned. "Well, I already decided I was through with that Dark Circle stuff. It wasn't really getting me anywhere."

Mimi's short attention span, Claire thought, might well be her best protection. She and the Chelseas would be safe now; that left only Donna, and she was smart, so it shouldn't be too hard to persuade her to drop out of the Circle. But Josie would go back to her warlock friends for help and advice on getting even with Claire. Their conflict hadn't ended with the encounter on the roof, after all. There would be more trouble ahead, and her shoulders sagged at the thought of it. She could not face this alone.

✧ ✧ ✧

After homeroom she went to the school's pay phones and dialled up her doctor's number. "Dr. Ames's office," said the receptionist's voice.

"Uh, hi. It's Claire Norton speaking. I'd like to cancel an appointment I made to see the doctor."

"Ah, yes, here it is. Did you want to rebook?"

"No, that won't be necessary. Could you tell her I haven't had any more of those hallucinations I was telling her about? I'm fine now." Claire hung up and checked her watch. She had a spare period now, and she decided to spend it as she usually did, studying in the library. But as she settled into a carrel and reached into her backpack for her books, her hand encountered the loose pages of old Mr. Ramsay's notes. She threw a quick glance behind her, but saw only other students sitting at their carrels and the librarian at her desk. Slowly she pulled the sheaf of papers out and began to read them, poring over each sentence.

The longhand manuscript began as a memoir and then turned into a kind of journal, recording the last events of Ramsay's life. It started with the story of his first encounter with his familiar in Africa, back in the 1930s. A native witch doctor had pointed out to him an African grey parrot in a nearby tree and told him it was his spirit guide; delighted, he had taken the bird home with him and begun to research animal familiars and shamanism. A description followed of his subsequent visits to Africa and other countries, wherever the various forms of shamanism were practised. He explained his own experiments with meditation and self-induced trances, and his growing belief that the bird he had brought back from Nigeria really did harbour some kind of supernatural intelligence. He named the parrot Ben, and the spirit, or daimon, inhabiting its body, Benvolio.

The being was not confined to the parrot, but able to move from animal to animal. "On my last trip to the Pacific islands," Ramsay wrote on one page, "I obtained a young fruit bat, of the species called 'flying fox' for its sharp ears and muzzle. In addition to being as affectionate and docile a pet as I've ever had, the creature will serve very well as a nocturnal host for Benvolio. My daimon has told me many times how he dislikes predators—hence his choice of a fruit-eating bird for his primary host. But I need him to do some night flying, and most animals that fly at night are hunters, like bats and owls. Benvolio's so tender-hearted he can't even bear being hosted by an insect-eater, so a fruit-eating bat is the perfect solution for him. Also this species does not use sonar, but relies instead on its large keen eyes to find its way about in the dark, which makes it perfect for spying.

I must find out who these other daimons in the neighbourhood are, masquerading in the bodies of wild animals. Exactly what are they up to . . . ?"

A shadow passed over the page, and Claire's head snapped up and around. But it was only another student walking past, books in hand, heading for the circulation desk. The study carrel blocked her view on three sides, providing cover for anyone who might want to sneak up on her. She stood, pretending to stretch her legs and back muscles, adding a yawn for effect. There was no sign of Josie anywhere in the library, and she sat down again, hunching over the handwritten pages. She really should not be reading these papers here, where Josie might see, or someone else from the Circle. But having read so far, she desperately wanted to continue. She had to know more. What about Myra? She had been reading his writings—Claire knew this from Myra's Post-it notes stuck to some of his pages—so she must know most or all of his story by now, but did she believe any of it, or had she dismissed her late uncle's claims as insane? The more Claire considered this, the more she came to doubt it. No, Myra would never shrug off his accounts. She was much too open-minded, and she'd known him too long and too well. And there was her own interest in Wicca. She might not understand everything about magic, but she'd certainly be intrigued by her uncle's findings.

Besides, she had looked so startled when Claire first used the word "daimon" in her presence. She wouldn't have reacted that way if the word had meant nothing to her.

Finally Myra's name showed up on one page: ". . . I purchased a companion for my African parrot, a female of the same species. I call her Tillie, after my old Aunt Matilda, and joked to Benvolio that he could now have a lady daimon to keep him company. He reminded me seriously that daimons have no gender, although some tend to prefer hosts of a specific sex—just as a man might prefer leather jackets to tweed, for example—and may even come over time to see themselves as masculine or feminine. And it appears the female parrot is, indeed, inhabited by a daimon! This spirit seems to me to have a feminine personality, mischievous and wry and knowing, like an impish old woman. It is very attached to young Myra, and will sometimes make Tillie fly onto her shoulder, much to her delight; I begin to wonder if it might be her very own daimon-familiar. How I long to tell her all I know! But she'd just think her old uncle had gone dotty. 'You say you're a shaman, Uncle Al? You learned all about magic in Africa, from an old witch doctor? And there's a sort of invisible being who lives in Ben the parrot and talks to you inside your head?' Out of the question, of course. A pity, as we're so close, and if she could be made to understand it all without fear she would probably think it wonderful. When she's older perhaps—but at times I doubt I'll ever be able to tell her, or anyone. I can still hardly believe it myself . . ." And then, many pages later, the name leaped out at her once more: "It is such a relief that Myra knows the truth at last. She suspected a good deal of course, being an intelligent woman—but while a part of her wants to believe, another can't quite accept it yet. She says her own familiar has not spoken to her. But she is showing increased interest in the paranormal and modern mysticism, and I expect she will find her own way to the truth in time."

So Myra *did* believe at least some of her uncle's story. And she knew too much—more than was good for her, or safe. Did the Dark Circle shamans know how much she knew? Claire's head was beginning to ache, and she put down the notes for a moment to massage her forehead. One thing was clear: the van Burens were dangerous. They would do anything to anyone, break any law in pursuit of their goals. She had met people like them before, in her life in Scotland: the brutal witch hunters Edward Morley and Anthony King, who had put her to the ordeal by water and so caused her death.

Claire did not linger after school. Mrs. Robertson was still away tending her sick mother, and the school library had none of the materials she was looking for. She needed to learn how to summon her own daimon-familiar at need, and also to repel any attacks made on her by an evil one. Al Ramsay's notes gave no clue as to how either of these things might be done.

She caught the bus and took it as far as the downtown core. Here she got off and walked the few blocks to the Books & Magic store. A wave of atmospheric music—pan-pipes and seashore sounds—greeted her as she went in, along with the tinkle of the chimes over the door. She did not browse the shelves, but went straight to the cash desk. Incense sticks burned there, sweet and pungent, in front of a Dancing Shiva who shared the counter with a Laughing Buddha, two stone inukshuks, and a large pewter figurine of a butterfly-winged fairy clasping a crystal ball in her arms. Ojibwa dream catchers hung like outsized spiderwebs from the ceiling. Claire tapped the bell on the counter, and from behind a clinking bead curtain came a girl with bright magenta hair and matching nail polish, wearing an ankle-length black gown. She gave Claire a languid smile. "Can I help you?"

"Um, maybe. I'm trying to find out about . . . daimons." If this place had no books on the subject, then no store would.

"I don't know," the girl said, glancing towards the jewellery counter. "We've got some semiprecious gems, and some quartz crystals for channelling, but no—"

"*Daimons,* not diamonds. They're a kind of—well, I guess you could call them spirits. The Greek philosopher Plato wrote about them."

The girl shook her head, making her long dangly earrings sway. "Never heard of them. Sorry."

Old Mr. Brown, the co-owner of the store, suddenly emerged from behind a bookshelf. He was wearing his usual outfit of mud-coloured sweater and trousers and his usual expression of glum disapproval. "As either of you would know," he grumbled, "if education was what it used to be, you will find daimons mentioned in the story of Er, in Plato's *Republic*."

He went and rummaged among the bookshelves, and held out a paperback to Claire. She took it and thanked him. She might as well buy it, she decided; there was probably a copy in Myra's own library, but it wouldn't hurt to have one of her own.

"It's at the end of the last chapter," he told her, and disappeared behind the shelves again.

Claire handed the book to the girl. "Oh—one more thing. Have you got any books about shamanism?"

"You mean natural magic?" the girl asked.

"I guess so. I'm especially interested in those rituals shamans had for summoning their spirit guides. Like the ones the Ojibwa did—what did they call them?"

The girl nodded. "Dream quests," she said, moving out from behind the counter. "I know a book you'll find useful for that. Hang on a sec and I'll get it for you."

Claire stood alone at the counter, gazing into the clear depths of the fairy's crystal. Was there something to those ancient shamanistic practices? *Could* a daimon be summoned by some sort of ritual—perhaps even against its will? The only way to find out, she thought, was by trying. She could not defy the

Dark Circle and protect Willowmere all on her own. She needed the help and advice that only her familiar could give her. Somehow, she must learn why Leo had stopped speaking to her and persuade him to join forces with her again.

Chapter 3

STOOPING SLIGHTLY under the increased weight of her backpack, Claire walked along Lakeside to Willowmere, deep in thought. As she passed the warlocks' house she heard a voice call out her name, and her heart missed a beat. She made no reply, but set her jaw and quickened her pace. *Whatever you do, don't show any fear,* she reminded herself.

But at the sound of approaching footsteps she had to turn. The elder Mr. van Buren was walking a few paces behind her. "Leave me alone," she snapped at him.

"Miss Norton. I truly regret that incident last night with the girl Josie," van Buren said. His voice was smooth and polished as always. "She is very willful, and forced the confrontation against our urgings."

She turned again. "Oh, really? And what were you and your nephew doing there? Not to mention all your nasty pets?"

His grey eyes were cool and steady, despite his contrite words. "You don't suppose we were there to make trouble, do you? On the contrary, we went along merely to ensure there was no harm done to either of you. We did not wish to trespass on Dr. Moore's property, but the situation had the potential to become dangerous. We are very relieved that neither you nor Josie was hurt. We were really more concerned for her than for you, Miss Norton. We knew she was no match for you." He was walking by her side now, and able to lower his voice. "Your powers are considerable—the strongest I've ever seen in someone your age," he said softly.

Claire quickened her pace. "Powers? I don't know what you're talking about. Just tell Ms. Sloan I'll call the police if she turns up at Myra's place again. And that goes for you and Nick as well."

"You don't need to pretend," he said, still dogging her. "We saw the owl fly to you and snatch her familiar away—at your command, was it not? Come now, we both know what you are."

Claire stopped dead. Her heart skipped another beat, and her pulse seemed to be pounding inside her head. "*What* I am? What do you mean?" *He knows,* she thought in sudden panic. *He knows I'm the reincarnation of Alice . . .*

"Don't look so alarmed!" he said. "We both know you're a witch. There—I've said it." He smiled.

A witch . . . just a witch? Then he doesn't suspect who *I am?* Her racing heart slowed.

"And one with remarkable talent. I would consider it an honour to train you." He took a step towards her, his eyes intent. "That is why you sought out Dr. Moore and her Wiccan friends, is it not? You weren't just after love potions like those other silly young girls from your school, or even special powers like Josie. It was knowledge you wanted: knowledge of the Craft and an explanation for the hidden potential you've always sensed in yourself. But you won't find it at Willowmere, Miss Norton. The old man is dead, and his talents were never very great to begin with."

"Old man? You mean Mr. Ramsay?"

"Alfred Ramsay, yes. I told you I'd met him once. You've seen his papers, perhaps? I understand he wrote a lengthy account of his experiences for his niece." Claire was acutely conscious of the notes concealed in her backpack. Information that would betray her and put her life in danger, within easy reach of his hands . . . She retreated as he advanced another step. "No doubt they discussed these matters when he was alive as well. But he was a dabbler in the Craft, no more. So is Myra Moore—she hasn't even her uncle's feeble grasp of magic; she only guesses dimly at the powers he once commanded. If you are hoping to learn all you want to know from Myra or her uncle's writings you will be disappointed. And her Wiccan friends are no use to you either. If you want magic, true power, there is only one place to learn about it—and that is my coven. I hope that you will consider joining us. We could use a talent like yours."

"If you don't go away," said Claire through her teeth, "I'm going to start screaming, and everyone in the neighbourhood will think you're harassing me."

That made him pause. "A formidable young woman," he said after a moment. "All right then, I will let you alone from now on. But please do consider my offer, Miss Norton. My door will always be open should you decide you want to join us." And with that he turned and walked away, leaving her staring after him.

✧ ✧ ✧

Claire did not relax until she got back to the house. Much to her relief, Sister Helena had come through on her promise to contact the telephone company: the phone line had been restored. It was reassuring to have a link to the outside world again. She let Angus out for his run, watching as he tore across the lawn after the ball with his tail flying like a flag behind him. The grounds looked tranquil in the mellow October light. Everything seemed so normal, she thought. Deceptively, treacherously normal. She looked around for the barred owl, but could not see him anywhere—either Leo had relaxed his vigilance, or he was using another animal host. Van Buren and his allies had their own daimon-spy to watch the grounds of Willowmere; it came in the body of another owl, a great grey owl much larger than Leo's host. It must have been sent to spy on her, not Myra, for it had continued to hang about the property after Myra left for her tour. But Claire had not seen the bird for a while now. Perhaps the enemy daimon was using a different host too.

She whistled for Angus and he gambolled back towards her, the ball clenched in his jaws, tail wagging. It was hard to believe that Nick van Buren had been able to make this dog turn on her yesterday, snarling and baring his teeth at her. No doubt the young warlock had called on a daimon to possess Angus—and if he could do that once, she thought, he could do it again. If only she could find a way to block the warlocks' powers! Van Buren's suave politeness had not fooled her. He and his nephew had no intention of leaving her alone.

At five o'clock Claire fed the dog and cats their evening meal. When she went into the aviary the birds screeched and cackled their welcomes, and Koko the cockatoo flew onto her shoulder. "Hello," he said in a loving tone, and playfully nipped her ear. But all of Claire's attention was on the African grey parrot, Tillie. She recalled the words of Al Ramsay's diary: ". . . it appears the female parrot is, indeed, inhabited by a daimon! . . . It is very attached to young Myra . . ." Was it present within the parrot now?

"Are you there, daimon?" she asked aloud. But Tillie just sat on her perch eating seeds, and paid no attention.

Claire finished feeding the rest of the menagerie—an iguana, some tropical fish, and a pet peacock that lived in an outdoor pen—and then went to the library, where she settled in a chair with the two books she had bought. As Mr. Brown had said, she found the story of Er near the end of the last book in Plato's *Republic*. It was about a man who had supposedly been found lying on a battlefield and taken for dead, only to revive on his funeral pyre and tell others all about his experience of the afterlife. According to his account, souls were reborn many times, sometimes in human or animal form; in the afterlife each soul was assigned a special "destiny." On a hunch, Claire got up and checked the volumes on the study shelves. There was an old leather-bound copy of the *Republic,* heavily annotated in Al Ramsay's strong handwriting. Yes—in this older version, "destiny" was translated as "daimon." Ramsay had put asterisks beside each use of the word, and beside the last one he'd written "daimon—demon—familiar: check *A History of Witchcraft*."

There was a loud buzzing noise from the kitchen, and she jumped and dropped the book. It must be the intercom at the front gate: Myra seldom used it, preferring to leave the gate open for her friends. Claire wondered if it was Mr. van Buren again and debated just ignoring it. But it might be the housekeeper, Mrs. Hodge, returning from looking after her sick aunt. Claire went to the intercom and asked cautiously, "Who is it?"

"It's Mrs. Brodie, dear. Silverhawk."

"Oh," Claire said, surprised. Silverhawk must have decided to check on her, despite Sister Helena's visit. "Hang on, I'll come let you in."

Claire went down to the foot of the driveway. A small red car was idling outside the gate, and as she drew near Myra's friend leaned out the driver's window and waved. Claire opened up the gate and the car rolled in.

"Hop in," Silverhawk called, stopping the car.

Claire slipped into the passenger seat. The woman next to her looked as reassuringly normal as Willowmere itself: plump and silver-haired, with wire-rimmed glasses and a wool knit sweater over beige slacks. No one would have looked at her twice on the street. Certainly no one would have dreamed she belonged to a spiritual movement whose members called themselves witches. Would the van Burens view her as a threat? Would she be in danger of some kind of retaliatory attack if they saw her helping Claire? She must be sent away from this place as soon as possible, for her own safety.

"It's good to see you," Claire said with feeling. Then she checked herself, trying to use a more neutral tone. "But you really didn't have to come all the way out here. That stuff I told you about last night, the people using black magic—it all turned out to be a hoax, nothing more. I'm sorry I freaked out on you like that."

Silverhawk drove up to the converted stable that was Myra's garage and parked the car. "It's all right, love. I know Myra wouldn't want you to feel spooked and lonely in her house. I was going to offer to stay overnight here myself and let you go home." She nodded to a small suitcase in the back seat.

"Oh, no, that's okay," Claire said quickly as they got out of the car and went up the front steps into the house. "I don't want to put you out at all. And I did promise Myra to house-sit for her. My imagination just got carried away, that's all."

"You're sure?" the older woman asked. She leaned over to rub Angus's ears as the collie ran up to her, grinning in delight. "That story you told me was pretty alarming."

"It was just this girl I know from school. Josie Sloan. She and her boyfriend are in this bogus coven thing and they keep trying to scare me, using all kinds of tricks. Most of the time I can see through what they're doing, but last night they did a—a kind of illusion I hadn't seen before, and it threw me a little. But I know now how they did it, and I'm not scared any more." At least some of this was true, so Claire hoped she sounded convincing. Witch or no witch, Silverhawk must not be drawn into this conflict. "I must have sounded like a babbling idiot on the phone." She put on a rueful smile.

"No—though you did sound scared. And I do try to keep an open mind about these things. I've always believed there's more to our world than we can ever see or know, even before I became a Wiccan."

"Yeah, or maybe there are some things we just don't completely understand yet. Well, since you came all this way I can at least offer you some tea," Claire suggested. She did not want to encourage the woman to stay, but neither did she wish to seem rude. Silverhawk accepted and they went into the kitchen.

The older woman raised her eyebrows when she saw the cardboard over the broken window. "They didn't do that, did they, the Dark Circle kids?"

"Josie did it." Claire went to get the teapot and some teabags.

"But this is serious! It's vandalism."

"Oh, don't worry, she won't get away with it. I left a message for Mrs. Robertson—the guidance counsellor at my school. She'll know what to do about it. Myra has some special herb teas—would you like one of those? Or there's orange pekoe."

"Orange pekoe will be fine."

They sat, drank their tea, and talked of ordinary things for a while. Claire found her anxiety starting to ease. Silverhawk spoke of Myra and her travels, and how she had met her at a conference on women's spirituality—"She was one of the key speakers on anthropology and the role of women in various societies," Silverhawk explained. "I was amazed at the breadth of her knowledge and the experiences she's had with indigenous peoples around the world. She told me all about her uncle, Al Ramsay—quite a fascinating person, wasn't he?"

"Oh, yes," said Claire. "He was." *If you only knew,* she added in her mind.

They talked then about Wicca and Silverhawk's own experiences with it. "We do get some people, especially young women who've watched too many Hollywood witch movies, who think it's all about making lightning bolts shoot out of your fingers and nonsense like that," the woman said with a rueful look. "But for those looking for a more spiritual experience it has a lot to offer."

"You said something last night about arranging for magic protection for Myra's place?"

"I was talking about warding—a ward is a spell of protection. Think of it as the opposite of cursing: a ritual intended to *save* someone or something from harm."

"You mean like praying for a person?"

"Similar to that, yes. A positive use of mental energy, directed towards a person or place. My coven would be happy to do it for Willowmere, and for you too if you like."

It was a rather comforting idea. And even if it didn't actually help, it would mean that Silverhawk and her coven members could offer aid while at the same time staying safely out of the main conflict with the Dark Circle coven. "Thanks," said Claire. "That's really nice of you."

The intercom buzzed again, and Claire jumped in her seat. Silverhawk noticed the reaction and stood up. "Would you like me to answer, Claire?"

"Uh . . . sure," she murmured. "If you don't mind."

"Hello?" Silverhawk said into the speaker.

There was a pause, then a voice spoke uncertainly: "Claire? Is Claire Norton there?"

Claire leaped up. "That's Mrs. Hodge."

Silverhawk nodded; apparently she too recognized the housekeeper's voice. "It's Sharon Brodie, Doris," she said. "I'm visiting. Claire will come and let you in."

Relieved, Claire set off down the drive again to let Mrs. Hodge in. While she was opening the gate Silverhawk drove up and parked for a moment as Mrs. Hodge's old blue car eased past hers.

"I'm sorry," Mrs. Hodge began, "about taking off like that—"

"Well, really, I should think you would be," interrupted Silverhawk indignantly, leaning out her window. "Leaving a young girl all by herself in that huge house! You might at least have told a neighbour to check on her or something."

"Oh, dear," whimpered the other woman. "I didn't think I'd be so long away. And I wouldn't have gone at all, except Auntie sounded so different this time. Not her usual self at all—she almost sounded frightened—"

Claire stepped forward. "It's okay, Mrs. Hodge. I don't blame you at all for going. Is your aunt all right?"

"Yes, thank you. It was rather odd: she just suddenly recovered last night and is quite herself again today."

"Maybe because you were there with her," Claire suggested. *Or because the warlocks and their daimons stopped playing with her mind,* she thought. It had been part of their ploy, she was sure, to get Claire all alone in the house.

"Yes, I'm afraid Auntie is a bit of a hypochondriac at times."

Silverhawk started up her car again. "Good. I'll leave you two together then," she said. "Goodbye, Claire. Feel free to call me any time."

"Goodbye," Claire called back. "And thanks!"

Silverhawk drove off, and Claire followed Mrs. Hodge's car up the drive.

The housekeeper was flustered and conciliatory for the rest of the evening, despite Claire's assurances. The sight of the broken window in the kitchen door also sent her into wails of dismay. Claire's explanation that it was only a classmate of hers causing mischief did not calm the woman, nor did a promise that the culprit would be punished appropriately. This further complication arising from her abandonment of her post sent Mrs. Hodge into throes of guilt. She said little during supper, and afterwards retreated to her guest room upstairs and shut the door.

Claire went back to the library and her purchases from Books & Magic. She wondered if there could possibly be any truth to the Er story. She had no memory of any kind of judgment or reckoning in the gap between her current life and the last one, but that was not to say it hadn't happened. Maybe she simply couldn't recall it. She picked up the book on natural magic. Scanning the table of contents, she noticed that one chapter was called "Summoning the Spirit Guide." She turned to the chapter and settled into a chair to read it. The author mentioned some modern rituals that were inspired by shamanistic practices; these involved deep meditation and attempts to visualize the spirit helper in animal form. There were also accounts of dream quests, traditional rites of passage for North American

Aboriginal tribes like the Ojibwa. These had been undertaken by young boys and involved bathing in pools or streams, followed by long periods of fasting alone in the wilderness.

Claire closed the book, absorbed in thought. Perhaps most people were like this man Er, never encountering their daimon-familiars until they died and left the physical world. But it was possible that some people did find a way to get in touch with these personal guardians while they were still living on Earth, and that was where all these rituals came from. Perhaps doing them placed the mind on some kind of higher plane, making communication with spirit beings easier. She might try one herself; they didn't seem terribly complicated. She had to know why Leo was holding back from her—whether it really was guilt over what had happened to her when she was Alice, or if there was some other problem that made him unwilling to contact her directly. If he wouldn't come to her, then perhaps she could somehow go to him.

The kitchen phone rang and she jumped for the third time that day. "Hellooo!" trilled a familiar voice when she snatched up the receiver. "Just phoning to see how everything is going."

For a wild moment Claire thought of telling Myra everything she had learned—about daimons and shamans, about the van Burens, about her own identity. It would ease her burden so much if she could only share it. But that also meant sharing the danger.

"Fine, Myra." Claire spoke in a voice that managed to be both light and firm. "Everything is just fine."

"I'll be back Sunday noon-ish, or perhaps a bit later. You don't need to stick around if you don't want to. Your father will be back soon from his own trip, won't he?"

"Yes, Monday afternoon." Claire felt a little tremor at the thought. Her father. For an instant the image of Dad, with his glasses and thinning dark blond hair, was overlaid with the image of another man, bearded and heavy-set, clad in Shakespearean attire of doublet and trunk hose: the father of Alice Ramsay. With an effort she banished the older image to the past. "I'm looking forward to seeing him." *But am I?* she wondered in sudden anxiety. Would her relationship with Dad ever be the same with the shadow of this strange dark secret between them? A secret involving reincarnation, and witches and warlocks and the spirits that aided them—things that her father, with his disciplined, rational mind, could never accept.

"And to sleeping in your own bed again, I'm sure. Well, it's very good of you to house-sit for me and keep Doris company. I'll see you both soon. Bye for now!"

"Goodbye," said Claire and hung up the phone. *And I can't tell her either; not because she won't believe me, but because she will. As long as she and Silverhawk and the others don't get involved in this business, they and their families should be safe from the warlocks.* Claire felt determined, but also horribly alone.

She locked up the house and climbed the stairs to her own guest room. There was a line of light under Mrs. Hodge's door, and she wondered what the housekeeper's return meant. The sudden recovery of her aunt freed Mrs. Hodge to go back to Willowmere, ending Claire's solitude. Did the warlocks not intend to mount another attack tonight, then? Or would they just go ahead despite the additional witness? She hoped the former explanation was true.

Claire went to her room, flung herself down on the bed, and closed her eyes. Her head throbbed with tension, and her eyes were so tired they stung. She pulled her glasses off and set them on the nightstand. Her hand met cool metal—of course, the dagger; she'd better hang it up on the wall again before Mrs. Hodge noticed its absence and started asking questions. *Later,* she promised herself. For now, a dull lassitude had fallen over her limbs, and moving seemed too much of an effort. Even her thoughts were slow and torpid, and she felt as though she were sinking down into darkness.

And then she recognized the sensation of dizziness that had come to her before, always when she was about to experience a particularly powerful memory from her previous life. With this one there came a sensation of heat and light, an image of a flat tawny plain . . . Not Scotland. Some other place, much farther away both in distance and in time. A place without a name . . .

She was aware of a great heat; a harsh light came with it, beating down from above. Sunlight, that was what it was—but brighter and fiercer than on the hottest summer day she had ever known. There was a strange landscape around her, brown and blurred at its edges with heat distortion. She looked down, and saw that the body she inhabited was not her own. It was dark, a deep brown-black as though it had baked in the glaring sun. Only a strip of animal hide clothed it, hung about the loins. There were a few other people standing nearby, also dark-skinned with scant clothing of animal hide.

She heard a low rumble in the distance and turned to see thunderheads looming on the arid horizon, their soaring heights dazzling white in the evening sun, their bases dense grey with concentrated moisture. Beneath them the sky was streaked with vertical shadows of falling rain. Thunder boomed out of their depths again, and a wind stirred the dry dust of the plain and sent it spinning through the air.

She stood with her family, gazing in joy and relief at the advancing storm. Rain: they could almost feel it on their parched lips. Birds circled in the wild air currents above, crying out in excitement. The old wizened sorcerer Mamba cackled and capered about, waving his bone staff. "There, you see? Did I not tell you I could bring rain?" he crowed. "You obeyed me, and now I shall reward you. Even those of you who denied my power." His eyes belied his words, full of malice as they turned to her.

She met their black gaze with her own and said, "I still do not believe it."

The adults and children in her tribe began to murmur in consternation, and the one surviving baby cried. They all moved away from her, half-unconsciously removing themselves from her vicinity and the reach of the sorcerer's wrath.

She spoke again. "If you can bring the rain, old man, why did you wait so long? Our people suffered from thirst and famine, and two of the children died, and still you did nothing. If you can make rain, then I say you were wicked to withhold it and cause them to die. But I do not believe you had anything at all to do with it. You are only a man, a little old man, and the sky is greater than you. The winds and the clouds are greater than you. How could you command them? Tell me that."

Mamba advanced on her, holding out the staff with its mongoose skull; she made herself stand firm as her adopted family cried out in fear. Let them see me stand up to him, *she thought,* and perhaps they will find their own courage.

"Flower-in-a-drought," her foster mother cried. "Please, please, you cannot do this. It is the heat that has turned your head. Wise one, forgive her!"—to the sorcerer. "She is sun-touched. She does not know what she is saying!"

"She knows," rasped the old man. His own voice was brittle with thirst, his lips as parched as the fissured earth at his feet. "This one has never respected me, never! But have a care,

drought-flower, or I will wither you. I will hold back the rain. Yes, yes—even now I can turn it away, stop it falling, if I am angered!"

"Flower!" her foster mother wailed. "For us, please, do it for us! Ask his pardon!" The children wailed.

Her heart was wrung with pity for them. But their fear was baseless; she had to show them that, or they would dwell in its shadow for as long as this evil man lived. "Stop it then," she told Mamba, ignoring the gasps and moans of the others. "If you can do that, then do it. We have had only words out of you so far. Show us this magic."

A silence fell, punctuated only by the sonorous voice of approaching thunder. The storm was nearly upon them. At the dried-up water hole nearby the few surviving animals had ceased to paw at the mud and were moving about: hyenas, jackals, warthogs, a few buffaloes and gazelles, some great cats, all of them pacing and snuffing the air. The energy of the advancing storm seemed to have gone into them. The rain would come; the old man could not stop it. The tribe would see that he had no real power.

His dark eyes flickered; he too realized this. At last he said, "I choose not to stop it. I will not punish everyone for your disbelief."

She raised her chin. "You have no magic. If you had, you would stop the rain to show your power." A clap of thunder followed, almost like a confirmation of her words. The rest of the tribe looked from her to Mamba and back again.

He glared at her for a moment in impotent hatred. Then with the shrill cry he said, "I will show you my power!"

He pointed with the bone staff at the bed of mud. A leopard that was lying at its edge raised its head, then rose to all fours and came padding towards the group.

"Kill her!" the sorcerer shrieked, pointing to Flower-in-a-drought.

The leopard growled low, its yellow eyes glinting. It stalked towards Flower. She stood, the blood beating in her ears, her heart lurching about in her chest. Screams came from behind her as her family retreated. But she could not seem to move.

It is true: he has magic, *she thought in the slow seconds as the leopard crouched to spring, muscles bunching under hide, an enmity in its eyes to match its master's.* I was wrong, he is a sorcerer after all; and now I will die . . . *The air was heavy with heat and dust; she could not catch her breath. A grating roar split the air.*

But it was not the leopard roaring.

The great cat leaped sideways out of its crouch, startled. On the other side of the mud bed another tawny shape reared up, blotched with the dirt in which it had lain. It was the young lion with the half-grown mane. Across the distance her eyes met his and her mind pleaded, Help me.

The lion roared again, shook his shaggy head, took a step forward. The leopard spun to meet the larger beast, snarling its defiance. The sorcerer yelled and waved his staff in frustration.

And the lion charged. Across the dead dried remains of the pond he ran, ears flat, eyes blazing, his great mouth open to show its yellowed fangs. The leopard did not try to meet the charge but wheeled away, a blur of black on gold, speeding in panicked flight over the plain. The lion came on, not swerving to follow its fleeing opponent, but straight on towards Flower-in-a-drought.

Still she stood unmoving. There was no time for fear or amazement. The great beast came right up to her, slowed, then turned about to stand at her side, flanks heaving. His teeth no longer showed.

Do not be afraid, *a voice said in her thoughts.* I am your friend.

Filled with wonder, Flower-in-a-drought laid her hand upon the thick tufts of the lion's mane, and the huge beast leaned into her caress. With a wail of rage and defeat the sorcerer fled after the leopard. The rest of the tribe stood motionless, too fascinated to flee, watching as she stroked the lion's head.

My friend, my spirit, *she thought.* I always knew we belonged to one another . . .

With another rolling boom the heavy clouds swept over their heads, shutting out the glaring sun; and the rain fell down upon the wasted land . . .

◇ ◇ ◇

Claire came back to herself with a sudden jolt. For a moment she looked in bewilderment at her surroundings, at her own body still sprawled on the bed, the images blurred at the edges with myopia. Then her head sank back onto the pillow.

Another memory, another life. How many times had she lived, and in how many places? *Who am I?* she wondered again, and she reached out with her mind for her friend, for the only one who had been with her in all those lives and lands. The one constant. "Leo!" she whispered. "Was that our first meeting? Is that how it happened?"

There was no reply. But from far away in the night came the hooting call of an owl.

Chapter 4

THE WEEKEND PASSED UNEVENTFULLY, much to Claire's relief. There were no more visions or other unnerving manifestations, and the warlocks remained out of sight. Her last two days at Willowmere were bright and clear with no wind; the sun was warm, and the trees in the garden were kindled with colour. Golden and red leaves floated on the pool above the swimming carp and lay scattered on the lawns. The lake was Mediterranean blue, flecked here and there with the white sails of pleasure craft: some local sailors, taking advantage of this autumn's unusually warm weather, had not yet taken their boats out of the water at the marina. Claire spent much of her time outdoors, exercising the dog, walking on the shore. She noticed dozens of crows cawing and circling over the warlocks' property next door; occasionally a few would break away from the spinning mass and fly over Willowmere, then return to the main flock. She forced herself to ignore them. Let the van Burens' spies see her living a perfectly normal life, she thought. That was a victory in itself: showing them that she was not going to be intimidated.

But normality was the last thing on her mind. She thought a great deal about the new memory the previous night had brought her. *Where was that place? It looked like Africa. But in what time?* Somehow, she felt certain that this other, more ancient life was the key to understanding both her later life in Scotland and her present existence. But there was nothing about it in Al Ramsay's writings. Disappointed, she returned to that part of his journal that described Alice's reincarnation into a new life and body here in suburban Willowville. No names were mentioned in these notes—perhaps Al Ramsay suspected that an enemy might one day read them—but certain details pointed to Claire's family: the death of a pet cat from a wild dog's attack (Claire's own cat, Whiskers, had died just that way), and the mother's seeming abandonment of her family. "I understand that she has left town, and that the rest of the family has not followed her. Perhaps she told her husband the story I told her, and he wouldn't believe it, causing a rift between them. Or she may want to pursue a relationship with her own daimon-familiar, but does not wish to expose the rest of her family to danger." Her mother and old Mr. Ramsay had met. Why hadn't she said anything to Claire about the meeting? They had always told one another everything. Had she been too frightened to talk of it, perhaps? How had Ramsay managed to convince her of the veracity of his outlandish story and the threat to her daughter? Claire needed to know so much more. She read on: "I feel very sad, for the reborn Alice is now at an age when girls need their mothers most. I cannot help feeling somewhat responsible. If I did not know that her spirit guardian Leo was still watching over her I would be worried. But of course he's more careful with his animal hosts now, since the cat was killed."

Leo . . . Yes, he was watching her. But if only he would talk to her! She needed a friend, a confidant, and she dared not expose another human being to the danger of the warlocks.

✧ ✧ ✧

Myra returned early on Sunday afternoon. Claire and Angus ran out to meet her yellow Beetle as it trundled up the drive, tooting its horn merrily. Myra emerged from the car looking rumpled but happy, and was almost bowled over by the collie, so huge was his joy at seeing his mistress again.

"Down, Angus MacTavish, down . . . I had the loveliest time, dear, everyone was just wonderful to me. Yes, please, I would love a hand with the luggage—I swore I was going to pack light for this trip but it's not like going to the jungle, you can't get away with two or three casual outfits . . . Down, Angus! And of course I bought a few things while I was away, not that there was much time for shopping with all the interviews and things . . . Angus, will you please calm down!"

Claire could not help stealing little side glances at her as they walked to the front steps. She looked relaxed and happy—not in the least like a woman bearing the burden of a strange and terrifying secret, the knowledge of the existence of otherworldly spirits and the frightening powers they conferred on some human beings. But perhaps she had borne her knowledge of these things for so long that it no longer showed as a physical stress; perhaps she had simply grown used to it. At any rate, she gave no sign that anything weighed more heavily on her than the suitcase in her hand.

"I'm back, Doris! You're free to go, my dear," called Myra as she entered the front hall. Mrs. Hodge came down the stairs with her own small suitcase and threw a sheepish glance at Claire. The girl said nothing. She would have to explain the broken window, but not until Myra saw it. Let the poor woman at least get her luggage inside and put her feet up, Claire decided, before hitting her with anything else.

As she crossed the hall with some shopping bags in hand, Claire's eye fell on the portrait in the drawing room. For an instant the painted eyes seemed to lock onto hers, and she felt a tremor go through her; it was as if her past self tried to reach across the centuries to her present one. Alice and Myra were blood kin—distant, separated by many generations, but still offshoots of one clan. *Don't let anything happen to Myra,* the portrait seemed to say. *She is family* . . . And Claire felt this was true; though there was no genetic link between her present body and Myra's, still she felt a great affection for the older woman, a bond that ran even deeper than friendship. She felt responsible for her safety.

They unloaded the car and carried all the bags and suitcases upstairs to Myra's room. "There!" said Myra. "I won't unpack them just yet. I'm exhausted, and you must be too. How about a cup of tea or something before you go? Let's go down to the kitchen!"

Claire drew a deep breath. "Myra, there's something I've got to tell you." As they descended the staircase she explained about Josie and the break-in. "I guess cursing and hexes weren't getting her anywhere, so she went for some more obvious intimidation tactics instead."

"Oh, my," Myra said when she saw the window. "That really is carrying things too far. You say you saw the girl do this?"

"Well—I didn't actually see her," said Claire. "I was upstairs. She broke in and came inside the house, and she—sort of confronted me. Tried to scare me."

"How awful! And Doris, where was she? Did she tell the girl to leave?"

Claire hesitated. "Mrs. Hodge wasn't here. She went to see her old aunt. It was an actual emergency this time, so she really did have to go."

"You don't mean to say you were all alone?" Myra looked appalled.

"Oh, it was no big deal." Claire shrugged. "I would have been alone at home, too."

"But how did this Josie girl know you were by yourself? It sounds almost as though she'd been spying on you."

"She was. Believe me, Josie is major trouble. But she stepped over the line this time. I'll see that she's punished for this and pays for your window."

"It's a pity Doris wasn't here to provide an extra witness. Not that your word wouldn't be accepted over Josie's, I'm sure. Anyone can see you have a better character."

"There'll be fingerprints too. Myra, I'm so sorry I brought all this trouble into your place. I really hate that it happened here. Josie didn't steal anything, at least—I checked, and nothing's missing."

"Goodness, Claire, it's not your fault. I really should have a burglar alarm in this house. There are some quite valuable things in Al's collection, and the parrots are worth a lot too. Angus alone isn't enough of a deterrent. My uncle never bothered with a security system, but it's clear I'll have to do something about it. Now how about that tea? And maybe a snack as well—I'm famished."

✧ ✧ ✧

After she and Myra had some tea and sandwiches and some more perfectly normal conversation, Claire packed up her things and cycled home. Her father was catching an early flight Monday morning and would go straight on to work before returning home in the late afternoon. So she would have one night on her own at home. But she doubted Josie would try anything, remembering the look of fear in the girl's eyes.

Still, the Dark Circle was another matter. She glanced out the front window at the maple tree. No barred owl was perching there—but there wouldn't be, not in broad daylight. He'd be using another form, probably a small one that wouldn't be too obvious to any of the warlocks' own spies. But Leo was watching over her, she was sure. If only he would talk to her!

She went to her room and stood gazing around her. It was strange to think of the girl who had left this bedroom at the start of the week—a different girl entirely from the one who had now returned. Nothing, she thought dismally, would ever be the same. She glanced at her nightstand. A paperback by one of her favourite fantasy authors was still lying where she had set it aside, back when she was still just Claire Norton and seeking excitement in books. She picked it up and stared for a moment at the cover. It was a moonlit scene: a girl in a gauzy, glittering dress was dancing with a handsome prince on a lawn jewelled with flowers. A marble fountain shaped like a dragon sent up a misty plume of spray in the background, and in the distance was a lamplit palace with fantastical pointed turrets. Above this in medieval lettering was the title, *A Princess of Faerie*. Claire had been drawn to the book mostly by its cover and had been quite enjoying the story. Now she put it down, wondering if she would ever finish it. Why read fantasies of fairies and knights and quests when your real life made them seem tame by comparison?

Suddenly some words came into her head from another book, the one on natural magic that she had bought at Books & Magic: "The dream quest began with a rite of purification, usually a long bath in a river or lake. Having endured his immersion in the frigid waters, the boy would then go out alone into the wilderness, far from the tents of his family and community, there to observe a fast that might go on for many days. At the end of the fasting period, according to tradition, the spirit guide would then speak to him or perhaps appear in the likeness of an animal."

A dream quest. She knew what a quest was, from reading all those fantasy stories. It was a journey you undertook to search for something—like King Arthur's knights setting out to find the Holy Grail. In a dream quest you were supposed to be in search of some form of spiritual enlightenment. The spirit guide was just that—a guide, a helper who assisted you on your way. That tied in with the Er story, and with what Myra had once told her about the ancient Greek concept of the *daimon:* a being who led you to your proper destiny in life. *Could* there really be something in all those old stories? Might performing a ritual like the Ojibwa one somehow compel her guardian daimon to speak to her, to come to her? Claire pondered the idea at length. She was desperate enough to try anything, she finally decided, to get Leo's guidance and advice. To have someone to talk to, someone that the warlocks couldn't hurt . . .

A purification ritual—bathing in cold water and fasting in the wilderness . . . how hard could it be? Feeling a little foolish, but also with a firmer set to her jaw, she headed for the bathroom.

✧ ✧ ✧

Instead of her usual quick hot shower she took a long and cold one. The purpose of immersing yourself in the chill waters of a lake or river, according to the book, was to test your endurance, prove yourself the master of your own body. The fast achieved the same. With the flesh subordinated, the mind took over, and sometimes the result was a sacred vision. Perhaps there was something to it; who could say? People in modern times never really tested their physical limits, beyond the occasional bit of exercise. They were accustomed to comfort, free to pamper their bodies, eat as much as they liked, fuss over their skin and hair. Claire wasn't quite as self-indulgent as some girls her age, but as she stood shivering in the frigid streams from the showerhead it took a greater effort of will than she would have thought possible not to spring out of the tub and run for a towel.

At last she turned off the water and stepped out onto the bathmat, her teeth chattering and her head aching from the cold. So far, she thought, this business of "rejecting the flesh" had only made her much more aware of it. When she towelled herself off, however, her skin began to tingle and she felt a warmth deep within her limbs and torso. As she dressed again that internal radiance seemed to spread and fill her entire body. Was this what the ancient practitioners of the dream quests had felt?

First, purification by water. Then fasting—that wouldn't present any problems, though she hoped it wouldn't have to go on for days. Dad would certainly notice her not eating and start fretting about anorexia in his overprotective way. Since lunch wasn't too long ago, she decided to wait until five o'clock when the first little hunger pangs started in her stomach. Then she put on a light jacket, locked up the house, and walked across the street.

One block to the west lay Birch Street, the main north–south road running through the centre of town. She walked through a little lane and onto the east side of Birch, the one that had a sidewalk. Across the street lay the ravine, with Willow Creek at the bottom. The houses on the ravine side were popular and highly valued; they had a view of the creek and in some cases flights of wooden stairs leading down to it. More houses had been built since the days of Claire's childhood, but there was still one place towards the top of Birch that was undeveloped. Claire had often come here with her best friend Ainsley Wayne. They would cycle from their former homes on Elm Street, leave their bikes by the road and scramble down through the trees and shaggy undergrowth covering the slope. At the bottom lay a strip of flat, muddy ground bordering the wide, slow-moving creek. In the summertime, with the leaves thick on the trees, the houses on both sides of the ravine were screened from view and even the high rises at the west end of town couldn't be seen. The place seemed utterly wild. She and Ainsley had once spotted a muskrat swimming near the shore and a pair of swans nesting in a bed of reeds out in the middle of the stream.

She hadn't returned to this place since Ainsley moved away, four years ago. Now she stood gazing around her thoughtfully. It wasn't perhaps a real wilderness, but it was as close as she could come to one in the suburbs of Willowville. And autumn was when the ravine was at its best. The willows' falling curtains of fronds were turning from green to gold, the oak leaves were like beaten copper, and the maples were every shade from buttery yellow to orange to deepest red. Their colours reflected in the placid surface of the creek. The reed beds had lost their vivid summer green and were now the same dull brown as the flats of mud on which they stood, but the stands of sumac along the shore were brilliant scarlet. Many of the trees were shedding their leaves, turning the ground beneath their boughs to a multi-coloured patchwork; the birches had already lost most of theirs, and against the brilliant autumn hues their branches stood out white and bare as bone. But there was still enough foliage to hide the houses behind and preserve the illusion of wildness. No one was out canoeing or kayaking today; nothing moved on the water except a flock of Canada geese paddling slowly downstream. It was as if she had gone back in time and was looking at the creek as it would have appeared hundreds of years ago.

Claire found a fallen tree not far from the edge of the water and sat down on the rotting trunk. She had no idea what was involved in meditation, but she knew it was more than just sitting and thinking. You had to empty your mind and relax completely at the same time—go into a sort of trance. Claire had to wonder how fasting would help to achieve that. All she could think of when she closed her mind was how very empty her stomach felt. The cool breeze blowing across the water made her shiver again. The internal glow had vanished from her body, and the bark of the dead tree felt clammy through her jeans.

Concentrate, she thought. *Centre yourself.* She tried to shift attention from herself and her bodily discomfort to the sounds of the ravine: water flowing, trees stirring in the breeze, chirps of sparrows and other small birds. The air was full of a smell of decay that was yet wholesome: rich, earthy, organic, the aroma of leaves returning to the soil. She breathed it in, felt the warmth of the sun's rays on her upraised face. It was so hard to shut out the world. Maybe she shouldn't even try. Maybe she should just let her consciousness blend with it—become a part of it, experiencing each sensation but not giving any thought to it. She must have no thought but one.

Leo, she called out silently. *Leo, come back. Talk to me. Show yourself to me. I need a friend.* She tried picturing her guardian spirit as the various animal hosts he had inhabited: her old grey-and-white cat Whiskers, the barred owl, the white cat of Alice's day, the lion on the African plain. People had once believed that witches' familiars were shape-shifters, able to take any animal or human form. But Leo had explained to her long ago that he had no body of his own, and entered into the bodies of living things and then left them again, so it merely appeared that he was altering his form over time. If he came to her here, would it be in the body of the owl or some other creature? How would she know him when she saw him?

There was no answer except leaf-rustle and birdsong. In the distance she heard the hum of traffic on the bridge and on the road above.

This is useless—useless! Claire opened her eyes and sprang up from the log. *I'm just wasting my time* . . .

Then she froze where she stood.

He was very small and almost the same colour as the leaves, reddish-gold, so she didn't see him at first, not until he mewed softly. Then she gasped and stared. Could it be . . . Was this the answer to her rite? Claire squatted down in the leaves and held out her hand. The kitten neither retreated nor approached, merely held its ground, considering her through large amber-coloured eyes. Then it mewed a second time and finally took a step towards her hand, sniffing at her fingers. It did not show the timidity of a stray, but it had no identifying tag and collar. It might belong to one of the homes in the ravine, but who would be so irresponsible as to let a tiny kitten wander loose with no tag—especially with foxes and coyotes on the prowl in the woods along the creek? The kitten mewed again, and Claire came back to reality. Whether he was her familiar returned in an animal host or had just shown up by mere coincidence, this animal was all alone and in need of food and shelter.

"You'd better come with me, kitty," Claire said. "If you stay here something's going to munch you up come nightfall. Here, just let me come a little closer—that's it . . ."

She used a soothing voice, and the kitten uttered a faint meow as she picked him up carefully in both hands—a sound that might have meant pleasure or protest at being handled. But he did not struggle, and when she held him close to her chest she felt a purr rumble through his tiny body. She began to climb the slope back up to the road, clutching twigs and tree trunks with one hand and cradling him in the other.

The kitten consented to all of this, much to her relief; she had been afraid he would squirm out of her grip and run away again. Once she was clear of the ravine she held him with both hands, talking to him in a calming tone as she crossed the street and headed for home.

"Isn't he adorable!" exclaimed a woman passing by on the sidewalk.

"He isn't mine, actually," said Claire. "I found him wandering in the ravine, down by the creek. I wondered if maybe he belonged to someone around here."

"Well, I live in the neighbourhood and I've never seen him before," the woman said. "He might be a house cat that got loose. Better take him to the Humane Society."

Claire nodded and walked on. The Humane Society would have to wait until tomorrow, when her father came back and could drive them there. For now, she would have to look after the kitten herself. If no one claimed him, she was going to keep him. Somehow, she felt certain that no one would claim him. His arrival was too coincidental—too magical—to be anything but part of some plan of Leo's.

Once she was in the house she set the kitten down. He stood still for a moment, ears and whiskers twitching, then began to explore. He went into each room, sniffing the carpet and furniture, jumping up onto the sofa in the den. Then he hopped onto a windowsill and stared at the view with interest.

"No way," Claire said. "You're staying inside, fella."

She went into the kitchen and he jumped down again and followed her. She wondered when his last meal had been and what he could have found to eat. He looked very thin, and she had felt all his little ribs as she carried him in her arms. But he had plenty of energy and didn't look sick. Tomorrow a vet would examine him, but if he showed any signs of illness today she'd call a cab and take him right away.

His appetite was healthy, anyway. When she opened a can of flaked tuna and set it on the floor in an old clay ashtray, he pounced on the food at once and gobbled it down. She was afraid for a moment that she'd given him too much and he would throw it all up, but it stayed down and he showed no sign of discomfort afterwards. Claire set down another saucer full of water, but he ignored it and went sniffing around the kitchen instead. She opened the cupboard under the sink and he darted inside, thrilled at the sudden appearance of this new cave.

Claire knew that her father used kitty litter in the winter to sand the ice on the front path and driveway, so she went down to the basement and fetched what remained of last winter's supply. It was probably too much to hope the kitten was house-broken, but she filled a shallow cardboard box with litter anyway and set it on the kitchen floor not far from his dishes.

She smiled to herself. Already she was thinking of things as being "his." He *was* male, that much she knew; she had read somewhere that a solid marmalade colouring occurred only in male cats. She would come up with a name for him later. As Claire made her own dinner in the microwave she went over all her arguments in her head: "First of all, Dad, he's a stray so he's free . . . Yeah, I know there's no such thing as a free kitten, there'll be vet bills and a licence and stuff, but I can pay you back in summer when I have a job . . . and he'll be fine on his own all day, cats can stay in the house and they're low maintenance, they amuse themselves and they don't have to be walked . . . And anyway he'll be company for me . . ."

The kitten sat by her chair as she ate her macaroni. He tried leaping up on the table, but she was quick to discourage that, setting him firmly down on the floor again. He looked up at her so imploringly that in the end she gave him a little bit of macaroni, which he sniffed at and abandoned in disgust. She talked to him the whole time in a quiet voice, partly to make him feel at home, but also reflecting all the while that it was nice for her to have someone to talk to even if he couldn't answer back. It was impossible to feel truly lonely with an animal in the room. After dinner and washing up, the kitten followed her into the den and sat on her notes while she tried to do her homework. Then he climbed onto her lap as she watched TV, throbbing all over with a purr that seemed too big for his tiny body.

When she turned out all the lights he followed her upstairs and sprang onto her bed. "Uh-uh," she said, shooing him off.

"Not till I'm sure you're housebroken." But in the end she gave in, because he wailed so pitifully when she closed the door on him. He snuggled into the small of her back, warm and purring, soothing her. It was, she remembered, exactly what Whiskers had always done.

But despite that comforting presence, she didn't fall asleep. She had been lying there only a few moments when she had a strange sensation: it seemed to her that a strong light was beating against her eyelids. And she had a peculiar feeling that she was no longer lying flat, but drifting through space. She couldn't feel the bed beneath her, nor the blankets on top of her. After a moment she had the distinct impression that she was standing upright, with a hard level surface beneath her feet. The light on her lids grew brighter.

Alarmed, she opened them—and found herself staring out onto another world.

Chapter 5

THIS WAS NO MEMORY, dredged up from a past life, nor was it a dream. She was standing all by herself in a place she had never seen before. The ground was paved and flat, as flat as a chessboard, stretching in three directions to a knife-sharp horizon. It had a pattern of pale tan squares, several metres across, separated by darker grey lines. Directly in front of her stood a group of buildings. The architecture was all of an old style, with classical pillars and arched colonnades, but the buildings themselves looked new, spotless and perfect. Indeed there was about the whole scene a perfection that was somehow unsettling. Not a roof tile was missing, not a wall stained or chipped; there were no marks anywhere of weathering or use, no dirt on the neatly ordered squares of pavement. In front of the buildings stood two rounded stone structures that looked like wells with steps leading up to them; they were exactly alike and were spaced in such a way as to balance each other perfectly. The sky was a very dark blue, with only a few small grey-white clouds in it. The clouds did not move, and there was no sign of the sun. A soft diffused light came from somewhere to the left, casting grey shadows.

Claire swallowed. She wanted to call out, and yet she was afraid to. There was no one in the town or whatever it was, no sign of a human being, or a dog, or a pigeon, or anything alive except for a few stiff and artificial-looking plants in window boxes. There were no trees, no grassy lawns; the porticoes and arcades of the buildings were surrounded by the pavement. Nothing moved or made a sound in all that unnatural landscape.

Claire began to walk towards the buildings. To her relief, she could actually hear her footfalls on the stone surface; she had begun to fear she had gone deaf. On she went, passing between the two wide-spaced wells, and entered the broad plaza. In the very centre of the clump of buildings was a round two-tiered structure, something like a huge wedding cake. The lower tier was tallest, with pillars crowned by leafy Corinthian capitals; the upper storey was not so high and was smaller in diameter, with shorter pillars ringing its circumference, and the round roof slanted up to a sort of small cupola with a pointed top. A "lantern," perhaps, intended to shed light on the interior. There were windows in the top storey, but not the lower one; that had only a high-pillared doorway whose doors stood ajar, opening inwards.

Claire stood still in front of the doorway, wondering if the open doors were intended as an invitation. It looked very dark inside. She glanced around at the surrounding buildings; their windows, too, opened onto darkness. She could stand the silence no longer.

"Hello?" she called. "Is anyone there?"

There was no answer; her voice echoed back unnervingly from the stark stone walls surrounding her. Then she heard a faint sound. She turned back to the dark doorway. Something crouched on the threshold, something that had not been there before.

It was a kitten. *The* kitten, with the marmalade fur.

She stared. All right, then, this must mean something. If it wasn't a dream—and it didn't feel like one—then the appearance of the kitten could only be linked to the ritual she had performed this afternoon.

She squatted down, as she had done in the ravine, and held out her hand to the little animal. "So," she said, "what's this all about, kitty? Can you tell me? What is this place, and how did we get here?"

The kitten mewed and rose to all fours. Purring loudly, he went up to her hand and rubbed his flank against it—she felt his warmth and his soft fur, as real as they had been before. But none of this could be real. Was it some sort of vision or hallucination? Or was it an illusion? Daimons could do such things, Al Ramsay had written, by a process called nerve induction. They could make you see or hear or feel whatever they wanted.

The kitten sauntered away again, tail in air, still purring. He moved out of her line of sight and she got up and turned, looking for him. But she found that he had gone. In his place stood another figure, human, somewhat taller than she. It was a boy of about her age or slightly older—dressed in strange medieval-looking clothing: a sort of long flared tunic nipped in at the waist and ending at the knees, hose and short leather boots, all in shades of gold and tan. His hair was ginger-coloured, a mass of soft curls falling to his shoulders, topped by a tan cloth cap; his skin was slightly olive-toned, and his large eyes so light a brown that they looked almost amber. He was gazing at her with a quizzical expression, one eyebrow raised and his full lips curving into a half-smile. He looked—she struggled to find a word—impish, puckish, human but with a hint of something else, some alien quality she could not quite identify.

"Who *are* you?" she asked, backing away a little.

The smile broadened, showing the tips of perfect white teeth. "I think you already know the answer to that." His voice was pleasant, low in pitch and gentle. She had the impression that he was trying to soothe her with it, as she had soothed the kitten in the ravine.

Claire was not soothed, however. "Don't play riddle games with me, please! I'm not in the mood."

"But you really do know," he insisted. As she stood watching him, he strolled over to the steps leading up to the door and sat down on them. "One of the things I have always loved about you is the way you think your way through everything. You enjoy using your mind, and that is becoming a rarity in your time. Tell *me* who I am."

Claire stood silent for a moment. "You were the cat a moment ago. You changed your shape."

"Yes. And what does that tell you?"

"That you're not human, for one thing. A human being can't—change like that."

"Both those statements are true," the boy said with a roguish grin. "I am not human, no—and humans can't alter their forms in what you call the real world. But the truth is, anything is possible here, even for human beings. So my shape-shifting doesn't prove I'm not human; you were correct there only by accident." His amber eyes laughed up at her. "Now, what can you conclude from all this?"

She stared back at him. "You're telling me this place isn't real," she said slowly. "Not my kind of reality, anyway."

"Exactly."

"But—*where* is it?"

"It isn't anywhere. 'Where' is a word that belongs to your own dimension, where physical distance separates things from one another. You have—well—crossed over, you could put it, into a reality that is utterly separate from your own. A nonphysical, immortal realm."

"Immortal? This isn't . . ." Claire was beginning to be frightened. "Have . . . have I died?"

"Oh, yes," said the youth. "More than once, actually; you seem to make quite a habit of it. But your present body is alive. You're not in Heaven, if that's what you meant."

Claire went and sat on the steps beside him. He looked utterly real to her, if a bit too flawless: there were no blemishes on his skin, and his features were as perfectly proportioned as a mannequin's. She touched the step underneath her; it felt cool and hard to her fingers, like real stone.

"You're Leo, aren't you?" she said.

"Of course I am." He smiled.

"But you don't really look like this." She indicated his figure and clothing with a wave of her hand. "It's a kind of—disguise. A costume."

"Right again. I don't really look like anything in my own reality. To have a physical appearance you must have a physical body, a solid surface for light rays to bounce off and so create an image in your retina. I have no body. I am all mind. My essence is consciousness, and this plane on which I exist is composed of the shared thoughts of many entities. Are you following me so far?"

"Yes, I think so. You're saying that this whole place"—she waved her hand at the unnatural sky, the eerie, perfect buildings and limitless plain—"is all in our minds?"

"That's correct. Does that disturb you?"

"No, but . . . Couldn't you have made it, well, realer-looking? That sky is so weird, and the buildings—it all looks like a painting."

"It *is* a painting. This simulation is based on a work called *Ideal City* by the Italian Renaissance painter Piero della Francesca. Many painters of his day created such scenes to demonstrate their skill at the art of perspective—which was still fairly new back then. In this simulation we've taken the concept of imaginary space one step further, turning two dimensions to three. We have other simulations that you cannot distinguish from your own world, so great is the attention to detail. But I thought it best to bring your consciousness first to a simulation that was obviously artificial, so you could more easily accept that it wasn't real. I didn't want to confuse you too much at first."

Claire pinched herself. "Ouch!" she exclaimed. "How can I feel pain if this isn't the real world?"

"Your *mind* feels pain. An amputee's subconscious mind sometimes conjures up a phantom limb to replace the lost one, and actually feels pain in that limb—even though the real one no longer exists. One might say the pain is all in his head, but he experiences it nonetheless. Your mind may be on this plane with me, but it hasn't broken loose and drifted away; it's still attached to your living body and brain."

Claire reached out, touched his long loose sleeve. It swayed, rustling. "You feel real. That cloth, I—*moved* it."

"This is mental space," Leo told her. "It responds to your mental form as the physical world responds to physical stimuli. But because it's a world of thought, it's a little more—malleable than matter."

She stood and began to walk around the circular structure. “How big is this place? Are those hills I see over there in the distance?”

“Yes—we call them the Ideal Hills, as they are rendered in a stylized painterly fashion. They are largely conjectural, since the buildings in della Francesca’s painting block most of the view of the countryside beyond. They lie to what you would call the north, if this place were on a planet with poles. The paved surface stretches to infinity in the other three directions, as the painting gives no idea where it ends, but we have added a curve to suggest the shape of a round Earth.”

“Do those buildings have interiors?”

“Yes, they do. Of course in mental space we’re not limited by the physical constraints of your material space, and so in some of our other simulations a building may be bigger on the inside than the outside, for instance. We have some amusing ones based on prints by Escher. But here in the della Francesca simulation we adhere strictly to the spirit of the original painting and aim for high realism.”

Claire turned back towards him. “Leo, tell me more about you—about daimons. Are you really just loose, floating minds without bodies?” she asked, sitting down again.

“You could put it that way,” Leo said. “Why should that seem strange to you? After all, you humans have known or suspected from earliest times that you share your world with other entities, beings immortal and invisible. We show up in your folklore and mythology as demons, Jinni, fairies, totem spirits, familiars. The human friends of daimons have been mythologized too, as shamans, wizards, and witches. Many stories have been embellished, others made up, but in all these traditions there is a tiny kernel of truth.”

"And that Ojibwa-style ritual I did today—was that really magic? Did you *have* to come to me when I did it?"

"No. Let me explain: we daimons decided long ago that we would not meddle with human beings and their lives. But we agreed that we *would* come to any human who reached out to us on the plane of consciousness. That's what you're doing in such rituals: raising your mind to this higher plane, where your kind and mine can mingle.

"We are unable to enter your physical universe directly, and so we manifest ourselves to you as projected illusions, or by using the bodies of animals as hosts. We don't *possess* the bodies of animals, like the evil demons of your folklore; the relationship is a symbiotic one. The animal provides the daimon with a material form that can navigate your material world, and five senses that relay information about it. We daimons are fascinated by your physical universe, and always eager to learn more about it. In return, we care for the animals that are our chosen hosts, helping them to avoid danger, nudging them towards shelter and food sources that we have learned about from other daimons . . .

"It wasn't always like this. In the beginning we were conscious only of ourselves. We had no true identity, no individuality, and nothing separated us. We thought only in abstract concepts. Mathematics, mostly; we knew all about numbers, of course. Irrational numbers in particular fascinated us."

In spite of herself she began to smile. "Poor you. I'm not bad at math, but I wouldn't want to spend my whole life doing it. So you daimons just floated around in your mind-universe, doing stuff like calculating pi and exploring the Mandelbrot set?"

"We had philosophical thoughts, too, not unlike those raised by some of your great thinkers. *Cogito ergo sum:* 'I think, therefore I am.' But then something peculiar happened. We began to receive signals from minds we couldn't identify—vague impressions that made no sense. There were images, too, of darkness and light, of inanimate objects. We had no idea such things could exist. What we were sensing were the first flickerings of consciousness in the first sentient beings in your universe. Arguments broke out in our dimension. It appeared there was another universe, a different one from ours, but until primitive minds arose within it there was nothing to bridge it with ours. A *physical universe*. How could that be? Things like rocks and plants made no sense to us. How could a thing exist if it wasn't *aware* of its own existence, if it didn't know itself? But at last we came to accept your reality, to study and explore it."

He stood up, and she also rose to her feet. "Have I been here before?" she asked. "Not that it looks familiar or anything, but I'm just wondering. I don't recall anything like this from when I was Alice Ramsay."

"You have been to my dimension before," he said as he walked on through the paved space between the buildings. "Not to this particular simulation, but to others. Between incarnations, when your consciousness was freed from its physical limitations, you enjoyed exploring our re-created environments."

"I don't remember any of that."

"Memory loss is usual for a revenant. A physical brain, after all, cannot be expected to store memories that predate its own existence."

She stopped walking and stared at him. "*What* did you call me?"

"A revenant."

"And what is that?"

"A term we've borrowed from your language and culture. Technically, it refers to folkloric figures such as ghosts, or to the living dead: people who were believed to return from the grave to avenge past wrongs or settle other kinds of unfinished business. But I believe the word can apply just as well to an individual like yourself, whose consciousness returns to the physical plane and re-establishes itself in a new body."

"Reincarnation, you mean?"

"That's another word for it. We use *revenant* because that word comes from the French *revenir,* 'to return,' and implies that there is reason for that return. Revenants actually aren't all that common—at least, as far as we can tell. It's rare for a mind that returns to be fully aware of its past lives. For that to happen, the memories must be accessed through your daimon, who safeguards all your past experiences for you. And few are the individuals who can communicate with their daimons.

"Some sense of purpose seems to guide most revenants."

"Then there are others like me? Who are they?"

"I can't tell you. Sorry. Some information is privileged, and we must respect the privacy of others."

"I bet Al Ramsay was one."

"Now you're fishing." He laughed.

"But he's dead. Privacy can't be an issue there."

"He is between lives. For all we know he may return again, as you have done."

"Well, what other lives have I lived? Come on, you can tell me that. It's my own business."

"Of course. Just the two, not counting your current life. We first met when you were Flower-in-a-drought. That was your very first name, in a time before history, before myth and legend, when you lived in the far off deserts of Africa—which was not yet known by that name. When you defied the evil old shaman Mamba and his daimon ally, Phobetor would have slain you using the body of the leopard that he controlled. But you summoned me, and I came to your defence."

She nodded, recognizing the new memory. "By taking the body of a lion."

"Yes. I foiled Phobetor by driving his leopard host away, and Mamba was filled with fear and fled, and your people were delivered from the fear of him, for they saw that you were stronger. The girl with the lion spirit! You became the leader of your people, until you died at the age of twenty-six."

"I did? Leo, this is scary. Am I doomed always to die young or something?"

He smiled. "Actually, twenty-six was a ripe old age for those times. And you had many children, healthy, robust children who survived as you did and raised offspring as strong as they. In fact, your line was so successful that it survives to the present day. There are in your world countless people of many races and countries whose genetic ancestry can be traced back to Flower-in-a-drought. You are a mother of millions. Perhaps that's why you have such protective feelings about your species."

A mother. Claire processed this statement in awed silence. She had been a mother, once—had had a husband and children. More than that, she had descendants living in the present day—not merely relations, like Myra Moore, but direct descendants of her former body . . .

"The time of Flower-in-a-drought was a perilous one for the human race," Leo went on. "Due to climatic conditions in the African continent, vast numbers of the newly emerged *Homo sapiens* perished—in fact the entire human population dropped to mere tens of thousands. Your species came quite close to extinction back in that age of drought. But it survived, thanks to the strong will to live and adaptability of the remaining groups. That's why modern humans all over the Earth are so similar genetically: all are descended from those few survivors in prehistoric Africa.

"Your own genetic line—Flower-in-a-drought's—continued right through the mass migrations and long pageant of history that followed. And then, many thousands of years later in the seventeenth century, a curious thing happened. A young Scottish woman named Anne Strachan told her family that she had had a vision in which a voice told her she would give birth to a child with 'a lion's spirit'—"

Suddenly Claire understood. "My mother in Scotland—Lady Anne! Of course! I see it now: Malcolm Ramsay must have heard about her prophecy and thought it meant her child would grow up to be king of Britain. Lions are symbols for royalty. So that's why he married her!"

Leo nodded. "His dream was to have an heir who would claim the throne. But in fact the 'vision' was a communication from Anne's daimon and really meant that Flower-in-a-drought was going to be born again—the girl whose daimon first came to her in a lion's form."

Claire sat still for a while, absorbing these things in wonderment. "Why," she asked Leo presently, "didn't you tell me all of this before?"

"We don't like to interfere in such matters. Your memories were for you to rediscover; it is usual to come to them gradually. But a part of you knew, or suspected—for when you were Alice you named me Leo, the Lion." There was a pause, then he continued: "I watched the Ramsay family for centuries after your death, saw your half-sisters marry and their lines die out, until only the line of your half-brother, Wallace Ramsay, remained—the little brother you never knew. I saw his descendants cross the sea with the relics of their old estate, including your portrait. They settled in the New World, in the town of Willowville that had just been founded back in 1821. You were with me in the daimon realm then, and you told me wistfully that your kin had fulfilled your long desire to live in the western lands. You said you would like to be reborn in that town, near the people you still thought of as family. But still you lingered on this plane, hoping that William Macfarlane would also be reborn someday, somewhere, so you could be reunited with him. While you waited I continued to watch the Ramsay generations grow up. I saw young Alfred Ramsay become a world traveller and ultimately a shaman in full contact with his daimon, while his sister Edith married a man named Moore and had one child, a daughter who never married. Alfred never married either, and as he and his niece Myra grew older I suggested you re-enter the world while they still lived, since they were all that remained of your family. And Alfred might have been able to help you."

"Help me with what? Why was I sent back? What am I supposed to do?"

"You weren't *sent* back. A revenant chooses when and whether to return. Some have specific deeds they want to accomplish; others want to teach and guide their fellow humans. You always seem to pick an interesting age to be reborn in: a time of growth, of innovation, with steadily expanding knowledge and frontiers. In your present time, space is being explored and genes are being decoded and new discoveries are being made every day. In your second life, the New World was being explored and settled and advances were being made in medicine and physics and astronomy. But unfortunately the Renaissance was also a time when superstition was rife."

"The witch trials," commented Claire.

"Yes. You choose times when there is danger too, no doubt because you wish to steer your species onto the right path and help them to avoid mistakes. Buddhism tells of the *bodhisattvas*—people who turn back from the bliss of nirvana and choose reincarnation so they can enlighten others who are still living. You are rather like that. In the Renaissance, knowledge and ignorance hung together in a precarious balance, and you returned to Earth to fight the ignorance just as you had fought and defeated it in ancient Africa. Sadly, you only became a victim of it in Scotland. After your death you waited for centuries, hoping that your William would be reincarnated and thinking of nothing else. But at last you set that hope aside, choosing instead to become incarnate in the present time and share your insights with others. For fear is rearing its head in this age, too. It may not be as widespread and blatant as the witch craze, but it is there nonetheless."

"The van Burens and their daimon allies," said Claire. "I see. I came back to fight them, to stop whatever it is they're trying to do to my world." Another little silence fell between them. Then she spoke again. "Leo—do you think William will ever be reborn? Will I get to meet him again?"

"I can't say for certain. I know you still love him, even though he's long dead. But this is a new life you have, here and now. Don't deny yourself a new love should it come to you. Or perhaps you won't need one at all. You may have a life like Myra Moore's, travel all over the world and have a brilliant career. It's for you to decide. But think how you would have loved having these opportunities back when you were Alice Ramsay or Flower-in-a-drought. In those lives you hadn't a fraction of the freedom you know now."

Claire said nothing for a moment. She glanced back at the round building. “Is there anything inside that?” she asked, pointing. “Or is it just empty?”

“We were able to extrapolate an interior based on the building’s design,” Leo told her. “The decor is of course conjectural, but in keeping with the period of the painting. One of my colleagues has been making use of it.” He held out a hand. “Would you like to see it?”

She took his hand—it felt exactly like warm, real flesh, even to the hardness of the bones within—and walked with him to the building’s entrance. It was not, after all, as dark as it had first appeared. The light from the deep blue sky slanted down through the windows of the upper level and from the lantern in the ceiling. Inside it was all one vast circular chamber. “The Rotunda, we call this place,” Leo said. “You may be familiar with the architectural term. It just means round.”

“Uh-huh—as in ‘rotund.’” Claire looked around the interior of the building. It was a library, with circular shelves crammed with books—all ancient-looking tomes apparently bound in calfskin to fit the time period. There were wooden ladders reaching up to the higher, less accessible shelves. The floor was paved with white-and-gold tiles in a pattern of concentric rings. A desk of dark, carved wood and a matching chair stood in the centre of the room.

Perched on one of the ladders was an elderly gentleman with long, untidy grey hair falling to his shoulders, an even longer beard, and a high scholarly forehead. He was dressed in medieval-looking robes of sombre hues, dull beige and brown. A pair of round-rimmed spectacles without earpieces perched on the bridge of his nose. He was reading a book, and he glanced up with a frown as they drew near. Claire was suddenly reminded of old Mr. Brown at the bookstore.

"You again!" he grumbled at Leo. "Come to disturb my peace once more, have you? And who is this you've brought with you?"

"This is—well, her name's Claire at the moment."

The scowl deepened. "Are you bringing your ward to our plane again? You know this is highly irregular."

"Irregular yourself! You know perfectly well she's a special case, Vecchio."

The old man snorted and came down from his ladder. "Well, well, get on with what you're here for, whatever it is, and don't disturb me any more than you have to." He went to the wooden desk and settled into the chair with his book.

Leo chuckled. "Don't you mind him. He likes you—always has."

"He knows me?"

"From your previous visits. You've forgotten, but you actually met Vecchio before, in other simulations where both you and he looked different. He approves of you because you have an inquiring mind."

"He called me something—"

"My ward. That's the term we use, when we're speaking in your language anyway. A ward is—"

"I know: for Wiccans it's a protective spell. But it's also used for a person who somebody else is looking after, protecting. Like when a person adopts some kid they're not immediately related to—the kid is their 'ward.' Is that what you do, Leo—look after me?"

"I try to. But a familiar isn't supposed to interfere too much. Our main duty is to stand guard over the minds of our wards and ensure that no other daimon attempts to get access to them. We take the notion of privacy very seriously. A human being's thoughts are personal and sacrosanct. We stand at the door, as it were, to drive away any daimon who might try to come spying. Not all daimons are that scrupulous, you see."

"But you can see into my mind, can't you?"

"No," he explained. "It would be just as wrong for me to do that as it would be for any other daimon. If you reach out to me, call on me, then I can join my mind to yours and share what you are willing to share. But humans who are aware of their familiars and consciously attempt to contact them are, as I have said, very rare."

She glanced with curiosity at the books on the shelves. History, poetry, mathematics, travel books—she was reminded of Al Ramsay's well-stocked and eclectic library. Leo smiled as he watched her pick up a book and read from it. "This is Vecchio's little hobby. He always liked the idea of books as a means of storing information, and so for this simulation he's catalogued all his own knowledge into book form. Not all daimons have wards, you know. Vecchio is one of those who just like to talk to other daimons and learn all the things they've learned. Like all of us, he's quite fascinated by your world and wants to know all about it. This human form is just one of many guises he takes in many simulations, but it's his favourite and the Rotunda has become his special haven."

Claire looked around. "And these books are his thoughts? So in a way I'm literally reading his mind?" Hastily she put the book back on the shelf.

"Oh, don't worry about privacy with us daimons," laughed Leo. "It's different for us; we're accustomed to sharing our thoughts with one another. Old Vecchio's perfectly happy to give you access to his knowledge. He likes to act the curmudgeon, but he's really quite fond of you."

"I wish I could remember more. Leo, this is really weird. It's like one of those stories where the main character has amnesia and has to learn all about their past again from other people."

Leo smiled at her fondly. "I've missed you."

"I missed you, too. Well—ever since I remembered you." She looked into his eyes. She could see tiny reflections of her face there in the irises . . . *Even reflections!* she marvelled. "Leo, why did you cut me off like that? I really needed to talk to you!"

"I'm here now," he said. He sounded a little evasive, Claire thought.

"But you weren't before—well, except for getting the owl to attack Josie's rat. That was brilliant. But then you backed off again. You don't have some crazy guilt complex, do you? You weren't to blame for what happened back in Scotland."

"Wasn't I?" he said in a quiet voice. "I got too close to you, at a time when it was not safe to do so, and the result was that you were branded as a witch. Most daimons oppose close involvement with mortals for this very reason—we don't suffer the ensuing consequences, but you do. And it prevents you from leading normal lives. I should have been more careful in Scotland. I was too impatient, too eager to help you in your new incarnation. But as you say, all that is past now. I had decided merely to keep an eye on you in your current life—until you were actually in danger. Since it's no longer possible for you to live a completely normal life in this time, I might as well reveal myself to you."

"So—you're going to keep in touch now?"

"If you wish it."

"I do!" Claire said. "I've been alone so long, and I can't tell my dad any of this—he'd think I've lost my mind—and I don't want Myra to know too much about any of it either. It's not safe for her, with those warlocks around; they're getting suspicious about her as it is. I couldn't bear it if they hurt her or scared her. But if I can talk with you, Leo, and ask you for advice now and then, that would help a lot."

"Very well. Whenever you want to talk to me, call me—in your mind, of course, not out loud—and I will answer you. And if you want me to see you as well as speak with you, let me know, and I will borrow the eyes of the kitten."

"It was you who brought him to me, wasn't it?"

"Of course. Just as I brought the stray cat Whiskers to your parents' home when I knew you were soon to be born. Just as I brought you the white cat when you were Alice. Daimon-familiars favour cat hosts because the animals are often semi-wild, staying in humans' homes but also roaming free at will. For daimons that wish to watch over their wards, but also to keep an eye on things happening outside the house, a cat offers the best of both worlds. In each case I found a homeless animal and gave it a safe haven in return for the use of its senses at times. That little marmalade fellow had been wandering the ravine for weeks. I did my best to keep him fed and out of the reach of predators."

"Lucky I thought of going to the ravine."

"I was bringing him to you in any case. But you sensed my intent and met me halfway. Yes: you sensed *me*. For the fact is I don't read your thoughts; you read mine. You sensed my wish for you to go to Alfred Ramsay's house and read his writings and learn all about your past life—why do you think you always longed so much for Willowmere?" Again he smiled his perfect smile.

She gaped at him in sudden understanding. But before she could speak, the interior of the Rotunda with its shelves and books and dusty light grew dim and indistinct, and faded away from her sight. Claire blinked and found she was once more lying in her bed at home. The marmalade kitten purred beside her.

Chapter 6

CLAIRE WENT TO SCHOOL the next day with a lighter heart. Her world had changed irrevocably, but she had now grown used to that change and even begun to feel excited about the possibilities it presented. And now that Leo was back with her again she felt ready to face anything. She whistled to herself as she headed for the bus stop. The kitten was using his litter box—no doubt Leo had something to do with that—and she felt safe leaving him alone in the house. But she knew she'd have to be home early today, or her father would just walk in and find the animal without Claire there to offer an explanation for its presence. So she decided that she would see Mrs. Robertson—if she was back—before the start of classes rather than after school.

With a wave of anger she remembered Josie sitting in the guidance counsellor's office, leaning back in her chair and sneering as Claire read the note from Mrs. Robertson explaining that she had to go look after her ailing mother. She remembered, too, the girl's gloating words: "Funny thing, all these elderly relatives getting sick lately. Almost makes you wonder if there's something going around." With the power of telepathic suggestion, Josie and the warlocks and their daimon allies had caused three people to fall ill: Mrs. Hodge's aunt, Mrs. Robertson's mother, and one of Claire's father's co-workers. As a result, all had had to leave town, the housekeeper and counsellor to tend their relatives, and Mr. Norton to attend a convention in his co-worker's place. And so Claire had been left on her own, without any adults to turn to when Josie stepped up her "magic" attacks. She knew now that the magic wasn't real, that the long tongues of flame that had seemed to burst from Josie's hands were only an illusion. But that first time she had been terrified, much to Josie's satisfaction. Had she not recalled a part of Al Ramsay's notes that explained the daimons' ability to cause humans to hallucinate, she'd probably be cringing in terror still. She decided she would also talk to Mimi and the other girls who had attended the Dark Circle gatherings, and learn as much as she could about what had gone on in the van Burens' house.

Claire went first to the guidance counsellor's office and saw that the light was on and the door ajar. It had better not be Josie in there again, she thought grimly as she went up to the door and looked inside.

Mrs. Robertson was sitting at her desk, reading some papers. When she glanced up and saw Claire she smiled. "Hello, Claire."

"Hi. How's your mom?"

"She's much better, thank you for asking. Come on in and have a seat." Claire shut the door behind her and sat down. The counsellor moved the stack of papers aside and looked directly at her. "Your teachers have noticed that you're skipping lots of classes lately, and that's not like you. You've always been a good student, no matter what's going on in your life. We've got a little while before homeroom starts, if you want to talk about it."

"Well," said Claire, "there is something I'd like to talk to you about, but it can wait if you're busy."

"Not at all. Let me guess. Is this about Josie Sloan?"

Claire stared. "You know about that?"

"I dropped by the school late on Friday afternoon to check for messages, and found Josie and her mom waiting to see me. They told me the whole story—at least, Josie's mom told me what her daughter told her. I'm sure you can add a lot more. The long and the short of it is, she's going to write you an apology and leave you alone from now on. Her mom asks that we not get the police involved if possible, but of course that's up to you."

"Well, it isn't really," replied Claire. "It's your friend Dr. Moore who's the injured party. Josie trespassed on her property and smashed a window in her house and cut her phone line."

"I talked to Myra on the phone last night and she says a written apology from Josie will be enough for her. She was more concerned about you, and so am I. Claire, how long has this been going on?"

"I only met Josie this fall. We got off on the wrong foot from the start, and it's just gone from bad to worse since then."

"Josie said you made fun of her religion."

"Her what?"

"She's a Wiccan or something, according to her and her mom."

"Her mom *knows*?" exclaimed Claire in disbelief. "But—she can't know, not everything anyway. Josie's not a Wiccan, never was. She's gotten involved with—with some other kind of movement, not quite a cult but not witchcraft either. I've met real Wiccans at Myra's, and Josie and her friends have nothing to do with them. Anyway, this other group has recruited some girls at this school—though those girls have quit the group now. I tried to talk some of them out of going, but in the end they all just left of their own accord. They said they weren't getting what they wanted out of the group. If Josie is smart she'll give it up, too. I don't think they're very nice people."

Mrs. Robertson tapped her pen thoughtfully on her desk. "I can see there's a whole lot more to this business than I thought. Can you tell me anything else about this—movement, as you call it?"

"No." Claire met the other woman's eyes steadily. "I wish I could. But I can't." She hoped the guidance counsellor wouldn't press the issue. Her elderly mother had already paid the price for Mrs. Robertson's connection to Claire. The counsellor must not get involved with the warlocks.

Mrs. Robertson's dark eyes dwelled on Claire for a long moment. "Can't—or won't?"

"There's a lot I still don't know about them," Claire hedged. "Josie could tell you more. But I doubt you'll be able to get it out of her."

Another long pause. "Okay, I won't pursue this line of inquiry any further—for now." Mrs. Robertson straightened her shoulders and sighed. "Josie's mom has asked if she and her husband could meet with your dad, with you and Josie present. A kind of two-family conference here at the school after class. I said I'd leave it up to you and get back to her. I think Mrs. Sloan's hoping to clear the air and avoid charges being laid against her daughter. We can give it a try, or not—whatever you feel comfortable with."

Claire pondered a moment. It was useless to involve the police, she was sure, but neither did she think that much would come of such a meeting. Josie didn't want reconciliation; she wanted revenge. Still, there was a chance her parents might curtail her activities. If they grounded Josie that would stop her from meeting with the warlocks and other Circle members. And her parents would be more cooperative if Claire and her father didn't press charges.

She stood up. "Okay. I'll talk to my dad and get back to you. He comes home tonight."

✧ ✧ ✧

Claire made a point of attending all her classes that day. It was part of her plan for returning to normality, for taking back her life, and as she listened to the teachers and jotted down notes, she found it surprisingly easy to push everything else to the back of her mind. If Leo was watching over her she saw no sign—no owl perched in the trees outside the window. Josie didn't seem to be at school today either; at least, Claire didn't see her anywhere in the halls or in the locker area.

She went to the library in her spare period and looked at a book on Renaissance artists. She couldn't remember the name of the painter who had done the city picture and had to look up the painting's name instead. She half-expected not to find it, but there it was in the index: *Ideal City,* page 41. She turned to that page and sat for a long time staring at the photograph of the painted buildings, the round central structure, and the empty plaza. It was in colour, and all was as she recalled it from the night before, even to the hues of the pavements and the deep blue of the sky. But all of it was flat, two-dimensional, forever visible only from one angle. She gave a little shiver and closed the book.

She saw nothing of Mimi and the Chelseas until biology class later that morning. They were doing dissection, which meant working in pairs since there weren't enough preserved frogs to go around. This left one of the threesome without a partner, and as Mimi and Chelsea happened to be sitting together Claire was able to slip into the seat next to Chel. It wouldn't be hard getting her to talk, she knew. With Mimi and the Chelseas, the problem was usually getting them to stop talking.

"Gross," commented Mimi as the frogs were handed out. "Why do they always make us do this before lunch?"

"Better than after lunch, I guess," said Chel, wrinkling her nose at the smell of formaldehyde. "If we had food in our stomachs we might upchuck in the lab."

Claire looked up from the photocopied diagram of frog organs. "It could be worse. I hear we do rats next term. Speaking of rats, has anyone seen Josie?" The girls all shook their heads. "Just as well. I was wondering if you guys could tell me more about that Dark Circle thing. What it was like."

Chel turned to her in surprise. "Why are you interested now? I mean, we've all left it."

"I'm just wondering how Josie got involved in it and whether it gave her this attitude problem. What kinds of things did you do there?"

"Well, like we said, Nick did hypnosis tests to see what our past lives were like. He says most people are reincarnated, they just don't remember it. And the old man gave a talk once on magic and the spirit world. To tell you the truth, after the reincarnation stuff it just got kind of boring."

"Do you remember what the old—what Mr. van Buren said? About spirits and all that?"

Chel opened her mouth to reply, but at that moment the biology teacher glanced at them. "How about a little less talk over there and a little more work?" he said.

The girls all fell silent and returned their attention to the dissection exercise. When the bell finally rang for the end of class Claire quickly brought up the Dark Circle again. "You can't remember anything more about the van Burens and what they taught?" she asked Chel as they left the classroom.

"'Fraid not."

"Oh, well, that whole Dark Circle thing sounds pretty lame. No wonder you left." Donna Reese was walking by at that moment with her friend Linda, and Claire raised her voice for them to hear.

Donna's head turned. "Yeah, well, I'm still going," she said with a scowl.

"Do you really think they can help you with—" Claire searched for a tactful way to say *your weight* "—your problem?" she finished.

Donna shrugged. "I don't know. But it doesn't really matter any more. If I can't get thin now, I can always be reincarnated as someone gorgeous. Mr. van Buren says in the future everyone will look the same: tall and thin and beautiful. I personally can't wait." She and Linda walked on.

"I'm thinking of going back to the Circle," said Chelsea.

Claire swung around to look at her. "Going back? But I told you, the whole thing's bogus."

"So Josie was lying about having magic powers," said Chelsea. "That doesn't mean the other Circle people were. Maybe they can fix things up between me and Dave."

Claire cleared her throat. "Uh—Chelsea? Using spells on Dave was what got you into trouble with him in the first place."

"I know. But I've tried everything else. He won't talk to me. And I really like him." Chelsea's lip trembled and for a moment Claire feared she would start to cry right there in the hallway. "You'd understand if you loved somebody."

Unwillingly, Claire recalled William Macfarlane, his face and voice and touch. What would she do to get him back? she wondered. *Anything,* her Alice-self replied. *Anything* . . .

"I know someone who likes Claire," said Chel, throwing her a sly glance.

"What?" said Claire, distracted out of her reverie. "Who?"

"Brian Andrews." She pointed.

Claire shot a quick glance towards Brian, who was standing at his locker. She knew him only by name and sight. He had sandy-coloured hair and wore glasses, and he was rather quiet, an A student who spent all his spare periods studying in the library as she did. But they had never exchanged a single word, to her recollection. As she stared at him he looked her way, saw her and quickly turned his gaze back to his locker. Was it indifference—or shyness? "No way," she said, uncertainly.

"Yes way. I've seen him looking at you, in class and in the hall. You're both smart, so why wouldn't he like you?"

With an effort Claire forced her mind back to the subject of the Circle. "They didn't teach you about cursing or—or casting illusions? The van Burens, I mean?"

"No, nothing like that. What does it mean—casting illusions?"

"Never mind." Whatever the van Burens might have taught them, it was clear the girls had absorbed very little of it. Which was probably a good thing, for them; but it didn't help Claire. She still had no clear idea of what the warlocks were up to. She hoped Chelsea wasn't serious about returning; and Donna still needed to be persuaded to leave. What had van Buren meant by that odd remark about everyone being beautiful someday? Had it just been a way to satisfy Donna, since he had no real power to make her tall and slim in this life? Or did it mean something more?

✧ ✧ ✧

She returned home at around three-fifteen, after dropping by a convenience store on Lakeside to pick up some milk and a couple of cans of cat food. The kitten was lying sprawled on her bed; at the sight of her he sprang up and began to purr.

"So how are you guys doing?" she asked.

"The kitten is doing very well, thanks to you," said Leo's voice in her mind.

"And you. After all, you brought him to me." Claire stroked the kitten's back and his purring doubled in volume. She dropped her backpack on the floor and sat on the bed beside him.

"And how are you doing?"

"Oh . . . fine." She told him about her conversations with Mrs. Robertson and the girls. "Leo, how did the van Burens convince Mimi and the Chelseas they were reincarnated? Were those 'memories' they had really some sort of illusion?"

"Probably. It's not likely that they're all revenants—and it's a simple matter for a daimon to make a person hallucinate, as you know."

She explained to him about the planned meeting with Josie's parents. "It may not help, but it's worth a try. We can't keep her away from daimons, but we can prevent her from hanging out with the Dark Circle bunch. Then they can't use her for their dirty work."

"There have always been daimons who collaborated with humans to do mischief. Have you ever wondered why so many tales of sorcerers and witch doctors paint them as evil? The girl Josie is not, of course, a true shaman. At the van Burens' instigation she surrendered her mind to the daimon that controls the

white rat. In addition to corrupt shamans, there have always been people willing to be duped by them and their daimon allies in exchange for the promise of power. Like the so-called witches of Berwick, who quoted King James I's private conversation with his bride aboard their ship. It would have been easy for a rogue daimon to possess a ship rat and listen in on their talk, then link to a human conspirator and relay the information. We think that's what happened there, though of course we can never be sure.

"Fortunately most of us daimons aren't like that. We want your world to be left free to develop on its own, without interference from us. We wish to observe the experiment, not tamper with it and alter the results."

"Is that all we are to you?" exclaimed Claire. "Just some big experiment?"

The kitten nuzzled her hand. *"Of course not. As soon as your kind arrived on the scene, we knew we were looking at something special. Your adaptability and your talent for innovation especially enchanted us. But that only made us all the more determined not to spoil things by interfering with you."*

"But couldn't you have helped us? You're super-intelligent; you could have solved a lot of our problems."

"Why? You're doing very well on your own. It may seem a long time to you, but the human species has only been around for two hundred thousand years, and your history is in cosmic terms a blink of an eye. Yet look how far you've come. Despite your wars and other troubles, you've advanced to the point of cherishing high ideals like freedom and cooperation and peace. We may have planted the occasional hint to certain individuals, but most of what you've achieved has been on your own. That is, we firmly believe, the way it was meant to be.

"In any case, we couldn't have helped you with things like diseases, for we perceive your world only through the animal senses of our hosts and know no more about it than you do. That's why we're so eager for you to explore and to do research. As you learn, we learn through you. We were very eager for you to go to the moon, for instance. We were curious to see what it looked like, and there were no living things on it to show us. Thanks to your Apollo missions we now have a very detailed moon simulation, complete with lunar gravity. I must take you there sometime—"

"But you still know much more than we do. I mean, you've actually witnessed our past. You saw Julius Caesar and Shakespeare and Socrates. You know what the dinosaurs looked like. Leo!" She gave a yelp of excitement. "You know if there's life on other planets!"

"Sorry." The kitten yawned and stretched its forelegs. *"Privileged information. If we just tell you humans everything about your universe, what's the point? Your species might well develop time machines and spaceships that travel faster than light if we leave your curiosity intact and unsatisfied."*

"You could tell *me,*" Claire wheedled. "I wouldn't tell anyone else. I promise."

"Rules are rules. Besides, how do I know you aren't the one who will invent the machines?"

She lay back on the bed for a moment, staring up at the ceiling. She felt almost dizzy with knowledge, with the sudden expansion of her universe and the changes to her own ideas of self and identity. All day she had found herself staring at other people—on the bus, on the street, at school—and wondering if they were descendants of Flower-in-a-drought. *I might even be my own descendant—how weird is that?* But there was still so much more that she needed to know. And one question above all others dominated her mind. "Leo, tell me one thing. Why did my mother leave me? Do you have any idea?"

"I think so. I couldn't read her mind, of course, any more than I can read yours. But she must have always been close to her own daimon, though not as fully aware of its presence as you are of mine. When she was a young woman, your mother told her fiancé why she wanted to have children: she believed she'd lived before, been a mother before, and she felt destined to have a child again. In both of two earlier lives, she said, she died before her child could know her. That remark was overheard by a number of daimons, and it attracted my interest at once. For I knew you had decided to be reborn in this time, and I wondered if your mothers in your two previous lives might also be one person—a revenant, brought back again and again by the desire to see and know her child. As for your mother's fiancé, he was charmed by her statement—when your father was younger he hadn't such a resistance to ideas of this kind, and of course he was in love. They married, and I brought the cat Whiskers to the door of their new home so that I could watch over you when you were born. But daimons who were . . . less scrupulous than the rest of us were watching her, too."

Claire sat up. "Let me see if I've got this straight. My family was under surveillance by bad daimons?"

"Yes. They didn't yet know you were a revenant as well. But they had their eyes on your mother—they knew that your mothers in both your previous lives had died before you could know them—and she lived in Willowville, where the last descendants of Alice Ramsay's family lived. Phobetor has never forgiven you and me for humiliating him in Africa. For a daimon, a hundred thousand years and more isn't too long

to carry a grudge, and he's been seeking you out ever since. So as long as your mother was with you, you and your father also came under some unfriendly scrutiny. Finally, my cat-host was killed by one of their dog-hosts, as a threat and a warning, and I knew your mother had to be told of the danger to her family. Al Ramsay learned of it from his own daimon, as you've read in his notes, and he decided to approach your mother. I think in the end she felt she had no choice but to leave—to draw the malevolent daimons' attention to herself, and as far away from you as possible. To pretend that you were not, after all, the child she had felt destined to have—the child that might be Alice reborn."

Claire was silent. *"Your mother loves you,"* said Leo. *"Never doubt that. I don't, and I have known her far longer than you have. Look!"*

Claire had a sudden picture in her mind: her mother, looking much younger with her hair down around her face, sitting in the living room of their old house on Elm Street. The scene looked strangely dichromatic, all dull yellows and blues, like a photograph that has faded after being exposed to too much sunlight. Her mother held a blanketed bundle in her arms, and sang softly as she rocked it back and forth.

"You," said Leo. *"That's one of my own memories, seen from the cat Whiskers's eyes—hence the limited colour spectrum. But you see how she loves you."*

The mental picture vanished again. "That was then. But now—she's stopped writing and everything . . ." It was hard to keep a quiver out of her voice.

"How do you know she's stopped?"

"Nothing ever comes any more—no letters, no packages, nothing. Not even on my birthday."

"That doesn't mean she hasn't sent them. The rogue daimons would take a keen interest in anything she might write to you."

Claire gaped. "Daimons can interfere with the *mail?*"

"No. But the humans who serve them are another matter."

"But then—she must think I'm getting her letters, but not writing back. That *I* don't want to talk to *her*." She sprang up and began pacing. "This is horrible! How can I get in touch with her? I don't know where she is!"

"Neither do I, at the moment. You may have to wait. If I know your mother, she won't be able to keep away much longer, even if she thinks you don't want to see her. She'll need to see you." The kitten raised its head, ears swivelling. *"I hear someone coming up the front path."*

Claire stood still, listening. "I don't hear anything."

"The cat's ears are keener than yours."

Claire left the room and went down the hallway, her pulse racing. There were definitely footsteps on the concrete path outside; they continued up the front steps to the door. And then there was the sound of a key in the lock. She sprang forward, relief flooding through her.

"Dad!"

The door opened, and there he stood, looking rumpled and tired—but so safe, so familiar. Seeing her, he smiled and stepped forward to meet her. Then suddenly he stopped dead, his briefcase still in his hand, staring not at her but at something behind her. Claire, turning, saw the kitten standing in the middle of the hallway, waving his marmalade tail in an amiable fashion. She cleared her throat.

"Uh—some things happened while you were away," she said.

Chapter 7

CLAIRE AWOKE THE NEXT MORNING to the smells of toast and bacon. When she made her way to the kitchen she saw her father seated at the table with the kitten next to his chair. Dad hadn't objected as much as she'd feared to the new addition to the household; in fact, he was feeding the kitten bits of bacon from his plate. She stood in the doorway gazing at them. Claire hated keeping secrets from her father, but she knew it was no use; he would not believe her story, could not believe it. He wouldn't think she was lying—he knew her too well for that—but he'd think there was something wrong with her. It would just worry and upset him.

She joined him at the table. "Morning," he said. Their usual muttered salutation.

"Morning." *(By the way, Dad, I've discovered I'm a shaman.)*

"I'm having fried eggs. Want me to put one on for you?"

"No, don't get up. I'll do it myself." *(I have a familiar named Leo, and I've been reincarnated twice.)*

"Got any plans for the weekend?" he asked as she moved to the stove.

"Not really." *(Well, I might be fighting evil. You see, there are these warlocks in Willowville who practise black magic . . .)* No, it was hopeless. He would never understand.

Claire cracked an egg and plopped it into the pan. But she couldn't stop stealing side glances at her father sitting alone at the table, the early sunlight shining on his thinning hair as he stroked the kitten's back. *Cats remind us of her . . .* She felt a twisting pain deep inside at the thought that he didn't know, that he hadn't the comfort of Leo's reassurances. And then it came out suddenly, a burst of words, without thought or preamble:

"Dad, Mom didn't run away."

He froze. She stood aghast, unable to take the blurted words back. It was no use; she had to keep going now. "From us, I mean. She didn't run away from us."

Still he said nothing. Then after a moment he looked up. "Your egg's burning."

Claire yanked the pan off the burner and turned to face him. "Dad, I want to talk about this. I need to talk about it. I'm positive Mom didn't want to leave us. It was something she had no control over, that she didn't want to do."

"How do you know that?" he asked, his voice ominously calm.

"I just—know. I know *her*."

He stood and began clearing his dishes away. "Your mother," he said, still in that low, even voice, as if discussing the weather, "chose to go away. Her personality changed radically, overnight, for no reason. She began having paranoid fantasies about being watched, but she couldn't say by whom. She didn't say anything to you at the time, not wanting to upset you. But she told me. She rejected all my suggestions that she see a therapist. Then she started hanging around with some strange types: practising witches, swamis, mystics. Finally she ran off to some place on the West Coast to live in a commune of shamans. A cult."

Shamans . . . ! "Dad, shamanism isn't a cult. There's nothing new about it—it's one of the oldest forms of religion around."

"Traditional shamanism, maybe. These were New Age wackos."

"How do you know? Did you ever meet any of them?"

He faced her at last. "Claire, denial can only take you so far. Mrs. Robertson went over all this with you a year ago. There are some things in life we have to accept. Truth is always better, even when it's painful."

"I know that, Dad. But I also know Mom would never *choose* to walk out on us. That is the truth, the one fact I can be certain of." Her heart was beating fast. She felt almost ill. Why had she raised the subject? She hadn't comforted Dad; if anything she had brought a new tension between them. Her secret hovered before her, a barrier invisible to the eye but almost palpable. If only she could break through that barrier, tell him all she knew!

"She hasn't phoned or written."

It was futile; she was just digging herself deeper, but she couldn't seem to stop herself. "Phone calls could be tapped. And mail can be intercepted." Worse and worse; as she watched he passed a hand over his face.

"Conspiracy theories now? You think your mother's on the run from organized crime or something? Claire, I'm sorry, but you can see for yourself where this is going. Your explanations just aren't rational. You love your mom and you don't want to believe any wrong of her. Someday you'll understand, but for now—" He straightened up. "I can't talk about this at the moment. I'll be late for work, and you'll be late for school. Eat your breakfast, and I'll give you a lift."

They said little during the drive, and none of it was about Mom. At last, as they neared the high school, her father turned to her and said, "It's my fault. I should have known that you couldn't just get over a trauma like that. You've only been internalizing it."

Claire couldn't answer. Between her frustration and her anguish for her father, she was close to tears. *I can never explain it to him, never. He'll never understand. And now he'll just worry about me. I've ruined everything*. She tried to swallow the lump rising in her throat.

After a moment he spoke again. "Will you see the guidance counsellor again? I want to help, Claire, but I know my limitations with this kind of thing. Maybe Mrs. Robertson can recommend a professional therapist."

I don't need therapy! I need you to listen, the way you wouldn't listen to Mom! To believe what I have to tell you . . . Then Claire recalled her last meeting with the counsellor. She forced down the lump and said, "Dad—about Mrs. Robertson. I forgot to tell you she wants to set up a meeting for us at the school. That girl I told you about, Josie, has been bothering me again. Mrs. Robertson thought we could get together with her and her parents and talk it out."

He sighed. "Yes, you did mention the girl. I didn't know it was that bad. All right. Tell Mrs. Robertson I'll be available for a meeting any night of the week. You don't need problems at school as well."

He looked worn and tired, and old—older than she had ever seen him. All the lines in his face seemed to have deepened, and the greying hair at his temples was more noticeable. Claire opened her mouth again, but could find nothing more to say. She slumped in her seat, utterly miserable.

It was about twenty past eight when he dropped her off at school. Lots of teachers were in the building at that hour, but not many students. As she walked down the half-empty hallway on her way to her locker she heard voices coming from inside the computer lab, and paused for a moment, listening.

"What about this one? Should I try it?"

"No, no, man—not that door! There's a troll with a battleaxe behind it. I tried it before. Take the other one, on your left."

Hearing the excited voices made her feel lonelier than ever. After a second's hesitation she opened the door and peered in. At once the students in the room all turned towards her, relief showing in their faces when they saw her. *Did they think I was a teacher?* Claire wondered. *What are they up to?* Donna Reese and her friend Linda Kwan were there, along with Earl Buckley, Jaswinder Singh, Brian Andrews, and several other computer-science students. They were all crowded around one of the monitors. It looked to Claire as though they were playing a video game of some kind, with virtual reality graphics depicting a long stone tunnel lined with shields and torches and other medieval paraphernalia. Wooden doors were set in the walls on either side. As Earl debated his next move Claire found herself watching, drawn to the scene despite her own preoccupations. Earl double-clicked his mouse on the left-hand door, revealing a pile of treasure—gold cups, gems, ingots, and so on. "Ha! Paydirt! How much of this can I carry, though?"

"You'll have to find a magic-user to do a strengthening spell on you," Brian suggested, leaning over his shoulder.

Several of the spectators glanced up again as Claire entered, closing the door behind her, and Donna frowned. "Well," she said, "out with it."

"Out with what?" asked Claire.

"Your usual lecture. How we shouldn't be playing video games on school equipment, and should stop wasting time and go develop our minds or something. Go ahead, say it."

Claire shrugged. "Why? You already did, better than I could. And anyway that's not what I was going to say." She hesitated again, then pulled a chair up to the computer table and sat down. "Is that really the way you see me? As someone who's always lecturing?"

"Aren't you?" Donna turned back to the monitor.

Claire sat and digested this for a moment, then looked up again. "What's the game? I like fantasy."

"Warrior Quest," Brian answered, turning towards her. "Earl's playing against some guy in California."

She met his eyes, noticing for the first time that they were a clear grey-blue behind his glasses. His expression was friendly, with no trace of self-consciousness. *Thanks a heap, Chel—now I'll never be able to feel normal around this guy, I'll always be wondering whether he really does . . . like me*. She could still hardly believe it, but she had to force a casual tone as she asked him, "You mean it's on the internet? A kind of two-way game?"

"Not just two-way. There are hundreds of players in this thing. See, you can be any character you want. A dwarf, a warrior, a wizard: anything. You just pick an avatar—an image of a character—and that's what the other player sees on their screen. And you see their avatar."

"Oh, I get it. So if you see a dwarf or a wizard or something, it's not just part of the scenery? It's actually being operated by another player somewhere?"

He nodded. "Yeah. The whole thing's totally interactive."

He looked back at the screen again. The scene on it had changed to an open green field. In the distance a herd of centaurs galloped across the turf, whacking at a ball with long wooden mallets. In the foreground a group of characters stood, having some kind of conference: knights, Viking-like warriors, a dwarf, and a tall blond woman whose close-fitting white gown showed off unnaturally perfect body measurements.

"See that? That's me," Donna told Claire, pointing to the woman. "That's my avatar in the game, Laradonna of Kirinor. To the players who've never seen me, that's who I am: this perfect beautiful woman. They don't get to judge me on my looks in cyberspace. They get to know me as Laradonna, and someday when they actually get to meet me, they'll accept me because they already know me from our games together." She turned her gaze to Claire. "And before you can say it, no, I *won't* go off alone to meet some stranger off the net. My friends will go with me. I'm not gonna bother with all that Dark Circle stuff any more. I've found my group. So, any more questions?"

Claire shook her head. "The centaurs playing polo are kind of cute," she offered. Another thought struck her. "Tell me, guys: what would you do if you came across a really cool game like this on the net, but you couldn't play? Even if you badly wanted to join in?"

Earl turned his pale, acne-spattered face away from the screen and grinned at her. "I'd try to hack my way in, of course," he said. "Take over someone else's avatar and use it to play the game. All I'd need would be their password."

"Our world is a game they play," Claire murmured, quoting Al Ramsay's notes on the daimons. They all stared at her.

"What did you say?" asked Linda.

"Nothing. Just talking to myself," said Claire.

"You're weird, Claire," said Linda with one of her nervous giggles.

"Yeah," said Donna, "and coming from *us* that's probably something you should worry about."

They returned their attention to the screen. Claire got up and left the room, shutting the door behind her. If the game kept Donna away from the van Burens, then that was just as well. But it had set her thoughts upon another track. For the rest of the day she forgot all about Brian and the others, and even about the troubling exchange with her father, as she returned to pondering the daimons and their world.

✧ ✧ ✧

"Why do they call it a city?" Claire asked, leaning back on her elbows in the soft, springy grass—softer and greener than any real grass could ever be. She pointed to the small clump of buildings out in the middle of the paved grey-and-tan plain below. "It's so small. It wouldn't even make a very big town."

She was lying on the slope of one of the Ideal Hills, under the perfect, unchanging blue sky. Looking around, she almost fancied she could see brush strokes in the scene around her. Leo, in his human form once again, was sprawled a little distance away from her. He stretched lazily, flexing imaginary muscles. "We just use the name the artist gave his painting," he explained. "We could have posited more buildings, of course, as we posited most of these hills—but we preferred to keep to della Francesca's vision as much as possible."

Claire lay flat and gazed up at the blue sky. It was a perfect day—but of course it always was, here. Rainy days never came to this place, nor winter, nor even nightfall. There was no sun in the sky to make her eyes blink and water; the light, as always, came from an unseen source to one side—on the right, from her current position. And the place was, as ever, silent and oddly still. No birds were singing amid the stylized greenery of the woods, and no wind stirred the trees. There was no other figure to be seen anywhere. No doubt Vecchio was puttering around in his library down there in the Rotunda—she could see the round roof of the city's central structure from here, gleaming in the soft light. But no other daimons seemed to come here. Perhaps it wasn't interesting enough for them.

On returning home after school, she had asked Leo to take her into his mind-dimension once more, partly because she wished to talk to him without any fear of interruption, and partly because—honesty compelled her to admit—she felt a need for escape.

She sat up again. "Leo, you say there are other . . . simulations, and some look realer than this one. Could I see one of them?"

"Of course—if you like." He rose to his feet and, holding out one hand, helped her to hers.

"How do we get there?" she asked him—and then the words died on her lips, for suddenly the scenery changed. In the blink of an eye she and Leo had gone from the painter's flawless hills to a dense and very realistic forest. There were groves of identifiable trees—oaks, maples, silver birches—as well as a thick undergrowth of ferns and little saplings. Sunlight poured through gaps in the thick summer-green foliage above. There was the sound of birdsong everywhere and of a river murmuring between its banks. As she stood staring around her, a wind gusted through the branches above and she felt it lift her hair.

"It's so real!" she exclaimed, walking up to a tree and laying her hand on its firm, solid trunk. The bark felt rough beneath her phantom hand. "Every last detail—I'd swear I was in an actual forest. What a lot of work you put into this!"

"We are fascinated by your world," Leo said. He was, she noticed, dressed now in more modern attire of denim jeans and a white shirt, and his face, though still attractive, showed some freckles and other minute flaws. "In fact, we've come to long for it, since we view it always from afar. Do you remember how you used to peek through the hedge at the Willowmere estate, wishing it could be yours?"

Claire nodded. She well remembered that yearning, and her delight when her acquaintance with Myra Moore gained her entry at last into the coveted house and grounds. She could certainly understand the daimons' longing for a place they could glimpse but never really enter.

Leo continued: "We marvel at its great variety of environments, and by the creatures whose senses we borrow to perceive those environments. We have simulations for every kind of terrain and geological feature on your planet. Some would look strange to you, since they're rendered from an animal's perspective rather than a human's. You might find yourself in a simulation that's all black and white, for instance, because its creator used the visual impressions of an animal that can't see in colour. Others use sounds you can't hear with your human ears. There are many other Earths aside from the one you are familiar with."

Claire recalled her conversation with the gamers and turned to look straight at him. "Leo, you told me that not all daimons are as scrupulous as you and your friends when it comes to dealing with our world. That there are lots of . . . evil ones too.

Like that one who hates me, the one who helped old Mamba—what did you call him?"

"Phobetor." Leo's cheerful expression faded, and his features took on a solemn cast. She wondered if this seemingly human change was unconscious or the result of deliberate effort on his part. "I'm afraid so. You see, when we first began to explore your universe there were no fully intelligent, self-cognizant beings in it yet. We thought of living organisms as primitive creatures, not equal to ourselves, and so had no compunctions about using them—even occasionally manipulating them into dangerous situations, for of course we didn't really understand the idea of danger, being immortal and immaterial ourselves. Then when the emerging signs of intelligence began to make us reconsider our treatment of living things, some daimons were at odds with the rest. To them your universe was just a very interesting playground—"

"Our world is a game they play," Claire murmured again, thinking of Donna and the other gamers.

"—and so they didn't want to go along with the new rules, which required daimons to be more careful and respectful of the creatures they used to explore the physical realms. Some of these daimons were very careless—even cruel. They sometimes deliberately endangered their hosts, for they were fascinated by pain and death—those things no daimon can ever know. Some argued that the other universe wasn't real, but only a kind of illusion, and so nothing they did there had any importance. Others, like Phobetor and his followers, believed it was real but saw no reason why they shouldn't do as they pleased with it. These daimons began to plot together to take over the physical universe for their own. So we were divided, we who had always been as one. It all goes back to the time when we began to choose hosts from among the living creatures."

"*Daimon:* to part, divide, allocate, apportion," quoted Claire.

"Yes, the dictionary definition for us is certainly appropriate. Well, so it has gone for countless ages before your kind ever arose. We call these rogue daimons the Legion, because there are so many of them and because they're like an army, seeking to overthrow and occupy your world. We try to undo the harm they inflict and to guess what their schemes might be. We spy on one another's activities on your plane."

"Good and evil," said Claire, leaning back against the trunk. "Like in those fantasy novels I used to read. I really just read them for escape, especially after Mom went away. I couldn't bear the real world, and it made a change to sort of plunge myself into imaginary worlds. Dragons and elves and knights and castles . . . bad guys and good guys. I always thought Good and Evil were the same as magic powers—just figments of the imagination. But now . . ." She gazed long and thoughtfully at her daimon. "I believe you're good, Leo. That you stand for everything that I know is—well, right and true. I like you, and I want to be on your side." She paused, then gave a rueful smile. "Have I said that before?"

He returned the smile. "Not in so many words, but yes, something very much like it. You've always fought for the right, for truth, for Good as you call it—as Flower-in-a-drought and as Alice Ramsay. And always there have been those who fought against you. Two individuals in particular have set themselves against you, time and again. Phobetor, the leader of the rogue daimons, and Mamba. You see, the shaman is a revenant too. Not all revenants are good people, unfortunately. Evil shamans too can make the return. You met him again when you were Alice, and Phobetor as well. Morley and King, the witch hunters—or so they called themselves, but it was only a cover. Morley was Mamba, come back to live in the world again; and Anthony King was Phobetor in a human body."

Claire gasped. "They can do that? Take over human beings? I thought daimons only used animals."

"Most of us will not use intelligent beings for hosts. That's why we appointed familiars, guardian daimons, to watch over your minds and keep other daimons from trying to take them over. But a human who reaches out to our dimension can get past his guardian daimon and encounter a rogue daimon. He can ignore the warnings of his benevolent familiar and turn to the power that the rogue offers him—and so become enslaved. Mr. King was a would-be sorcerer who was taken over in this way. A man possessed. Phobetor used him to join forces with the revenant Morley, and together they set out supposedly to hunt witches and their familiars, like their superstitious colleagues—but in fact they were on a private campaign to seek out good daimons and their wards, and destroy them. They learned from other daimons that you were once more in the world, in Scotland, and they conceived a plan to get revenge on you for exposing and humiliating them in Africa long ago. It was hard for them to find you, for you yourself didn't remember that you'd been Flower-in-a-drought. But they found you in the end because I inadvertently led them to you." He passed a hand over his eyes. "They heard the reports of your extraordinary powers—or what seemed to other humans to be powers—and learned that you called your animal familiar Leo, the *Lion*. And so they guessed your true identity—and so you died."

"Oh, Leo. I told you I don't blame you for that."

"I blame myself. And now here you are again—and you're in danger again. For the shaman has returned, and his daimon too."

She looked at him. "Mr. van Buren—he used to be Mamba, right?" Leo nodded. "And that bad daimon, Phobetor—he's possessed the black wolf-dog, Rex. Hey—Rex is Latin for king, isn't it?"

"Another little joke of theirs, yes. They—and the rest of the Legion—have been watching out for you for years now, expecting you to return. They knew you'd want to be reborn in this time to stop their games, and they settled on Willowville—home of Alice's present-day kin—as the most likely place you would be reborn."

"But they don't know who I am yet."

"No. They may have their suspicions, but they don't know for sure. I don't wish to frighten you, Claire, but you must know they might eventually learn who you are. I may have exposed you to danger yet again, with that little display on the roof of Myra's house. At the very least, they now know you're a shaman with a daimon ally—though not necessarily that you're a revenant. They must not learn you are Alice."

"I'm not afraid, Leo. I'm angry. I can't begin to tell you how angry. All I can say is, they'd better steer clear of me in this life. Because this time around I intend to fight back."

"Well, don't allow your emotions to make you do anything rash. Keep your wits about you! You'll need them."

They were both silent for a moment. Then Claire spoke again in a calmer tone. "This whole thing—it's like one of those crazy conspiracy theories—"

"Only this one is real. The greatest conspiracy that ever was, with the fate of your world and your species hanging in the balance. For if the daimons of the Legion do succeed in their ambition to take control of your universe, you'll likely end as their slaves—though your enslavement would be beyond anything humans have ever inflicted on one another. They would take over not only your bodies but your minds; you would become puppets, playthings, without even the ability to dream of freedom. That is, if they allow you to go on existing at all."

Even in her phantom body Claire shuddered. "And what can *I* do?"

"I don't know yet. But you have certainly come back for this reason—to try to stop them."

She sighed as they walked on. "You know, you're really lucky to be a daimon. I mean, you're immortal—really immortal. You don't have to be reincarnated or anything, you can just always be *you*. Nothing can ever hurt you. You can never be separated from anyone you love . . ." Her voice caught in her throat. "You can never be lonely."

"All the same, we envy your kind. We envy you for being *able* to be alone, to enjoy the privacy of your own thoughts. To be individuals. There can be no true individuality when all thoughts are shared in common. We can screen our thoughts from the rebel daimons if need be, shut them out of our minds and so keep our own counsels secret from them. In theory, a daimon could even shut out every other daimon and so experience utter solitude. But none ever has; it could lead only to insanity. Your kind, by contrast, has the best of both worlds. You can commune with others on a daily basis, using the spoken word, yet at the same time keep your thoughts to yourselves. You are alone, yet not alone. With us it is all or nothing."

They had come to the river; it was a large one, too deep for her to see through to the bottom. They both stood on the mossy bank, gazing into the water. After a moment Claire said, "Just for once it'd be nice not to feel limited, though. You told me a human can do anything on this plane, Leo. What kinds of things could I do here?"

He made no reply, but grinned his playful grin. As she watched, his human shape shifted and flowed into another form—a white stag, tall and splendid with antlers like branching candelabra of ivory. *"You see?"* said his silent voice inside her head. *"Now you try it."*

"I don't know how."

"Your body is not really here. The body that you seem to see and feel is only a projection of your mind. Transform it as you wish; it has no physical reality."

She looked down at her legs and arms, her jeans and long-sleeved T-shirt, and willed them to change. *This is not real, it is only a phantom, an image in my mind* . . . She closed her eyes and imagined another form, a doe as white as the stag, slender and graceful.

She looked down again. In place of her own body, now there was a pale, softly furred breast and two slim forelegs ending in cloven hooves. She moved what should have been her right arm and saw the right foreleg bend at its knee joint. She moved her legs and knew by the feel of them that they had changed, become the curved hind limbs of a deer. Her eyes had more peripheral vision than before, while her ears had become sensitive, muscular organs that swivelled to and fro, seemingly of their own will. She swung her elongated neck around, saw a white back and the cottony tuft of a tail.

"But—how?" she asked, marvelling at the detail. *"I didn't imagine all of this!"*

"I helped you out a little—I know what a deer looks like. We daimons have photographic memories. You had but to specify what form you wanted, and I filled in the details."

Claire moved the legs that had been her arms, and the hind limbs that her legs had become. Slowly she walked forward. It wasn't like crawling on all fours as a human; these limbs and that long flexible spine felt no strain, but were designed for quadrupedal locomotion and horizontal posture. It was more like gliding than walking; it was fun. She bounded lightly to the river's edge and peered down at its dull green surface. A long, narrow face looked back at her, a face with quivering nostrils and dark liquid eyes and wide, flaring ears.

The stag strode majestically to the river and waded into it. And then there was no longer a stag there, but a tall white crane, walking through the shallows on its stilt-like legs. "*Change again!*" urged Leo's voice in her mind.

Joyfully she complied, calling up another image in her mind—no flimsy crane but a graceful gliding swan, like the ones on the duck pond at Glengarry Park. And then she *was* a swan—floating awkwardly on the stream, kicking with her strangely shortened legs and staring down at an orange-billed swan's face in the water. Her "arms" were bent backwards and folded along her back, which felt peculiar: she spread them out to either side, felt the long feathers flowing back from the bones. Wings: she really had wings . . .

"*Fly!*" The crane spread his own black-edged wings and rocketed upwards, spraying water in all directions. Claire tried to leap up too and found herself running instead—beating down the water until it lay beneath her paddle-feet like a floor of glass, pumping her wings and stretching out her long sinuous neck. How odd that her *arms* were now her strongest limbs and chief means of locomotion. She flapped them wildly, drew up her legs, and was airborne.

It was just like the dreams of flight she had often had as a child. She soared effortlessly over the river, seeing her swan reflection flitting along its surface. The crane was far ahead, his long legs trailing behind him as he flew. As she beat her wings furiously to close the distance, she caught sight of something else: another bird-shape spiralling down from the sky above, the light glinting on its outspread wings. It was a huge griffon vulture, with a black-plumed body and long, pale, featherless neck.

Seeing it, she faltered in her flight. As their flight paths converged, the vulture curved its snaky neck to look at her with a dead-black eye.

"Do you remember me also?" asked a mental voice, mocking and ironic.

Claire panicked, swerving away, calling for Leo. But now her bird form was fading, dissolving; she was falling down, down . . . She cried out silently. *"Help me!"*

Something flashed in the corner of her eye, a blur of feathers in sun; she thought at first that Leo had come back for her. But then she saw it was a smaller bird, a sharp-winged peregrine falcon. Its great dark eye looked into hers as it flew past her head. *"Go back, Claire!"* cried a silent voice. *"Return! You have the power. Go back to your own plane now!"* Then it shot upwards, folded its wings, and plunged at the vulture's back.

Darkness overcame her; and then out of that darkness came the voice she had desperately hoped to hear. *"Go back,"* said Leo, echoing the falcon's words.

She opened her eyes. She was safe: back in her home, her real body, lying on her bed. She gazed up into the amber eyes of the kitten, who was sitting on her chest, and gave a soft cry of relief.

✧ ✧ ✧

“Was it that bad daimon, do you think?” Claire asked Leo some time later, when she had calmed a little. “Phobetor?”

The kitten looked up at her as it lay on her bedspread. *“I’m afraid it was,”* Leo replied. *“How he knew you were in that simulation I don’t know, but naturally he wants to monitor your progress. He and Mamba are very curious about you.”*

Claire looked pensive. “And—the other bird, the falcon . . .”

“Who can say? Another daimon who saw that you were in need, perhaps . . .”

Claire shut her eyes, recalling the little bird’s fierce protecting presence. “I think,” she said, “I’m almost certain it was . . .”

“Yes?” prompted Leo.

Claire sat gazing into space. “My mom,” she said softly.

Chapter 8

CLAIRE SAT NEXT TO HER FATHER, looking around the classroom. It was empty except for themselves, Mrs. Robertson, Josie and her parents, and the middle-aged police officer who sat quietly in a corner holding a notepad and pen. The guidance counsellor sat at the front of the classroom and Claire's and Josie's parents sat in chairs to either side facing one another.

Josie sat glowering in her chair, her dyed black hair falling forward to hide most of her face, her arms crossed. She was dressed, not in her usual slinky black, but in a much tamer-looking print blouse and skirt. *Dressing for the jury,* Claire thought. No doubt at her parents' suggestion. Claire stared at Mr. and Mrs. Sloan, feeling a certain morbid curiosity as to what peculiar pairing could have resulted in Josie. They looked perfectly ordinary and unremarkable, Mr. Sloan with his beige striped sweater and slacks and his greying beard, Mrs. Sloan in a loose comfortable skirt with matching vest and silky blouse.

Her hazel eyes blinked behind gold-framed glasses and her hair was straight and mouse-brown, falling to her collar. Claire suspected Josie's real hair colour was the same, since they both had the same pink complexion.

Mrs. Robertson folded her hands on top of the binder in her lap and looked from one family to the other. "Well," she said, "shall we begin? For those of you unfamiliar with this kind of conflict resolution, we'll give both sides a chance to speak, and then see if we can come up with a solution to the problem. Obviously we can't let things go on like this. What started out as a personality conflict is clearly escalating, to the point where one party could wind up facing criminal charges. None of us should take this matter lightly, but it's still possible for it to be resolved if we act right now."

"She started it," growled Josie from behind her hair.

"Josie, you'll have a chance to speak later," said Mrs. Robertson. "No talking out of turn, please."

"It's a pity we couldn't ritualize this a bit more," put in Mrs. Sloan in her light breathy voice. "Like an Aboriginal sentencing circle. We should really start with a sweet-grass ceremony, to create a feeling of harmony, and then pass around a sacred eagle feather. Whoever holds the feather, you see, gets to speak. That way there's no problem with talking out of turn—"

"Yes, well," said Mrs. Robertson, "we haven't got any of those things, and as long as we all behave responsibly there shouldn't be a need. We're not sentencing Josie, just trying to reach an agreement on her future conduct. And Josie, if you don't want to cooperate, there's always Juvenile Court as an alternative."

Josie slumped lower in her chair and her parents looked dismayed. "Oh, surely there won't be any need for that, Mrs.

Robertson," said Mr. Sloan, leaning forward with an earnest expression.

"It depends entirely on Josie," the counsellor replied. "Claire, why don't you begin? Give us your impact statement."

With a feeling of futility Claire related the whole story—of the first meeting with Josie by her locker, Josie's sneering comments about Claire's mother and the resulting sharp exchange, her veiled threats and warnings as Claire publicly questioned Josie's claim to possess supernatural powers, the involvement of Nick van Buren and how he had harassed Claire by following her along Lakeside until she had to take refuge in the convent. Then she briefly described the two trespasses on Myra's property: the first one with Nick and then Josie's break-in leading to the confrontation on the roof of Myra's house. She didn't mention the other things: the bad dreams, the terrifying illusions, the way Nick had caused the dog Angus to turn on Claire. There was no point. No one would ever believe them.

As she spoke she noticed the policeman jotting down notes in his notebook. Josie saw this too; her face grew slightly paler and her jaw clenched. At last Claire said, "So you see, legally speaking, I'm not the injured party. It was Myra's house that got broken into, her grounds that were trespassed on."

The policeman looked up. "Actually, harassment is a pretty serious charge. Josie's behaviour wouldn't be tolerated in an adult and would result in criminal charges."

Mrs. Robertson nodded. "A good point. Josie?"

The other girl stood, throwing a hate-filled glance at Claire. "About Claire's mom. All I said was what I'd heard from some other people. As far as I knew it was the truth. And you say I threatened her, but I never touched her."

"You claimed you could harm her by magic?" asked Mrs. Robertson.

Josie shrugged. "She didn't have to believe that."

"You also made some vague threats, such as 'You'll be sorry for this,'" remarked the policeman, glancing down at his pad.

"I just said it so she'd leave me alone. She said things about me to other people. She told them . . ." Josie hesitated.

"What did she tell them?" asked Mrs. Robertson. Josie said nothing. "Is that all you have to say, Josie?"

She nodded and sat down again. Mrs. Robertson looked at Claire. "Did you say anything about Josie to the others?"

Claire shook her head. "I told them I didn't believe anyone could make things happen by magic. That was just my opinion, and I didn't mention Josie by name."

"Surely my daughter is entitled to free speech?" said Mr. Norton, shifting in his chair.

"Of course she is. So Claire told everyone she didn't believe in magic, and Josie took it personally," resumed the counsellor.

"It's my religion," muttered Josie.

"Yes," her mother said, "and it's very important to us that she should have these beliefs. We've always encouraged Josephine to adopt a belief system. Which one, we don't care. I myself am deeply interested in various forms of Native spirituality and eastern traditions like Buddhism, and my husband and I both take courses in meditation. So perhaps, you know, Claire might show some religious tolerance." She beamed benignly at Claire. "Because witchcraft—Wicca—*is* a religion."

"Yes," replied Claire. "I know quite a bit about it, actually. But Josie doesn't practise Wicca."

"She told us she does," Mrs. Sloan said.

"It's not true. Her . . . belief system has nothing to do with the Wiccan movement at all. Has she told you anything about the Dark Circle and what they do there?"

Mr. Sloan looked offended. "We don't interrogate our daughter. Our relationship with her is based on trust. Any young person will want to explore her world, test her limits, make mistakes and learn from them. We don't lay down the law; we listen to her. All we care about is that she has a good sense of self-esteem. And we're completely nonjudgmental, so she knows she can come to us any time if there's a problem."

"Yes," said Mrs. Robertson, "but young people can also benefit from a certain amount of structure. Rules like curfews help them feel secure and loved."

"I guess we have a different idea of love." Mr. Sloan reached out to lay a hand on his daughter's shoulder. She hitched her chair away, and there was an awkward little silence. Mr. Norton was staring at the senior Sloans with an incredulous expression.

"Well, this isn't really getting us anywhere," said Mrs. Robertson at last. "We aren't here to discuss parenting techniques, though I certainly think Josie could do with a little more parental supervision—before she ends up in Juvenile Court or worse." She paused a moment to let these words sink in. "But we still need a resolution. Mr. and Mrs. Sloan, will you see to it that Josie's behaviour improves? Otherwise we'll have to discipline her here, possibly with an in-school suspension from regular classes. And certainly she must pay for Dr. Moore's broken window."

"We'll take care of that," said Mr. Sloan. "No problem."

"No," the policeman said, closing his notepad and standing up. "Josie must pay—out of her own money. You can't bail her out like that."

"Exactly," said Mrs. Robertson. "She must learn from this. Grounding her for a while may help, with perhaps a curfew to follow later. You can extend that curfew gradually as she earns your trust."

"All right," said Mr. Sloan, glancing at the police officer and then at his wife, who nodded.

"Good. Claire, I suggest that you and Josie refrain from speaking to each other for the next little while, to give you both a chance to cool off. And now, if we're all in agreement, I think we can end this meeting."

Suddenly Josie stood up. "Listen, I just want to say I do realize what I did was wrong." Her voice had changed: it sounded lower, sweeter, more like her mother's. She threw a glance at the policeman. "It won't happen again. My feelings were hurt, and I guess I just freaked out. I'll pay for the window and anything else that got damaged."

Claire stared at her. What was this all about? Why was Josie all honey and syrup now, after being so defiant in the beginning? Did she really think she could fool everyone with this act?

"All right, Josie," said Mrs. Robertson. "If Claire and her father agree, and there's no repetition of your problem behaviour, we can consider this matter closed." She looked at the Nortons. Claire nodded, and her father grunted his assent.

"There!" exclaimed Mrs. Sloan with a radiant smile. "Now wasn't that easy?"

✧ ✧ ✧

"Idiots!" snapped Claire's father as they left the school. "Those idiots! Letting their daughter run wild, no rules, no questions asked. No wonder the kid's a little horror."

"And she doesn't even love them for it," commented Claire. "That's the sad part. Did you see the way she looked at them when they were leaving together? Sort of cold and contemptuous." A week had passed since her outburst about Mom, and a little distance had grown between her and Dad, a discomfort in each other's presence, a wariness on her father's side and increasing frustration on Claire's. But now, at the recollection of Josie and her parents, she walked a little closer to her father's side.

"It's certainly given me food for thought. I realize now I've been somewhat remiss in my own parental duties," said her father. "For one thing, it's high time I met this Moore woman."

Claire turned and gaped at him. "Myra? What for? You mean you want to see if she's respectable or something? Come on, Dad! She's a well-known travel writer, with all kinds of university degrees, plus all the honorary ones she's been given. And Mrs. Robertson knows her."

"All the same," he replied, "you've been seeing a lot of her, even staying at her place, and it's high time I was introduced to her."

"Well—as long as it doesn't look too obvious that you're checking her out. That would be really embarrassing."

"All right. How about inviting your Dr. Moore to dinner?"

Claire looked warily at her father. "You're not going to cook, are you?"

"No. Since she's your friend, I thought I'd leave that honour to you, so you can repay her hospitality."

"Fair enough. What should I make?" asked Claire, mentally running over her limited repertoire.

"Anything but Swill." Swill was their term for a dish consisting of anything they could find in the cupboard—canned soup, canned beans, canned vegetables—plus any suitable leftovers from the fridge, thrown together in a pot and boiled.

"Okay, no Swill. I'll see what I can come up with."

✧ ✧ ✧

Myra Moore accepted the invitation to dinner for Friday night, and Claire decided it would be a good idea to make some preparations. The house—a small, old-fashioned bungalow—looked clean enough at first glance, but closer inspection revealed a fine layer of dust on some of the bookshelves and on various light fixtures and furnishings. And there was a good deal of clutter, since both Claire and her father were in the habit of leaving books, magazines, and newspapers lying around on any convenient surface. Some tables and desks had built up impressive deposits that could be dated like geological strata; at the bottom of one Claire found a science magazine from the previous March. She launched into a frenzy of tidying and cleaning that week, at the end of which she had a new respect for her mother, remembering the spotlessness of their old home on Elm Street. Mom had been a neat freak, and Claire realized that she had probably spent much of her time picking up after her husband and daughter.

The kitten followed Claire everywhere, helpfully sitting on the magazine piles when she tried to sort them, tussling with her duster, and running behind the sofas when she moved them to vacuum. She managed to work around him and was rather glad to have him there as an occasional distraction from her chores. She hadn't realized how lively kittens could be. Since she and Whiskers had grown up together and his kittenhood lay far back in her own infancy, she had no memory of it, and she marvelled at this little animal's energy and agility.

Leo gave no sign of his presence and sent her no messages, and she was secretly glad, as she needed to focus on the job at hand.

The menu for the dinner was something over which she agonized a good deal, realizing that she wanted to make a good impression. Mom had just started teaching Claire to cook when she left, and the culinary arts were an area she had never mastered. Neither had her father, though in the old days he'd had to do his fair share: he and Mom had agreed that the first one home from work should put dinner on, and for years they had tried to outdo each other in tardiness—on more than one occasion the two of them had circled the block in their cars for nearly ten minutes before one of them finally gave up.

One of Mom's specialties had been chicken cacciatore—the spicy, tomatoey smell of the sauce still reminded Claire strongly of her and so, though it was first dish she had learned to make, she had avoided it ever since Mom had left. But after her visit with Leo in the virtual forest and the timely appearance of the falcon, a little of the hurt within her had eased and she threw herself into the making of the dish. She picked up some boneless chicken breasts from the deli on Lakeside, but couldn't find the recipe for the sauce and in the end had to improvise with chopped green pepper and some canned pizza sauce.

Dad came in the door after work with a couple of bottles of wine. "I got white and red, just in case. And this is for you," he added, holding up a bottle of cheap generic cola. "So what did you decide to make?"

"I call it pizza chicken," said Claire, adding some slices of mozzarella cheese. "It's kind of an experiment. If it works I'll come up with a fancier name for it."

"It looks okay," he observed, glancing over her shoulder. "Want me to make a salad to go with it? I got one of those ready-made kits."

"Thanks. I made some garlic bread, too."

She set the table while he got out the wineglasses. It had been a very long time since they had invited anyone over, she thought. In fact they hadn't really entertained since Mom's time. Her father hadn't wanted to see anybody, and they'd left their old neighbours behind on Elm Street. Most of them had been Mom's friends. Now Claire took this occasion as yet another sign of positive change, a slow return to the old ways. The fierce hope she had come close to discarding was alive again.

Myra showed up promptly at a quarter to seven, dressed in a smart suit of green tweed and carrying another bottle of wine, which she handed to Mr. Norton as she came in the door. Dad's eyes widened as he read the label.

"From my uncle Al's stock," she said. "He used to entertain a lot in the old days and kept a good wine cellar. There's still plenty of it left."

Claire took Myra's coat, and as she hung it up in the hall closet the kitten came running out from behind some boots. "Oh—here's the new addition to our family circle. Meet Leonardo."

"Isn't he a beauty! So you found another cat at last." Myra held her hand out and the kitten sniffed her fingers.

"He kind of found me, actually."

"His name reminds me of Alice's cat—Leo."

Claire had begun to worry that the name might be a little too obvious. Was that a searching glance Myra had given her before stooping to pet the kitten? "Actually, his full name is Leonardo da Vinci," she explained quickly. "I'm following your custom of naming cats after famous people."

"Your daughter is very bright," Myra said to Mr. Norton. "How many kids would name a pet after a Renaissance genius?"

He beamed. "Yes, she's always seemed old for her years."

You have no idea, Claire thought with a wry smile.

"Claire told me how much she missed having a pet," Myra went on.

"Yes, we were sorry to lose old Whiskers," he replied. "He was a special animal. When he was killed we couldn't bear to just replace him."

"Killed! Oh, my, how awful! I thought he died naturally."

"A dog got him," Mr. Norton explained. "Some irresponsible idiot let his pet run wild, and it killed ours."

Claire hastened to usher them both into the dining room. Whiskers's death was not a safe topic—not when Al Ramsay's notes mentioned the death of the reborn Alice's cat. The last thing she wanted was for Myra to start putting two and two together.

She was also anxious that her father and Myra get along. She hoped to revisit Willowmere one day, and preferred that it not be against his will. *Please, Myra, don't talk about Wicca,* she thought as they sat at the table together. *Or anything like that. Stick to plain old facts . . .*

So far Myra seemed to be doing well. "I did a double major, biology and anthropology," she was telling Mr. Norton. "Some of my friends thought I should narrow it down to one discipline or the other, but I've always been just as interested in human culture as in zoology. You might say humans are the most interesting animals of all."

"Yeah, tell him about your first research trip," urged Claire. "This is really interesting, Dad."

"The first trip." Myra smiled. "Yes, that was thrilling. I was still in my last year of university, and I got to go with my professor and some fellow students to seek out unknown animal species in the South American rain forest. We did actually catalogue a few previously unidentified subspecies of amphibians and one new insect. We started out in the Amazon river basin for six weeks, then travelled about a bit and ended up going through Central America to visit the rain forests of Costa Rica and Guatemala . . ."

She chattered on as Mr. Norton listened. Claire was pleased to see that his face showed keen interest. She let her mind wander a little as Myra told the familiar story of getting lost in the Guatemalan jungle.

". . . and I trudged for what felt like miles until I finally ran into some villagers—a group of children and an elderly lady who had never seen a white woman before and thought I was some kind of holy vision." She chuckled. "It's rather funny in retrospect, but it wasn't at the time. I can remember crying my eyes out, not so much from fear as anger—I was furious with myself for being so stupid as to get lost. Luckily there was one automobile in the village, and the driver was able to get me back to my base camp."

Claire said, "I'd love to be a nature writer like you, Myra. Maybe I could do a double major too, science and journalism, and then write articles for scientific publications. You should read her book, Dad—*A Journey through Gaia*. It's great. All about the ecosystem and the way different peoples view it all over the world."

Myra beamed. "Thank you, dear. If you really do want to follow in my footsteps, I'll be happy to give you some pointers. This chicken is delicious, by the way."

"I'm glad you like it. Hey, I've heard that whenever anyone eats something new and exotic they say it tastes like chicken. Is that true?"

"Well, I don't know that everything does, but certain types of snake and lizard meat do—especially iguana."

"You've eaten iguana?"

"Yes—along with a great many other things I'd rather not talk about." Myra made a face.

"So what are you working on now, Dr. Moore?" Mr. Norton asked, refilling her wineglass.

"Oh, call me Myra, please. I'm doing some articles about saving the environment, one of my hobbyhorses. When you see these fragile ecosystems, rain forests and coral reefs, it makes you want desperately to save them. I'm also helping to write and research a TV special on cryptozoology."

"What's that?" asked Claire.

"It's the study of bizarre animals that might or might not be real, like the Loch Ness Monster and Sasquatch. I'm reading about the Beast of Gévaudan right now. Have you ever heard of it?"

They both shook their heads. "Can't say I have," said Mr. Norton.

"It's really interesting," Myra said. "Gévaudan was an eighteenth-century French village that was terrorized by a mysterious animal. Supposedly it killed a hundred people altogether and wounded dozens. People who saw this Beast said it had a wolf-like appearance, only it was bigger and a strange reddish colour. It might have been a wolf–dog hybrid, because normally wolves don't attack and eat people like that. That would explain the size and peculiar colouring of the Beast. People were terrified of it; they even made up wild stories about it breathing fire and walking on its hind legs, and they said it could be in more than one place at a time. Some people thought it was the Devil, or that an evil sorcerer had summoned some kind of demon. It's said the Beast was once seen in the company of a man—isn't that strange? And *two* Beasts were once seen together."

"I guess that'd explain how it could be in two places at once," said Claire.

"That's right. The attacks of the Beast of Gévaudan stopped when two unusually large wolves were killed in the vicinity, so everyone concluded that the Beast was in fact these two animals. But the strangest thing of all is that something rather similar happened in Africa in 1898. Only in that case it wasn't wolves; it was two huge lions that ran amok in a place called Tsavo in Kenya, killing more than a hundred labourers working on the Uganda railroad."

"Oh, yeah—there was a movie based on that story, wasn't there?" said Claire.

"That's right. Now, lions don't normally behave like that, either. It made me wonder if there was some kind of connection between these two incidents."

"What sort of connection could there be?" asked Mr. Norton.

"I have no idea. What do wolves and lions have in common? Nothing I can think of. Except that in both cases people thought the animals were evil spirits. To quote a book about Tsavo I've been reading: 'So fearless were the attacks of these two abominable beasts, so endlessly resourceful and cunning their strategies for securing human prey, so uncanny their ability to evade and even, apparently, to detect the traps set for them, that many of the terrified workmen began to declare that the creatures were not lions at all, but demons in animal shape.' Doesn't that give you the shivers?"

She was looking at Claire as she spoke. *She's watching me,* Claire thought, *looking for my reaction. Does she suspect that I know all about daimons and animal hosts? Or even that I'm Alice? What if she tries to confide in me? Should I give in and tell her everything I know—or pretend I don't understand and keep her out of what's going on?* With an effort she kept her expression mildly interested and noncommittal.

"These things always turn out to have rational explanations," said Mr. Norton, oblivious to his daughter's dilemma. "Like your French Beast turning out to be a couple of wolves. Come to think of it, there's something quite similar going on right here in Willowville."

"There is?" Claire stared at her father, distracted.

"Well, not quite at the same level as that Gévaudan thing. But large wild animals have been seen locally, attacking people's pets and even following children. None of the witnesses can agree on whether they're coyotes or wolves, though they've been described as too big to be either. There was a really big one seen in the ravine a few nights ago."

"Again, probably a hybrid," said Myra. "Wolf–coyote, coyote–dog, or wolf–dog. Perhaps even a mix of the three. They can all interbreed."

Wolf–dog . . . Claire's thoughts immediately went to the van Burens' "pets." No doubt Phobetor and his fellow daimons roamed free in the ravine at nights, hunting smaller animals for sport, amusing themselves—and giving rise to rumours of wolves and coyotes in the town. "This big animal—was it black?" she asked, thinking of the dog Rex.

Her father raised his eyebrows. "Black? No—brownish with a darker colouring on its back. Why? Do you think you've seen it?"

Claire realized in horror that she had spoken without thinking. Both Dad and Myra were staring at her now. Had she given herself away? Did Myra know about the black dog, and would she guess the reason for Claire's query? She tried wildly to come up with another, perfectly ordinary reason, but her mind was blank. "Uh—seen it? No, I—I just wondered. Because wolves and coyotes are brown, so if it was another colour that'd prove it was a hybrid, maybe." Even to her own ears that sounded unconvincing.

"Anybody up for a second helping?" she added, rising in a hurry from her seat.

Chapter 9

LATE THAT NIGHT, after Myra had left and her father had gone to bed, Claire spoke to her familiar in the privacy of her bedroom.

"Did you hear what Myra said about the Beast of—what was that place called?"

The kitten jumped onto her lap and curled himself up into a marmalade-coloured ball. *"Gévaudan. I know it well. It was the site of what I believe was one of the worst daimonic infiltrations in history."*

"Infiltrations? I don't understand. What exactly happened there? And what has it got to do with that other place—Tsavo? Is Myra on to something?"

Amber eyes blinked up at her. *"I will show you, and you shall judge."*

Into her mind there came a picture: steep mountain pastures, strewn with boulders and fringed with dark forest. She was reminded of the image he had given her of her mother, but in this scene the colours were brighter and there was sound as well: she could hear the rustle of wind in tree branches, and in the distance the bleating of sheep. Then the angle of view slanted and tilted, showing her more of the mountain's lower slopes; sheep were moving in large flocks down there, and crook-wielding shepherds walked in the midst of the woolly bodies as if wading in rivers of fleece-white foam. Nearer at hand, some shaggy cattle grazed the turf while a pair of large heavy-muzzled dogs paced to and fro protectively. A young woman sat on a boulder nearby watching them. She was clad, like the shepherds below, in plain peasant attire: in her case, a dull brown skirt and tight bodice over a short-sleeved blouse. It was a thrill to think that this was no mere recreation of the past, like a movie with an actress in period dress. Claire was seeing real history, just as she had seen it in her Alice and Flower-in-a-drought memories. But this was a time and place unknown to her.

Suddenly there came a great rushing sound, a thrashing and crackling of snapped twigs from the direction of the forest, and out of the twilight under the trees a huge shape came bounding. At first she thought it was a bear—a lean, long-legged bear with russet-brown fur. Then she saw that its ears were sharper than a bear's, and it had a long tufted tail. It came on at a hard run, springing over the rock-strewn alp, heading in the direction of the cattle. They bellowed and scattered in panic. The two dogs ran forward to challenge the great red-brown animal, but it bared long yellow fangs in a savage snarl and they too turned and fled, yelping. The beast continued to charge—not at the cows and bulls, but at the girl guarding them.

The cries of the dogs had alerted the girl to the approaching danger. She stood for an instant frozen in fear, mouth rounded in a soundless scream; then abandoning her lowing and milling charges, she began to run, struggling and stumbling in her long skirts. The great beast pursued her, but was impeded by the mass of terrified cattle. Still it ignored them, dodging past and around them. As it drew closer Claire saw that it resembled a wolf, but with a shorter muzzle and a more massive build. It howled with rage, snapping at a bull that moved to confront it with lowered horns. In the meantime its prey fled down the mountainside, shrieking in terror.

The vista of pasture and mountain faded, and in its place there was Claire's bedroom with its old familiar furnishings. Claire realized her heart was beating hard. "What was it?" she asked, shaken.

"The Beast of Gévaudan–one of them, that is: there were two, as Myra said. This is the only known sighting we have, made by a daimon whose animal host happened to be in the vicinity at the time. That was the creature's very first assault on a human being. There were many more afterwards."

"That girl—did she survive?" Claire could still hear the frantic screams. She knew she'd never be able to forget them.

"Yes. The cattle got in the way of the Beast and she was able to make her escape. Most weren't so lucky. More than a hundred people in the area were slain. The Beasts of Gévaudan preferred human prey to livestock."

"What were they? That thing looked like a cross between a bear and a giant wolf."

"The Beasts were wolf–dog hybrids, we think, specially bred for size and strength. We have long suspected that the rogue daimons of the Legion are capable not only of controlling animals but of forcing them to breed, actively encouraging the stronger, fiercer ones to mate and produce even more powerful offspring."

"But why? Why would they do that?"

"To create better hunters, as you saw. These daimons are, as I said, fascinated by violence, and so they prefer hosts that are predators. Over the ages they've concentrated on these species and bred them to make them bigger and more fearsome—I have wondered at times if they might even have been responsible for those prehistoric species you call the Tyrannosaurus rex *and the Terror Bird."*

Another mental scene replaced the interior of her bedroom. This one was of a dry grassland, interspersed with thorn bushes and small trees, a landscape Flower-in-a-drought would have felt at home in. Two prowling forms were visible in the middle distance, shapes the same flat tan colour as the tall grasses through which they moved. Two huge, maneless male lions, their jaws hanging open in the heat to show their teeth and lolling tongues. One seemed to turn towards Claire, and she looked straight into its yellow eyes. They were not at all like the warm amber eyes of Flower's young lion, but were cold as stones, empty of soul and expression, intent only on the search for prey. Human prey . . .

Once more the image faded. "And those were the Tsavo lions," she said, "weren't they?"

"Yes. Those two animals held up the building of the Uganda Railway into Kenya for nine months by killing more than 130 labourers. It would appear that the daimons controlling them did not want that railway built. The African continent, with its variety of wildlife, has much to offer to the predator daimons and they may have resented the incursion of Europeans into their hunting grounds.

"Gévaudan is more puzzling. The slaughter there seems meaningless. I am struck, though, by the fact that so many

victims of the Beasts were women. Were the daimons after someone in particular? A shamaness, perhaps? They might even have suspected, Claire, that you had been reborn in that time, and set out to destroy you. For in these two Beasts I see the same culprits as before: a rogue daimon and a human who has learned with his help to control living creatures. That's the explanation for the two man-eating lions of Tsavo, the two rampaging wolf-beasts of Gévaudan. And also for the pair of witch hunters, Morley and King, who murdered hundreds of women, including poor Alice. And long before that, in the dawn of human history, a witch doctor with a leopard familiar in prehistoric Africa, who met you in your very first incarnation."

"And now they're back again, as van Buren and his wolf-dog. But what are they up to this time? And how can I stop it when I don't know what their plan *is*?"

"That's what I'm wondering. Exactly what is the source of van Buren's wealth and what business does he work at?"

"He's a diamond dealer or something."

"Is that all, or has he some other work on the side? I can't tell, limited as I am to the use of animal bodies."

"Maybe I can find something out for you."

"Don't take any risks, Claire. I don't want to see your life cut short again when it has such promise. We'll have to bide our time."

"Leo, I don't want to just wait until the bad guys move against me. Remember what they did to me the last time." Cold grey water seemed to close in around her as she spoke, sucking her down into lightless depths. She rubbed her arms and shuddered.

"They will not be as bold as that again. Your current era has its advantages, including your justice system and criminal

investigators. The daimon Phobetor may strike with impunity, leaving his animal host to take the blame. But Mr. van Buren must take care."

"Yes—even in Scotland he bought it in the end, when he was Edward Morley. You knew that Morley and King were executed?"

"Yes—for killing you, an innocent person. Phobetor wasn't harmed, of course; he merely left King's body when the man died. But Morley cannot have found his hanging a pleasant experience. No doubt he resents you for that as well as for what you did to him back in Africa. I'd very much like to know what he's up to now. Is he just searching for you? Or has he some other scheme in mind?"

"In a way it's too bad that Mimi and the Chelseas and Donna have all quit the Circle. I could've pumped them for more information about their meetings."

"I doubt you'd learn much from them. A lot of important information would slip past them, since they have no idea what's really going on. You need an informed, expert spy. I would do it, but I can't risk any of my hosts coming to harm. I and the daimons who are like me are against hurting or killing living things. The rogue daimons like Phobetor don't care about that sort of thing. His predations in Gévaudan and Tsavo caused his animal hosts to be shot dead, and I suspect he also killed the great grey owl that he and the van Burens were using to spy on Willowmere. Did you hear that the power failure that occurred when you were alone at Willowmere was caused by a large bird flying into a transformer? And that owl hasn't been seen since. Phobetor and his ilk are utterly callous about such things, and I will not allow myself to become like him—not even to gather necessary intelligence."

She smiled wanly. "You couldn't just be a fly on the wall?"

"I could, but I'd be limited to an insect's senses, which are nothing like yours. Yes, yes, I know that was partly a joke. But you do see why I can't help that way."

Claire nodded. She thought hard for a moment, resting her chin in her hand. "Van Buren saw me on the roof with Josie. And he saw your owl host too. He knows I've got a daimon on my side. He might know that my mom was aware of daimons—he may even have been the one to arrange the attack on Whiskers that scared Mom off. But there's nothing to tie *me* directly to Alice and Flower-in-a-drought. Not yet, anyway. Right now he just knows I'm a friend of Myra Moore's, and that *she's* descended from Alice's half-brother. That might look a little suspicious. But then, lots of other girls from my school went to Myra's place to meet Silverhawk and the other Wiccans, so as far as he knows I might just have gone to her to try to learn about the Craft, too. And perhaps I learned about her uncle at the same time, enough to be able to summon a daimon on my own. Because that's pretty much what *did* happen, after all. Myra and I haven't been doing anything together with our daimons—I've been really careful not to get her involved in any of this. All van Buren really knows is that I've been to her place, picked up a lot of stuff about daimons and learned how to call on them, and then used that knowledge to fight Josie."

"Yes—I think you're right. For the moment, he's not certain about you—just intrigued."

"So he wants to know more about me, and I want to know more about him and what he's up to." Claire went to her computer and turned it on. "Well, let's see what we can find out about him from the net. Klaus van Buren is an unusual name—

how many of them can there be out there?" She activated her search engine and typed the name in.

The kitten jumped up on her desk and sat next to her mouse pad, gazing intently at the screen. *"I can't quite make out the words. The print is too small. Cats' eyes aren't good at this kind of fine detail."*

"There's a special magnifying function for the visually impaired—there, is that better? Well, there's a Klaus van Buren, dealer in fine diamonds . . . That'll be our guy. And yes, he's a dog breeder too. He's still got some kennels operating in South Africa. Now, here's another entry. Some kind of biotech firm—looks like he's on the board of directors." She paused. "If this is the same man, that is."

"Biotechnology," mused Leo. *"The altering of living things through genetic manipulation. I can see how that might appeal to a daimon. That way they could create changes in animals in one generation without having to get them to mate. And the changes could be more dramatic and unnatural. Dogs already have supersensitive hearing and smell, but these could be improved even further. And they could be given greater strength and stamina, and their body size increased. In short, they could be made into perfect hunters. Some could be sold on the side for profit, as hunting dogs or police dogs. But the ultimate goal of such a program would be superior hosts for predator daimons."* The kitten looked up at Claire. *"I don't like this. I can think of some other possibilities too, very disturbing ones."*

Claire shut down the computer and stroked the kitten's ears. He jumped down onto her lap. "Well, they've been spying on us," she said presently. "Maybe it's time we did a little spying on them. If we can't risk an animal host, could we maybe find one that they won't be willing to harm? One of their own pets, for instance?"

There were footsteps in the hallway. *"Your father,"* Leo warned.

Claire raised her voice. "Who's my wittle kitty? My cyoot wittle kittycat?" she crooned. "Izzee the pwettiest kitty in the world? Duzzee want his tummy tickled?"

Dad's footsteps moved away down the hall and descended the stairs. "Okay," Claire said, her voice returning to normal, "Nick somehow managed to summon the bad daimon into Myra's dog, Angus. Why can't we pull the same kind of trick on them—but use it to spy on them, not attack them?"

Leo considered a moment. *"I would imagine most of their animals are in constant use as hosts by the rogue daimons. However . . . they have been making use of a flock of crows lately. You've seen them, perhaps, gathering in the trees next door."*

She nodded. "Yes. Looks like something out of a Hitchcock film. Al Ramsay's journal mentioned some crows hanging around the place; he suspected they were daimon-controlled. This has been going on long before the van Burens arrived in Willowville. There was the dog attack on poor Whiskers."

"Yes—though the van Burens could easily have controlled it all from Africa—distance means nothing to shamans and daimons. Now, I suspect the daimons who use the wolf-dogs' bodies for hosts are also using the crows, just to give themselves a change of pace. The dogs would have to be confined, at least in daytime, so the daimons turn to the crows and spend those hours flying free—and spying. They must come and go from the crows' bodies at will, switching from host to host as the whim takes them. I've seen them flying in and out of one of the upper-storey windows. They have access to the house."

"You couldn't take one over? Sort of like hacking into someone else's avatar on a computer?"

"Yes. But I would likely only get away with it once, I think; they may catch on rather quickly to what I'm doing. I'll have to choose a time with care."

"Leo, I'd like to listen in as well. I did it once before, didn't I—that night when I dreamed I was the owl. I was linked to you, wasn't I? I could see and hear and feel along with you."

"Yes, you were reaching out to me then, whether you knew it or not, and your mind touched mine while I was linked to the owl. But for you to link more directly to an animal would be dangerous. If any harm should come to my crow-host, I wouldn't suffer. But you would. Your nervous system would relay the same messages the host receives, causing you pain and trauma. Remember Josie and the rat."

"Teach me how to break off the link to the animal, then. I want to do this, Leo. I need to know what I'm dealing with here—to get a sense of what these people are about. Nick, for instance—how does he fit into all this? Is he daimon-controlled, too—or is he just like his uncle, bad all on his own?"

"All right then—but when I tell you to break the link, you must do it at once."

"Okay. Now what do I do exactly?"

"Just wait for me to contact you and tell you that the time is right. It's better for you to do this at a time when you can pretend to be asleep, because you'll have to go into a trance-like state."

She smiled. "Yes—if Dad sees me turn into a zombie all of a sudden he'll be pretty upset. And obviously I can't do this while I'm at school. It's the weekend now. Couldn't we try it in the next two days?"

"Perhaps. I'll keep a close watch on the enemy's house and try to choose a moment when they're both away. And then—we will learn what we will learn."

"I hope this helps, that's all." There was no answer. The kitten jumped suddenly out of her lap onto the floor and started to play with her shoelace. Leo had left him.

✧ ✧ ✧

Claire heard no more from her guardian until Saturday afternoon. The leaves were now falling heavily, and she and her father were out most of the morning raking them into piles. "Here's the deal," he told her. "We'll rake leaves until lunchtime, then later today I'll give you some very basic driving lessons. I know you've been wanting to drive for a long time, and I promise we'll get you a learner's permit. But in the meantime we can go to a quiet parking lot somewhere and I'll show you how to start and stop the car. It should be okay as long as we stay off the road."

"Deal," said Claire, pleased. She did not in the least mind raking leaves. There was something very calming about the activity; she was reminded of her childhood, of jumping into the fragrant, rustling leaf-heaps. The maple tree on the front lawn had surrounded itself with a thick scarlet carpet, and as she scraped the leaves up with her rake she couldn't help glancing at the tree, and especially at the little round hole halfway up the trunk that gaped like a tiny cave-mouth. She remembered the sensation of flying down to this tree on an owl's soft-feathered wings, seeking the refuge of the hole even as the talons of a larger owl reached out to seize her. It was a strange, fantastical memory, but it wasn't like recalling a dream.

She knew it had really happened—that she really had been linked through her mind to the owl Leo used as a host. But she hadn't known then how to pull free of her unconscious link to him and the bird, and only Leo's urging of the barred owl into the safe refuge of the tree's interior had saved her.

Would I have died if the owl died? she wondered, shuddering. In such mental links shamans' nervous systems actually reproduced all the animal host's sensations. That was why a witch would die suddenly if her animal familiar did; there would be no time to terminate the link. Claire began to doubt whether she really should take part in this new experiment. It seemed safe enough, given the choice of host. But she was starting to have misgivings.

When she went to her room after lunch Leonardo the kitten was sitting bolt upright on her bed, with an alert, intelligent expression she had come to know well. She untied her sneakers, kicked them off, and sat down on the bed beside him.

After a moment Leo spoke. "*I have made a search of the van Burens' grounds from the air with the help of a seagull flying over the estate. I picked up a stale French fry outside a restaurant, so that some other gulls would see and pursue me. A group of birds looks less suspicious than one.*"

"Clever," laughed Claire, tucking her legs underneath her. "You'd have made a great spy. So what did you find out?"

"There are, in addition to several dog runs and kennels at the back, some wire cages with crows in them. Of course, the birds that are under daimon control can fly free; when they're not serving as hosts, they must be kept in captivity until they're needed. I saw one crow fly out of a cage as I passed over. The daimons must be able to free themselves from the cages; otherwise, the van Burens would be busy all day letting them out and

shutting them back in. That means the cages have locks inside that a daimon can operate, but a crow cannot."

"It couldn't be too hard to outsmart a crow."

"You would be surprised. Members of the corvid family are very intelligent. But I digress. What I must do is choose one crow, figure out the lock on its cage and escape—then fly into the house. I can find van Buren's office and search his files and private papers, look for anything that might give us a clue as to what he's planning. I doubt he's here merely to take revenge on the former Alice. What, for instance, is this Dark Circle of his all about? Van Buren doesn't really believe in evil spells and curses; as a revenant he knows such things don't exist. This 'coven' must be a front for something. And what is the role of the boy, Nick, in this affair? These are the things I want to find out. Do you still wish to link to me and my host?"

"Yes," replied Claire after a lengthy pause. "I'm a bit nervous about it, but—two heads are better than one. This is too important for either of us to miss anything."

"I could try to persuade another daimon to help me instead. There are some on my side who might be willing. Or we could try to talk Myra Moore and her daimon into helping."

"I'd rather you didn't. I'm trying as hard as I can to keep Myra in the dark about this."

"She would be a good ally. She obviously learned much about the situation from her late uncle."

"No. This is my problem, not hers. If I'm your ward, then you could say that Myra's mine. I'm not dragging her into this. I'm—I'm warding her, and Willowmere."

The kitten gazed long at her, a gaze more lingering, more thoughtful than that of any animal. She could almost *see* Leo looking out of its amber eyes. *"You really have difficulty opening up to others of your kind, haven't you? A consequence of having so often lost people dear to you, I suspect: your mother, in both your previous lives and in this one; and your William. It has made you afraid to lose others, afraid to love them."*

"Thanks for the analysis, Dr. Freud, but I'm still doing this my own way. As for your daimon friends, they all have to depend on animals to learn things about our world. You told me it limits you in lots of ways. Leo, could you even use a computer if you tried?"

"I could probably use yours, having watched you from the kitten's eyes. Still, you have a point. When it comes to things like searching for files, you would be of more use. Anyway, we must make haste, if you're joining me. Your Mr. van Buren has gone off in his car, but Nick went out on foot and may be gone for only a short time. We must move now." The kitten nudged her hand with his nose. *"Lie down on the bed and shut your eyes. That way if your father looks in on you he'll think you're just having a nap after all that fresh air."*

Claire did as she was told. For some time she was aware of nothing but her own breathing and the pale autumn sunlight beating against her lids. Then a faint picture formed within the spangled patterns against her eyelids—dim, poorly focused, remote as a movie playing on a screen. There was a grid-like pattern, and through it she saw distinct shapes: trees, buildings, clouds in the sky.

She was looking out through a wire cage with the eyes of its occupant.

Chapter 10

A bird's-eye view, Claire thought as the image came into focus. *Literally.*

There was none of the otherworldly quality she had known in her link to Leo and the barred owl. The details in this mental picture were sharp and clear, amazingly so: she could see every leaf-edge wavering in the wind, every single blade of grass. And though her twin fields of vision didn't quite overlap at the front, her peripheral vision was greatly increased. Claire was reminded of the day when she was outfitted with her very first pair of glasses. She had lived so long with her increasing myopia that she'd had no conception of what she was missing. With all its blurred and softened edges removed, the world had looked almost unreal to her at first, too distinct, too precise. Now she had that same sensation: the scene before her seemed almost too clear and crowded with detail, and the colours—! They were brighter than the colours of her own familiar world, more vivid, luminescent, and jewel-like.

She called out with her mind. *"Leo, are you there? This is amazing!"*

"I'm here," his mental voice replied.

"I can't believe how clear and bright everything looks."

"Birds have the best eyesight in the world, far better than mammals. And they see in colour too—the ones that are active by day, anyway. Owls see a more limited spectrum, being night hunters."

The cage she was in was something like a rabbit hutch, with walls and roof of wire and a sawdust floor. There were many others surrounding it, some empty, some containing sleek black crows. Her field of vision tilted slightly as her bird-host cocked its head, and she saw more crows—a dozen at least—perching in the boughs of a tall tree several metres away.

"How do you do this—get inside an animal's head?"

"First of all, we're not inside the bird's head—it only feels that way to you. Your mind and body are still in your own room at home, and I am in my daimon dimension. We're both touching the bird's consciousness, which like all minds—even the faint, rudimentary minds of lower animals—intrudes into my mental universe. We daimons have learned to monitor all these mental signals, analyze the images within them, and determine what regions of your world they come from. We have mapped out your whole planet, just by comparing all the millions of mental images we receive from its creatures."

She tried to imagine that piecing together of a whole world, just from glimpses of mountains, seas, plains, seen from the eyes of the living things dwelling among them. And of course those geographical features would change over time. The thought filled her with awe. The daimons had memorized not one Earth but many, all the Earths of all the ages, including and preceding humanity's recorded history.

"Once we touch a mind, we try to learn all about the creature that possesses it—a quality you know as empathy. Reach out with your mind now, and feel the bird: its senses, its body, its awareness of itself. The rebel daimons seek only to control a host, to influence it, make it do whatever they wish. But I and those like me desire to understand living things, to forge partnerships with them. To do that, you must put the creature first—subordinate yourself to it. Think, Claire, of being a crow."

She concentrated, and little by little it came to her: not just the world as seen by the crow, but the bird itself. The quick, flickering impressions that made up its mind, the messages of its nerves that told her of the wings and flexible neck and strong, clawed legs on which it stood. She imagined what it must be like always to have this form, and how it must feel to fly free among the treetops, where the spreading network of branches made perches and nesting places and aerial roads for the swift-running squirrels.

Leo's mental voice sounded amused when he spoke again. *"There's a band on the crow's right leg—so that's how they can tell their own crows from any that might be used by our side. Very clever of them. And I see the lock, too. A simple hook-and-eye arrangement, high up on the inside of the cage door. You see it? Just a little higher than the crow might normally reach. The daimons lock their hosts in before they leave them and so ensure that the hosts stay in one convenient location until they're ready to use them again. Would you like to unlock the door, Claire?"*

"How do I do that?"

"Suggest to the bird that it do so. Draw its attention to the shiny metal. It's like riding a horse: you give the directions, and persuade the animal to follow them."

Claire turned her thoughts to the metal hook resting in its metal ring. *"Look at that,"* she silently urged the flickering mind of the bird. *"Look! You want to touch that thing. You want to fly at it and peck it and take it in your beak. Go on! Do it!"*

The bird's-eye view tilted again. The crow's gaze focused on the hook. It hopped forward, still gazing upwards, and half-spread its wings. A caw burst from its throat, which set some of the birds in the neighbouring cages to cawing as well. Then it sprang up at the hook.

The first thrust of the bird's beak dislodged the hook, but it merely flipped upwards and then settled back into the ring. *"Come on,"* thought Claire. *"Give it another try!"* The crow sprang again, striking harder. At last the hook dangled loose. The wire door swung open. And the crow, finding itself free, forgot the shiny metal and flung itself forward into the air.

Claire *felt* the sweep of the wings, the exhilarating skyward surge as the crow flew up, up into the boughs of the tallest tree. Then she was perching with it on a high branch with the autumn leaves all around her: ruby, emerald, citrine, a cascade of incandescent colour. Between gaps in the foliage the sky blazed like blue fire. She was filled with a heady, giddy excitement, and another sensation almost like joy—drunk on the mingled sensations of flight and enhanced vision. This was not the world she had known, as Claire or Alice or Flower-in-a-drought: this was a new realm altogether, vaster, richer, crying out to be explored.

"Keep your focus," cautioned Leo's voice within her mind. *"The open window—do you see it, Claire?"*

"Yes." The house loomed before her, huge in the crow's eyes, a giant's castle. There was a window in one of the turrets, tall and narrow, its pane opening outwards. Before the crow looked away from the house again she thought hard about the window,

suggesting to the bird that it was a good place to go to, safe, familiar; that there might perhaps be food in there as well as the shelter it offered. She felt the crow resisting the suggestion, wanting to join the other crows in the upper branches of the tree, but she kept gently prodding him and at length he opened his wings again and sprang off the twig. There was a sensation of plunging that made her feel as if her own stomach—back in her bedroom on Maple Street—was turning inside out. Then in one long, graceful arc the crow flew from the tree to the open window and landed on the sill.

It took her a moment to distinguish details in the room beyond—it seemed dark after the dazzling sun outside—but presently Claire could make out the shapes of furnishings and of pictures on the walls, looking huge from this perspective. It was a private office or study. There was a large grey desk with a computer and printer on it, some stacks of paper, and a few folders. Claire coaxed the bird, with a little help from Leo, to fly down onto the desk. A leather jacket hung on the back of the chair, she noticed—too big for Mr. van Buren; it must be Nick's. There were two doors, one opening on the hallway and one on an adjoining room. She made the crow fly on through this second door. There was another gigantic room beyond—a bedroom, sparse and Spartan-looking except for a few framed pictures and posters. These were dark, sinister paintings of shadowy figures and faces, of men and savage wild animals locked in gory battle. She felt repelled by them; if she had needed any proof that Nick was a disturbed and abnormal young man, those pictures were enough to convince her of it. But also she felt a twinge of unease, a sudden awareness that she was invading someone else's private space. She urged the bird to fly out the huge open door, and after a moment it complied, flapping down the hallway outside. Nick, Claire knew, had one whole wing of the house to himself, so if she wanted to see van Buren's office the crow must be made to fly to the opposite end of the building.

The hallway swept past, swaying a little from side to side as the crow veered in its flight. Now and then it hovered, wings beating furiously, searching for a perch. She and Leo together persuaded it to hover briefly in front of the doorway of each room it came to, and it obeyed, but afterwards had to be urged to fly on. They passed a bathroom, an upstairs laundry room, and another room that contained a number of cages and terrariums. There was a small owl in one cage, a large snake in another, but most of the cages contained white mice and rats. *"Food for the other animals,"* said Leo. *"So that's where Josie's rat came from."*

The crow was getting tired and uncooperative. It took both their urging to make it fly on. At last Claire said to Leo, *"There—that must be it!"*

A door opened on another study, larger and grander than Nick's, with a carved wooden desk and wall-to-wall bookshelves. There was a computer here too, as well as a fax machine and a small photocopier.

The crow flew down and landed on top of the desk, folding its wings. It looked around it, cocking its head to one side and then the other. They had a good look along with it. There were many objects on the desk, from small carvings and statues to jewellery cases.

"Can we get him to turn the computer on somehow?" asked Claire.

"I'm sure we can. He is a very intelligent bird, remember. Ideally we should motivate him with the promise of food—the

same method your species uses to train animals, from dogs to dolphins. But in the absence of any food, we'll just have to be gently persuasive."

"Well, maybe we can let him go wild in the kitchen later. In the meantime—persuade away."

Leo spoke to the bird—or rather, he sent little glimmers of thought through its mind, images and suggestions. He coaxed it to focus on the machine before it, hinted that the big box might hold something good—perhaps even something edible. The crow considered a moment, its gaze sweeping the objects on the desk but always returning to the computer. Finally it stalked towards the tower, and guided by Leo and Claire, poked at the power switch with its strong, sharp beak. After a few tries the system turned on. Next they directed it to the monitor and the smaller power switch there.

As the screen came to life a box appeared demanding a six-character password. Claire remarked, *"Well, there we are—locked out! Of course in movies the password's always something ridiculously easy to guess . . . What're you doing? Oh."*

Leo was making the bird peck at the keys. First he tried M-O-R-L-E-Y, then Y-E-L-R-O-M. After the second letter combination the words "password approved" appeared.

"There!" said Leo. They began to search through the files, one by one. There were drafts for speeches, reports, and various emails from business associates. After they had read through several of these, Claire spoke to her daimon.

"There's not much here about dogs, is there?" she said.

"No. This biotech firm seems to be mostly concerned with human genetics—improving human strength and agility," said Leo, *"but I see nothing in any of their documents about curing disease or improving human longevity."*

"Maybe they're just into athletics."

"Improving athletic performance might appeal to some people. But isn't most of the money in genetics in finding cures and improving overall health?"

"Yes. That is kind of strange."

"Perhaps not so very strange," mused Leo.

Before she could ask him what he meant, a loud bang echoed from downstairs as the front door of the mansion opened and slammed shut again. The crow, startled, instinctively opened its wings and flew up onto one of the higher bookshelves. Then came the sound of heavy footsteps in the downstairs hall, and a man's voice muffled by distance.

"Mr. van Buren," Claire said. *"He's back. But who's he talking to?"*

They couldn't hear a second voice. Was he talking into a cellphone—or perhaps communicating out loud with a daimon? *"We'd better get the crow to turn this machine off,"* said Leo. *"We can't leave it running, or van Buren will know someone has been here."*

The crow took some persuading, even with both of them working at it. The bird was clearly growing bored with its surroundings and was feeling hungry as well. It wanted only to leave the room now, and even when they succeeded in coaxing it off the bookshelf it went for the window instead. This was fortunately closed, but the crow hovered in front of the glass barrier for some time before it became convinced that there was no way through the transparent panes to the trees and sky beyond. It dropped and settled on the sill, cawing irritably.

"The desk! Go to the desk!" Claire urged the bird. She could hear van Buren's heavy tread on the main staircase. His study

was probably the first place he'd go to. *"Come on, come on—the desk! That big flat place! You want to go there . . ."*

Finally Leo had to lure it with a promise of food if it obeyed, sending mental images of foods appealing to crows. It flew to the desk. The footsteps were in the upstairs hall now, and the voice. They could now hear clearly what was said.

". . . a little patience, that's all I'm asking. You've waited this long, my friend. Is it so hard to wait a little longer?" There was a brief pause, as if van Buren were listening to some inaudible response, then: "Yes, yes, of course I understand. Very tiresome. But you know King was a special case. There just aren't that many human beings who reach out to your dimension nowadays. So many other areas to pursue, and of course most people don't believe the old lore. This is a highly sceptical age . . ."

"Food," thought Leo at the crow again, and Claire added her mental voice to his. The bird walked across the desk to the computer monitor and tapped the off switch with its beak. There was no time to shut down the system by command. The crow fluttered over to the computer tower and stood with its head to one side, regarding the main power switch.

The voice was closer, clearer. "The boy, yes, he knows all about it, and is venturing farther each day. No inhibitions there any more. But you know he's needed for this current business, and he's really the only person for the job. Trust me, my friend. You know what a fine hunter I am. The attack, the wounding and killing of the prey, that is where you excel and always have. But my forte is the planning, the strategy that precedes all of that. Sometimes your prey must be lured out of hiding. How, for instance, do you hunt a lion? You have had lion hosts, so you should know. You must make use of something that the lion wants. You tether a goat out in the open where its bleating can be heard, and you crouch down with your gun, and you wait . . . You wait until the lion, drawn by its hunger, emerges from cover—and you have it. You see? The boy is the lure, drawing them all here; we have only to reveal a little more information and we may have our quarry in our sights . . ."

Claire and Leo sent out a simultaneous urgent plea to the crow, and it sprang up again, wings beating, and jabbed at the round glowing button with its beak. Once, twice: the pressure was not enough. The green light would not go out. The system was protected against this kind of shutdown.

"The power bar," said Claire.

"The what?"

"That plastic bar with the switches, for surge protection. Over there under the desk. Quick, hit the red switch!"

The crow hopped over to the bar and stood beside it. Then it pecked hard at the switch. At once the computer turned off. *"There,"* said Claire. *"With any luck he'll think he accidentally hit the thing with his foot. All the computer will say when he switches it on again is that it shut down improperly."*

The footsteps entered the room. Peering out with the crow's eyes from underneath the desk, they saw van Buren standing by the door dressed in a suit with a briefcase in one hand. *On a Saturday?* Claire thought. *Where's he been?*

The black dog stood at his side.

So he had been talking to Phobetor. But there was no time to ponder further, for the crow, alarmed at the appearance of the dog and man, and further agitated by Claire and Leo's own unease, could no longer be controlled. It started out from underneath the desk, uttered a loud caw, and took wing.

The black dog jumped backwards, startled, then began to bark in fury. Claire felt a wave of vertigo as the room seemed to spin around her, walls looming up and falling away again as the crow circled in search of an escape route. Van Buren was still too close to the door for its comfort, and it kept flying towards the window, drawn to the vista of freedom it offered.

"Where did that bird come from? Is it one of ours?" van Buren snapped.

The crow alighted on the bookshelf again. Feeling safe on this high perch, it cawed its defiance at the two larger creatures below it.

"It is one of our own crows—I see the leg band," said van Buren, answering his own question. He looked disconcertingly huge from the bird's perspective: an evil giant looming below. "But why is it behaving like that? Is there no daimon using it? It shouldn't be indoors, if so. Something is wrong."

He moved closer. Leo spoke to Claire: *"We had best go now. He'll summon his other daimons, and if one of them links to this crow I'll be discovered. Go, Claire! Think of your room, and return there."*

The giant man reached up a monstrous hand, grabbing for the bird. An unreasoning terror seized hold of Claire. The crow, feeling it, jabbed with its beak at van Buren's fingers, drawing blood. With a bellow he recoiled, glaring.

"Blasted bird! I'm going for my gun." He headed for the desk, and reaching in his pocket, he took out a key. The dog moved closer to the bookcase, glowering up with malevolent, tawny eyes.

Leo spoke again, his mind-voice filled with urgency. *"Claire! Let go and return! You must let go!"*

Through the fog of fear that had overtaken her mind, Claire realized what he meant. Leo was safe, but she was bound to the bird, and if van Buren killed it she too would die. Desperately she strove to withdraw, to pull away from the crow's mind and body, retract the tendrils of thought that tied them together.

Van Buren unlocked the drawer and took out a small handgun.

"Fly!" Leo commanded the crow. It launched itself forward, flapping off the shelf and swooping down across the room and through the open door. The black wolf-dog barked in fury and leaped as high as it could, teeth snapping together in the air, then spun and followed the crow out the door. As the panicked bird glided back down the hallway, Claire caught a glimpse of van Buren, carrying the gun in his hand. Frantic, she thrust hard at the bird-mind, shoving it away from her, picturing instead the safe interior of her bedroom. Her vision began to swim, to fade.

There was a great, shattering report like thunder.

Claire gasped—and sat up.

She was lying on her bed again, looking around at her own safe, normal-sized room. Her heart was racing, and her chest heaved as though she had been running for her life.

Chapter 11

CLAIRE SPENT THE REST of the afternoon recuperating from her experience and wondering what was happening over at the warlocks' mansion. Van Buren was bound to figure out that someone had been into his computer files. The improper shutdown could only have happened while the system was up, and he'd have no memory of any such thing happening while he was at the computer. Even so, he might have dismissed it as a glitch or his own faulty memory had it not been for the panicked flight of the crow.

"I managed to get the crow to the open window in Nick's study," Leo told her. *"Apart from losing a couple of feathers, it should be all right. That's the closest I have ever come to losing a host since Whiskers was killed. I don't want to risk another host."*

"It's my fault, really. I panicked, and that got the bird all excited. But why would van Buren try to kill it? Why should he even suspect it was under someone's control? I mean, a crow could get all agitated on its own. And he grabbed for it—any bird would try to defend itself."

"What worried him was that it clearly wasn't being controlled by one of his own daimons. Why should a daimon take its crow-host inside the house and then abandon it to fly about on its own? Was it an accident that the bird got into his study, where all his private information is stored? Naturally his suspicions were aroused. There was one way to know for sure: take out a gun and see what the bird did. If it remained where it was, it was just a bird ignorant of its danger. If it reacted to the word 'gun' and to the sight of one, it had to be hosting a daimon or a shaman, who would understand what these things meant."

"So we gave ourselves away."

"He would have found out in any case. The rogue daimons will tell him that none of them freed the bird from its cage, and only an outsider daimon or shaman could have taken control of it. One thing is for certain: even if I were willing to borrow one of their crows again, the rogues would likely challenge me. They will monitor their hosts more carefully now."

"And we didn't even learn that much," moaned Claire.

"You think not?" he replied. *"I'm very interested in what we found out about van Buren's company."*

"The files said only that his company is doing the kinds of things other companies like that do—improving human genes and so on. There was nothing about making giant killer dogs or anything like that."

"They wouldn't be likely to commit such things to the internet, where anyone might see them. And they said little enough about their human research, but what I saw made me suspicious. A biotechnology firm that has no interest in improving human health or longevity?"

"Why exactly does that make you suspicious?"

"Because it appears to me that the concerns of this company are not human concerns. They want to make better human bodies—strong and agile and athletic—but apparently feel no concern about what may eventually happen to those bodies. Why worry about the health or lifespan of a body when you can simply discard it and move on to another if it sickens or dies? I suspect they're interested only in designing perfect humans to use as daimon hosts."

"Oh." Claire shuddered. "That's a nasty thought!"

"I might be wrong. But that's certainly how it looks to me. Though how it ties into this Dark Circle business is a mystery."

Claire sat in silence for a moment, gazing out her bedroom window. The day was still sunny and clear, the autumn trees bright. But the colours seemed to her muted, the images dull and unfocused, after seeing through a bird's eyes. "I'm not sorry I had that experience of linking to the crow," she said presently. "It was awesome. But I also have the strangest feeling that there was more to it than I can remember now. Leo, I swear I saw a colour that I've never seen before. It wasn't like blue, or red, or purple, or any colour I know. I keep trying to picture it in my mind and I can't. Could there be such a thing as a *new* colour?"

"New to humans? Of course. Just as dogs can hear sounds too high-pitched for the human ear, birds see more of the spectrum than humans do. They can see well into the ultraviolet, which you cannot. Colour, after all, isn't inherent to an object, but is produced by the observer's eye and influenced by its structure. To a bird certain flowers and berries, and the plumage of other birds such as starlings, reflect UV rays in hues that are invisible to your human eyes. In the past when I showed you things as seen by birds, I always had to mute the

colours a bit–to make them more understandable to a human. But this time you were directly linked to a bird, sharing all its sensations."

"It was incredible—just incredible. It wasn't like dreaming, it was like being more *awake* than I've ever been before. The world was a whole different place. If I could only show other people how to link to birds, it'd blow their minds. No one would ever bother with drugs any more after getting high on something real."

"Yes, indeed. Do you think it's a coincidence that shamans in all cultures are closely associated with birds? Many perform rites in which they dress in feathered or wing-shaped cloaks and go into ecstatic trances in which they dream they are flying. A relic of earlier times, perhaps, when human linking to birds was more common. Well, I must go back to watching over the van Burens–from a safe distance, this time."

"Okay. Take care, and let me know how it goes."

✧ ✧ ✧

After dinner Claire's father drove her to the parking lot behind the discount supermarket at the top of Birch Street, where they got out of the car and switched places, and he taught her the basics of driving. It felt strange to be not only sitting in the driver's seat—she had often sat there when the car was stationary, even as a child, just to get the feel of being behind the wheel—but actually to place the key in the ignition and feel the engine rev up.

"That's it—you're doing fine," he told her as she backed up, turned the wheel, and eased forward with a cautious pressure on the accelerator. It recalled to her an old Alice memory, of learning to ride for the first time on a small shaggy pony, feeling the animal respond to her commands. As she drove slowly around the lot—which was half-empty, as it always was at the dinner hour—Claire noticed a bright yellow Volkswagen Beetle in a parking spot near the front of the supermarket. *But it needn't be Myra's car,* she thought. There were plenty of yellow Beetles around . . .

Then as she passed it for the second time, she saw a magnificent collie raise his head and poke his muzzle out the half-open window. Angus! It *must* be Myra's car. But was her presence here only a coincidence? Claire wondered as she drove back to the vacant half of the lot and parked. Or had Myra somehow known that Claire was on her way here? *This is ridiculous,* she thought. *I'm getting paranoid.*

As she got out of the car and walked around to the passenger side, her father remarked, "Isn't that your friend Dr. Moore coming out of the store?"

She turned to see the familiar plump figure with its mousy grey hair approaching them. "Hellooo!" Myra called out, waving, and Angus gave a volley of barks from the car window. "Lovely evening, isn't it? And what luck to run into you two. I was hoping you could join me for dinner sometime soon. What about this Friday or Saturday?"

"That sounds wonderful," Mr. Norton replied, getting out of the car and smiling at her. "What do you say, Claire? Which day's best for you?"

Claire thought fast. If she was going to convince the warlocks that she'd stuck around Myra's place only to learn about daimons and shamanism, then surely it would look suspicious if she returned to Willowmere any time soon. To keep Myra safe, she should appear to discard her—at least for now. She replied,

"Oh, I'm sorry. I have a really big test coming up pretty soon, and I need to study for it."

Her father raised his eyebrows. "On the weekend?"

"Well, the test's Monday. And I've been kind of putting off studying for it," she said, getting desperate. "I need a whole week."

"Oh, that's too bad. Another time, then," said Myra. "So you're learning to drive, are you? What fun! I remember my own first lessons. Are you shopping too? They've got a sale on Halloween treats for the kids. I'm stocking up for next weekend." She held up her shopping bag.

"I had better get some too while I'm here, I guess," Mr. Norton said.

"You won't be doing the haunted house thing at Willowmere any more, will you?" asked Claire, feeling a little wistful. "Your uncle used to go all out, didn't he? When we were kids my friend Ainsley and I always wanted to go to Willowmere on Halloween night, but our parents wouldn't allow us to cross Lakeside. Killjoys." She threw a look of mock reproach at her father. "Still, I used to catch a glimpse of it sometimes when I went by in a car or a bus." She didn't tell Myra about riding her bike to the estate in daytime so she could peep longingly through the hedge at the house and grounds.

Myra looked thoughtful. "I didn't intend to do all that, but I'm starting to wonder if I should. The neighbourhood children would be so disappointed if I didn't."

"It would be an awful lot of work, though," Claire said. "Your uncle didn't do it all himself, did he?"

"No, that's true. He hired people to help him, especially when he got old and frail."

"Perhaps Claire could come and help you," offered Mr. Norton.

Too late, Claire realized she had trapped herself. What if the van Burens or their spies saw her entering the estate? She cast about vainly for an excuse, but could only manage a feeble "Well, if I get my studying done . . ."

"Forget the studying for an hour or two," said her father, exchanging a genial look with Myra. "Taking a break helps your concentration. You seem to spend all your time closeted in your room these days."

"Well, if you have the time for it, dear, that would be nice," said Myra. "I'm sure I could never do as good a job as my uncle did. But together we could give it a try. It wouldn't take the whole day, only part of the afternoon."

Despairing, Claire gave in. She couldn't do otherwise without hurting Myra's feelings, and it was obvious that her father considered the older woman a good influence. They were both looking at her and she had to give the expected response. But as she and her father made their goodbyes and walked towards the supermarket, she was filled with nervous anxiety.

✧ ✧ ✧

Claire went to school Monday feeling depressed. The school's decor didn't help her mood: the walls and bulletin boards were decked with black-and-orange paper decorations. Everywhere she looked there were ghosts, spiders, skeletons, black-hatted witches on broomsticks, grinning jack-o'-lanterns, and posters advertising the annual Halloween dance. The bristling black cats on these posters drew Claire's eye every time she passed one in the hall. Who would ever have guessed that the traditional witch's familiar had some basis in fact? *"Daimons have always favoured cat hosts . . . a cat offers the best of both worlds."* She felt lonely in her knowledge, cut off from most of the human race.

Mimi and the Chelseas looked at her with a new interest as they gathered around the lockers at lunchtime. "We heard about you and Josie," Mimi remarked. "She really got in trouble, right? I hear the police were there and everything."

Mimi's intelligence network, Claire thought, would put the daimons to shame. "It's all settled," she said in an indifferent voice. "Josie knows what she has to do now. If she leaves me alone I'll do the same for her. But I'd give a lot to know whether she's still sneaking off to the Dark Circle. She's supposed to be grounded, but her parents aren't likely to keep a close eye on her."

"If you really want to know if she's going there," Chel replied, "we could tell you."

Claire stared. "How would you know?"

"'Cause we're going to the meetings again. Chelsea decided to go back to the Circle. She's feeling totally bummed about Dave. So we said we'd go too, to support her, 'cause she doesn't want to go alone. And there's supposed to be a really important meeting Halloween night. So we're all gonna tell our parents we're going to the dance, then we'll drive on to Nick's place. Want to come? Then you can see for yourself what it's like."

See for myself . . . "I can't go. It's too far from my house, and I don't drive yet," Claire replied.

"I could pick you up in my car," said Chel. "You really should go at least once. It's cool. And then you'll finally know what we're talking about. C'mon, give it a try."

"Uh—thanks. I'll think about it," Claire said. "It's definitely an idea."

Instead of going to the library for her spare as usual, she decided to take a short walk. Her head was cluttered with uneasy thoughts and she needed to clear it. Putting on her jacket, she left the school grounds and walked westwards along the street. As she strolled down the sidewalk a grey squirrel kept pace with her, darting along branches high above her head and making acrobatic leaps from tree to tree.

"What is it, Claire?" Leo's voice said in her head. *"Where are you going at this time of day?"*

"Nowhere. I'm just walking. I need to think." She kicked a pinecone along the sidewalk.

The squirrel clambered down the trunk of a large maple, ran across a lawn, and scrambled up the trunk of another tree. *"You're being spied on, did you notice? A couple of crows are flying up ahead."*

She had seen them too: a pair of black specks circling against the sky. As she looked at them, they dropped and settled into the boughs of a big oak several metres in front of her. "Yeah, I'm getting sick of all this surveillance. Fortunately I've got my very own mobile security camera." She deliberately avoided looking straight at the squirrel as he sprang onto a telephone wire, watching him only from the corner of one eye. "Leo, there's a big meeting of the Dark Circle on Sunday night."

"You want me to spy for you? The risk to my host would be too great. I'd have to use another animal; they're monitoring all their crows very carefully now."

"I don't want you to spy. I intend to be there myself."

The squirrel halted in the middle of the wire. *"Be there? At the mansion?"*

"The girls are going—Mimi and her friends. Someone really should go along with them and see what these rituals of theirs are all about. I mean, why are they doing this anyway—putting on these magic shows for teenagers? What has that got to do with van Buren and his work? Did you hear what he said about using handsome Nick to draw them in? It sounds to me as though he's trying to attract as many girls as possible to the meetings. Why would he do that?"

The squirrel began to move along the wire again. *"Because he's looking for one girl in particular?"*

"Maybe. He could be thinking that if Alice started to be aware of her past she would want to know more about it. And if her familiar hasn't gotten to her yet, maybe van Buren can find her first. Witchcraft's all the rage with high school–age girls, so he invents a super-cool coven of his own and lets the word get out that wonderful things are happening in it. He gets his daimon friend to give the girls hallucinations of being reincarnated. Of course they'd get all excited and tell everyone about it, and the news would spread like crazy. That would catch Alice's attention, if she just has an inkling of her former lives and wants to learn more. He's hoping she'll come to a Dark Circle meeting and tell them about her own memories of living before, and then they'll know for sure who she is." A chill passed down her spine as she spoke. "He probably suspects me because of the Willowmere connection, but he doesn't really *know*—yet."

"I would have thought that would be all the more reason for you not to go to his house."

"But that's just it, don't you see? If I *do* go and I *don't* let anything slip, if I can somehow convince him that I'm not a revenant and I'm just interested in power like Josie, then he may decide I'm not the person he's looking for. It's too late to try to make him think I'm only an ordinary kid. But I can pretend I'm not Alice. And if I really was just after power for myself, the first thing I'd do would be to pay the Dark Circle a visit. By staying away from them, I'm actually raising their suspicions."

The squirrel reached the telephone pole on the other side of the street and leaped into the branches of a tree, where it perched and chattered irritably. *"This is not a good idea, Claire. Is there anything I can do to change your mind?"*

"Probably not," she said. "I'm going to that gathering to learn everything I can about it and the van Burens. And if they want to give me one of those fancy coven names of theirs, then they can call me . . . Mole." She walked on at a determined pace.

"Claire–"

"I'll see you later, Leo," she cut him off. "Take care—and stay off the bird feeders!" She strode on, leaving him behind.

✧ ✧ ✧

That evening Claire and her father went back to the supermarket for some paper decorations to put on the front door and more candy to replace what they had eaten already.

"We've got to stay out of the stuff this time," Claire said as they left the store and walked towards the car. "Maybe we should've bought something we hate, like licorice or peppermints."

"Then we'd be stuck with the leftovers," said her father through a mouthful of toffee.

"Um—by the way, Dad," said Claire, getting into the passenger seat, "I'm going out Sunday night."

"You? Out?" He turned and looked at her with a puzzled expression.

"Yes, me. That's why I was a little antsy about the studying. I'll be taking Sunday evening off. Some girls at the school invited me to go to the Halloween dance with them, and I was thinking maybe I should go. The student council's organizing it, and it's really going to be special. They've got permission to use the school gym, and some parents are volunteering as chaperones. So I thought maybe I should join in the fun for once." It was difficult to get the words out. Telling her father the truth had been difficult enough. Lying to him was harder still.

"I see." He started the car and swung out of the parking lot. "Well, I'm glad to hear you're socializing a bit more. But remember it's a school night. Don't be out too late."

"I'll try, but I can't really control when I come back, Dad. I'm not the one who's driving. Hint, hint," she added.

He sighed. "Okay, I'll see about some real driving lessons for you. I promise. Just tell the other girls you can't be late. Who are they, anyway?"

She hesitated, unwilling to tell yet another lie. "You're not going to believe this, but they're the same girls who were into witchcraft a while ago. Mimi and the two Chelseas. Remember? It turns out they were disappointed in the whole magic thing, and they're not doing it any more. They were just following a fad, that's all." Part of this at least was true, but she still couldn't look him in the eye and had to stare at the road ahead. The barrier that had grown between them was no longer thin and curtain-like; it had become a wall, solid and impenetrable.

"All right. I just hope they're not a bad influence on you. Trying to be popular can cause people to make silly mistakes."

She tried to smile. "Hey, Dad, maybe *I'll* be a good influence on *them*."

He thought about that for a moment, and then he nodded. "Fair enough. Just tell them you need to be home before eleven."

She agreed and lapsed into silence again. It wasn't going to be dangerous, she told herself. The warlocks were unlikely to try anything on her. There was really no reason for her palms to be sweating.

✧ ✧ ✧

When Claire arrived at Willowmere on Sunday afternoon she found Myra on the front porch. She had already strung some fake cobwebs between its white pillars and hung up a bedsheet in a good imitation of a floating ghost. Angus sat beside her, wagging his tail. "Ah, there you are, dear!" she called. "What do you think?"

"Wonderful!" said Claire, trying to sound enthusiastic. "The kids'll love it."

"I've got some pumpkins inside if you want to help me carve them."

Claire followed her into the kitchen, where several pumpkins were set out on the counters, and accepted a carving knife. Myra had already started one; she turned the huge, hollowed-out gourd towards Claire, showing off its slanting cat-like eyes and jagged grin. "I think I'll put this one on the porch. And look," she said, "here's a nice big carrot for the nose. I've made a hole for it, see? The goop from inside the pumpkins can go in those buckets in the corner; I'll take it out to the compost later. But pick out the seeds and save them for the birds."

Koko the cockatoo and Tillie the grey parrot were perched on the counters, snapping up the fresh pumpkin seeds that Myra had set out for them in a little dish. Koko glanced up at Claire's entrance and greeted her with a cheery "Hello!" Claire scratched the cockatoo's crest, then chose a large round pumpkin and cut into its rind. At the smell of its moist, stringy orange innards, her childhood came rushing back to her. It was all such innocent fun. She suddenly yearned to be ten years old again, looking forward to an evening of running through the shadowy streets, with Ainsley at her side in some outlandish costume (she had gone as a gorilla one year, wearing an old black fur coat of her mother's and a cheap dime-store mask that she'd had trouble seeing out of), and coming home with a sackful of sweet loot to be hoarded for weeks to come.

"I've got a witch hat," said Myra. "I picked it up at a party store today. I'm going to wear it, with a black dress, and carry one of the cats in my arm. I think I'll use Plato; he's the most docile one. And I've got tons of candy. Help yourself to some, dear; it's in those bowls over there on the table. I feel I must keep up the Ramsay Halloween traditions."

"What do your witch friends think of all this?" Claire asked, carving a pair of fangs into her jack-o'-lantern's mouth.

"Halloween? Oh, they think it's dreadfully tacky and commercial, of course," chuckled Myra. "Silverhawk and her friends will be gathering tonight for a solemn celebration of the Celtic festival of the dead, thinking about loved ones who have passed away, that sort of thing. But for my part, I adore Halloween—the children enjoy it so much, and some of their costumes are really quite ingenious."

They talked on as they worked; the topics of discussion remained quite innocuous, much to Claire's relief. She had been half-afraid that Myra would broach the subject of daimons—that her whole purpose in asking Claire to come here was to find out what she knew. But the subject never arose. They carved a half-dozen pumpkins to place at various points along the winding drive, encouraging any children who might be shy about venturing so far onto the property. Then they did two more for the front gate, to balance on the lions' stone crowns.

"I could put them up there with the help of a stepladder," said Myra. "I think there's one in the garage."

"I can do that for you," offered Claire.

"Thank you, dear, but I don't want to take up too much of your time. Are you doing anything fun tonight?"

Claire hated lying to Myra as much as she'd hated lying to her father. *Get used to it,* she told herself. *If you really want to shield this woman from everything that's going on, you're going to be lying to her a lot.* "I'm going to a dance at the school with a bunch of other girls. And then to a—a sort of party afterwards."

"Oh, I am glad to hear that! I know your father is anxious for you to make friends in your own age group."

Claire looked up from her pumpkin in surprise. "When were you talking to Dad about me?"

"I phoned last Saturday morning to thank you both for the lovely dinner, and your father took the call. We had quite a long chat. He's terribly proud of you, of course, but he wouldn't be a good parent if he hadn't a few worries. But there, you *are* making friends, so that's one concern he can lay to rest."

Claire felt a longing to tell this kindly woman the truth—the whole truth about the daimons and the Dark Circle. *Perhaps she knows the full story already,* Claire thought. *We could talk about it together, share our thoughts. Become a sort of anti-Circle, Leo and Myra and me . . .* The lies she had to tell created a distance between herself and Myra in place of the comforting closeness they had begun to share. She felt a wave of anger against the rebel daimons. *All of this is their fault . . .*

Myra carried her finished jack-o'-lantern out to the front porch as Claire sat putting the final touches on another. The African grey parrot, which had been perching silently on a chair all the while, fluttered over to the counter in front of Claire and sat eyeing her for a moment. Then, deliberately, it winked at her. "Clever girl," it said clearly and distinctly.

Claire dropped the carving knife and stared at the bird, her head reeling. The parrot gazed back at her with one little bright eye. Claire swallowed, remembering the words of Al Ramsay's diary: ". . . it appears the female parrot is, indeed, inhabited by a daimon! This spirit seems to me to have a feminine personality, mischievous and wry and knowing, like an impish old woman . . ." She moistened her lips and said, "Who are you?"

The parrot cocked its head. She found herself gazing mesmerized into its tiny black dot of a pupil. Then the bird's hooked beak opened. "No name," it said in its expressionless voice.

"Is this—are you Myra's familiar?" Claire whispered.

The bird scratched at its neck with one clawed foot, as if considering her question. "Myra's—yes," it squawked.

Claire took a deep breath and leaned forward. "Can you tell me what she knows? About you—and all of this?"

Tillie strutted across the counter and began pecking at the pumpkin seeds she had piled there. "Nope."

Claire stood up straight again. It was that "privileged information" business Leo was always going on about—of course Myra's guardian wouldn't reveal her private thoughts, not even to a friend. She cleared her throat and tried again. "Do you know who I am?"

The grey parrot put its head on one side. "Claire now. Others before," it said in its little tinny voice. "Alice before."

"Well, No-name, you know I'm not a bad guy, then. I want to help. But I want to shield Myra too. She's your ward, but she's my friend too and I don't want her getting mixed up with the warlocks. You know what's going on next door, don't you?"

The parrot opened its wings and flew up onto her shoulder. Leaning its head close to her ear it said, "Bad man, bad daimon. Fought them before, you did. Fight again."

"That's right. It's my fault they're even here; they're watching out for me to show up. Myra can't help being related to me—to Alice; it's not fair that she should be in danger because of that. But she is. Those guys totally suspect her; they figure the new Alice will inevitably find out about Willowmere, and that Myra will try to find out about her—about me. You understand? I'm scared they might hurt her or—or worse. Can you look out for her, No-name—keep her safe from them?"

"No worries, dearie. Watching always." The parrot nipped her ear gently, then flew back to the counter.

There were footsteps in the hall, and Myra came beaming and bustling into the kitchen. "There! I put the pumpkin on the top step. I can't wait to see him all lit up. That's a very nice one you've done, Claire. I love his expression!"

"Thanks," she replied in a faint voice.

The grey parrot cracked a seed in its bill, watching them both with its bead-bright eyes.

Chapter 12

AFTER DINNER, Claire went up to her room and dressed herself for the evening. She put on a fresh pair of blue jeans and the only black thing she owned, a cotton T-shirt with the logo of a local business on the back. Everyone dressed in black for the Dark Circle, she'd been told. She added a plain black headband to keep her unruly fair hair under control and made up her face a little so it would look as if she really were going to a dance.

As darkness fell she saw glimmers of light begin to appear on front steps and porches all over the neighbourhood: the glowing eyes and grins of jack-o'-lanterns. She flung open her window and leaned out. It was a beautiful night for late October, cool but not bitter, with no wind. The moon, a waning gibbous two days past the full, rode high and lent its silver brilliance to the surrounding clouds, so that the bared branches of the trees showed black against the sky. It would, she thought, be a wonderful night for trick-or-treating. She could see little groups of costumed figures running along the shadowy streets, and there was the sound of voices and laughter in the air. Once again she felt a little pang. Stepping back, she closed the window again.

The girls arrived late, parking out front and honking the horn twice. Claire looked out the living-room window and saw Chel's car at the curb, a second-hand midnight-blue BMW. She grabbed her jacket and yelled, "I'm going, Dad!" and rushed out the door. If only these could be real friends, who were taking her to a real party . . .

Mimi stuck her head out the passenger-side window. "C'mon, we're late!" she shouted, as if it were Claire's fault. "We still hafta pick up Chelsea."

They drove to Chelsea's place in the east end, then drove on to the high school, where they parked the car and went into the dance—"Just so we can say we did, and so people will see us there." The gymnasium was dark, with flickering strobe lights and jack-o'-lanterns everywhere, and music booming in their ears. A lot of people were in costume: the room was full of ghosts, pirates, monsters, princesses with sparkling tiaras. The girls wandered around, talked to a few of their friends, and then turned back towards the door.

"Let's go," said Mimi.

"Hang on a sec, I really love this song," said Chelsea.

"You're the one who wanted to go to the Circle meeting," returned Mimi. "Come on."

Claire followed them, also feeling reluctant to leave. A part of her yearned to remain in the gym with the other kids—to have just one happy, normal experience for someone her age. Brian Andrews was there, standing in a little group of other guys near the doorway. She wondered again if what Chel had said about him was true. If she decided to stay, would he notice her? Would he ask her to dance? Would somebody else ask?

But none of these guys was William. Once again his face and voice filled her memory and made her ache with loss. Who in this room could possibly measure up to him? William had been ready to risk everything to live with the woman he loved. He was a man; they were just boys. Claire turned away. She remembered Leo's words: *Don't deny yourself a new love should it come to you.* But she knew she would never love again, no matter what Leo said. William had spoiled her for anyone else. And in any case, she could never hope to have a normal relationship in this life. With so many secrets to hide, she could never open up fully to another person.

She trailed after Mimi and the Chelseas, feeling weary and despondent and not at all ready for what awaited her. Perhaps Leo was right, and she was making a terrible mistake. She said little as they drove down to Lakeside and turned west. The car passed Willowmere, and she saw the two jack-o'-lanterns perched in playful mockery atop the scowling lions' crowns, and the laughing lit-up faces of the others leading up the dark driveway. Goblin lanterns, warding off evil. Seeing them, she remembered that she was doing this in part to make the warlocks less suspicious of Myra. To keep her safe from them. *And anyway,* she told herself, *it's too late now to turn back.*

✧ ✧ ✧

There were several other cars parked in the circular driveway at the van Burens'. Claire moved to the back of the group as the girls walked up the steps to the vast, forbidding mansion and pressed the doorbell. A furious barking started up at once inside. Mimi and the Chelseas giggled. "Rex always does that," Chel told Claire. "Don't worry, he doesn't bite."

That was the least of Claire's worries, but she made herself stand still as the door opened. It wasn't the old man, but Nick van Buren who stood there, dressed in black jeans and shirt under his black leather jacket. He restrained the growling Rex with one hand and stared openly at Claire. "What the—? What are *you* doing here?" he demanded with a frown.

"Trick or treat," said Claire. "But wait a moment—*we're* supposed to be the ones wearing goofy masks, aren't we?" She was being immature, she knew, but Nick always brought out the worst in her.

"What's the idea?" Nick demanded of the three other girls. "Why's she with you?"

"You know her?" said Chel in surprise.

"Unfortunately, yes." Nick glared, along with the dog.

"Fine. If I'm not wanted, I'll leave." Claire, not without a sense of relief, turned as if to go. But then a shadow moved behind Nick, and Mr. van Buren's voice spoke.

"Now, Nick, that is no way to greet a guest." The old man moved to stand at his nephew's side. He, too, was dressed all in sombre black, a formal-looking jacket over a turtleneck and well-pressed pants. "Good evening, Miss Norton. Have you decided to join us after all, then?"

Claire affected a little shrug. "I changed my mind after talking to Mimi and the others. I thought I'd check your coven out, if it's okay with you. And with Nick," she added with a pointed glance at the younger man.

"But of course. Come in, all of you."

The girls entered. Claire thought the front hallway with its stuffed animal trophies even more eerie than on her first visit. But now that she knew all about hunter daimons, van Buren's fascination with hunting and killing things made sense. He had likely picked it up from the predatory daimon Phobetor. As the senior van Buren and the dog walked ahead, leading the group towards the living room, she looked at the glass-eyed antelope heads, the hides hung on the walls, and the display cases full of stiff, dead birds. Claire shuddered to think of the other hunts he and his daimon had been on—some of which had involved preying on humans . . .

"Did you shoot any of those animals?" Mimi asked Nick.

"Yes," Nick replied. "That buffalo head on the wall is one of mine. And the two leopard skins on the floor, and one of the gazelles in the living room."

"Cool," said Mimi. "You must be a really good shot."

"Yes," said Claire, "there's something thrilling about going up against the brute power of nature with nothing between you and it but an automatic rifle with a telescopic sight."

"So you're an eco-freak too. It figures." Nick gave her a withering look. "Wild animals aren't the cute cuddly things your kind goes on about. You wouldn't like them so much either if both your parents had been mauled to death by a leopard."

Chel gasped. "Omigosh! Did that really happen to your mom and dad, Nick?"

"Yes. I was only twelve at the time. My parents were game wardens, and part of their job was to drive around this national park looking out for poachers. They were killed by one of the animals they were supposed to be protecting. How's that for irony?" His voice was bitter. "It was Klaus who first taught me to hunt, after he took me in and legally adopted me. I enjoyed it. I'd had nightmares about what happened to my parents, but once I knew I could kill anything that attacked me the dreams stopped."

Mimi gave a sympathetic murmur and laid a hand on his arm. Claire said nothing. As before, when she had seen his room with the dark disturbing pictures, she felt a strange blend of pity and distaste. Whatever he might say, the young man still had serious problems.

Though he addressed his words to Chel, Nick's dark brown eyes remained fixed on Claire with a smouldering resentment. She struck a voluptuous pose as she passed in front of him. "If you keep on looking at me like that, I'm going to think you're interested," she purred.

"Hardly," he snapped, moving away. Good. That got rid of *him*. Claire walked on with the others into the large high-ceilinged living room.

There were several other dark-clad people gathered there. She counted five young men, who looked to range in age from about seventeen to well over twenty, and a larger number of girls—more than a dozen people in all. Josie Sloan was there, dressed entirely in black and talking to one of the other girls; when she saw Claire her face froze and she took an involuntary step backwards. Her eyes sought Nick's. He scowled, shaking his head, and she stood still with her hands tightening into fists at her sides.

The black dog went to a zebra-skin rug in one corner and lay down, his head on his paws. On the marble mantelpiece, next to some African sculptures in ivory and ebony, a crow perched as motionless as the stuffed birds in the glass cases. In front of the empty fireplace stood a long table covered with a red cloth, scattered with an assortment of peculiar objects. One gave Claire a creeping sensation: a human skull, very ancient-looking and lacking its lower jaw. As well, there were some animal bones and teeth, a glass goblet, a dagger, and several jewellery boxes.

Claire eased her glasses down the bridge of her nose and looked over the lenses as she scanned the room. Al Ramsay had warned in his notes that daimons could create illusions, and that only myopic people could distinguish them from reality; the false images always looked too sharp and clear.

"Why do you keep doing that?" Nick demanded, moving to stand in front of her.

Well, he looked blurry, so he at least must be real. "Just improving the view," Claire told the blur. She removed her glasses, dangling them from her hand. "Now if only I could make you inaudible as well."

The blur stalked away with a muttered and uncomplimentary remark. Claire took another swift look around the living room and then replaced her glasses. It appeared that all the people and animals in the room were real. She watched as Nick went over to stand beside the table, arms crossed, eyes still glaring under his dark forelock. His uncle went and stood in front of the table, smiling in a genial way at the assembled coven members.

"Ah, Draco, Orion, good to see you . . . Moth, Nightshade, Altair, I am delighted you could make it. And what a pleasure to see Catseye, Screech Owl, and Moon Shadow back with us again. Welcome to you all!"

"Welcome," added a harsh, high-pitched voice. Claire turned, startled. It was the crow on the mantelpiece that had spoken.

"It can talk?" she blurted.

"Yes, corvids excel at mimicry, much like parrots," van Buren said.

She stared at the crow. Was it merely mimicking, or had a daimon within it used its voice to speak? "They do? I had no idea."

"Well, well," observed Nick with a sneer. "Something Claire Norton doesn't know? Who'd have thought it!"

She longed to hit him but contented herself with a glare.

Van Buren continued in his smooth voice, "And we have another new member! Miss Norton, if you decide to stay you can choose your own coven name. We tend to use names that have a nocturnal theme: night creatures, for example, or the names of stars and constellations. My coven name is Mizar, and my nephew here is Rigel."

There was a brief, expectant pause; they were all looking at her. "Oh, I can't think of a coven name," Claire said.

"I will give you one, if you like." Mr. van Buren took a step towards her, then spoke a word. It sounded like "serious." She gazed at him in puzzlement for a moment.

"Serious? Oh, wait. You mean *Sirius*—the Dog Star?" she asked.

Josie sniggered, and Nick muttered, "Now *that* would be appropriate."

Claire seethed but remained silent. Van Buren threw a hard look Nick's way. "A good guess, Miss Norton. But I actually meant night-blooming *cereus,* the flower that opens its petals only after dark." He stepped back to the table. "For those of you who are new here, I will explain these objects on the table. The fossilized skull was found in Africa, along with these warthog teeth that were originally strung on a ceremonial necklace, as you can see by the holes bored in the roots. The skull is that of an ancient tribal sorcerer from prehistoric days, and the necklace belonged to him also. I found these relics all by myself, because I could not get any professional archaeological team to assist me in my search. Archaeologists, like so many modern professionals, can be terribly narrow-minded when it comes to psychic abilities. But in the end it was not really difficult for me to locate them—because, you see, I *was* the sorcerer in a former life, and though the shape of the land had changed over the millennia my visions told me where to find these relics of my past existence." He laid a hand on the skull. "I found my remains exactly where I knew they would be, and I took them to my home in South Africa to add to my personal collection of curiosities. It is rather fascinating, you see, to have mementoes such as these, reminders that the spirit is indestructible and can move from body to body, from age to age. You, too, can know this type of immortality if you decide to follow my teachings."

His audience sat in rapt silence. He was very persuasive, Claire thought, impressed against her will. Who wouldn't be fascinated by such a story when it was delivered in such a calm, quiet, matter-of-fact tone? Some of the story was nonsense, of course—all that about finding the site with "psychic powers," for instance. He had more likely been led there by his daimon, who would of course remember exactly where old Mamba had died and know how the land had changed in the intervening millennia. But much of his account she knew to be true, and his voice rang with the strength of conviction.

He went on, "We have a number of goals for this movement. The first and most important one is to serve as an alternative to all the other spiritual paths out there, most of which we find narrow-minded and repressive. Even many magic-based practices tend to be timid and conservative in nature, shying away from what we feel is the true goal of magic: the discovery, seizure, and enjoyment of power. To be a member of the Dark Circle is to grasp at things that have previously been shrouded in darkness and mystery—hence our name and the clothing we wear. It takes great courage to venture into the dark, but for those who make that venture, the rewards can be great."

And what you mean by that, Claire thought to herself, *is that you'll break any rule and stop at nothing to get whatever you want, no matter what harm you may cause to other people in the process.*

"Here we do not bind ourselves to others' rules and regulations. Here we are free to pursue any path we wish to the goals that we desire. Forget everything you've ever been told; this is the only route to happiness. Look at the natural world, where there are no rules except for survival. The ancient shamans considered themselves to be a part of the natural order and accepted its ways. Often, it's said, two shamans would fight each other for supremacy using their animal familiars. When one animal was finally killed by the other, its shaman died, and his adversary was the victor. Power is life, and weakness death. The only true goal for a witch or warlock is to be stronger than any other witch or warlock."

He moved his hand to an object on the table, a small jewelled casket. "As some of you know who have come here before, we screen our new members for any signs of a previous existence. I'm pleased to say we have in fact found many people who have memories of previous incarnations. It would be a rare gathering, actually, where no one had lived before; reincarnation is much more common than you might suppose. But most people cannot remember their former lives without assistance from a trained psychic. A few, very sensitive people have such memories, though they may not understand them, or else dismiss them as dreams.

"So, have any of our newcomers any memories or pictures in their heads that could belong to past lives?"

No one said anything. His eyes passed lightly over the group, but Claire saw them linger just a second or two longer on her. She forced her features to remain blank. "None at all? Don't be shy. There's no need to feel self-conscious here. Talk to the other members of the Circle, and most will tell you they have lived before, as I have—and as Rigel has."

"Nick's reincarnated?" exclaimed Chel. "He never said so before."

"I prefer not to talk about it," growled Nick.

"Yes, Rigel has a few memories, but his most recent past life was not a very agreeable one," his uncle said. "In fact it gave him nightmares as a child. He was a witch hunter in the Middle Ages, and he recalls watching the executions of accused witches."

Nick shifted his weight from one foot to the other and glowered at his uncle, but said nothing.

"Many people find their past recollections disturbing," van Buren continued. "And this is no doubt why so many are suppressed. We must remember that life conditions were very poor in ages past, and most people would have suffered from illness or hunger, or lived during wars and uprisings. This is always the danger of regressing your memory to previous lives—you might find the experience unpleasant. But speaking for myself, I would much rather know. It is always better to choose knowledge over ignorance."

"Knowledge is power," Nick mumbled. It sounded like a phrase he had learned and memorized.

"Exactly," van Buren said, unruffled by his nephew's sulky demeanour. "So, are you new members willing to journey back into your past?"

Heads nodded. Van Buren's eyes settled on Claire again and she grunted, "Okay." What were they going to do now? she wondered. It would be easy for them to create false "memories" for the newcomers by using daimonic illusions.

"Good." He picked up the little jewelled box and opened the lid. "Here on this table are several objects I would like each of you to look at in a moment. Tell me if the sight or feel of them arouses any strong feelings. But first," he said, setting the box down again, "you will have to go through an exercise designed to liberate your minds. It just requires a little meditation on your part, with some help from us. Before your thoughts can be freed to roam at will through the psychic realm, you must first pass something we call the 'guardian at the gate.'

"Beyond our universe is another, a realm of pure spirit inhabited by immortal, all-knowing entities. On that higher plane, which we can enter in our minds, we may encounter these entities and learn from them. That is how people we call witches and sorcerers and shamans get their powers. Most human beings live their lives without ever knowing about that otherworldly realm. Only to a select few comes the knowledge of its existence, and for these few the rewards are great: the gift of what we call magic and the ability to cheat death. You, too, can enjoy all these benefits if you can only pass the spiritual gateway that leads to it. And that gate, as I have said, has a guardian. A spirit whose sole purpose is to prevent you from passing its threshold. A jail-keeper, if you will.

"So I will ask you, now, to meditate. Find a chair or sit on one of the rugs, anywhere you feel comfortable, close your eyes, and centre yourself. Imagine that you are on a road or path with a gate ahead and a wall to either side. Picture that gateway in your head. Do you see it?"

There were murmurs from various parts of the room. "I'm picturing a brick wall," said one girl. "And the gate's made out of iron."

"Mine's a stone wall," a boy said. "The gate's wooden."

Claire visualized the gates of Willowmere, topped by their old stone lions, through which she had once gazed longingly.

"Very good. You want to get beyond the gate. Imagine that you are walking up to it and opening it with your hands. It's not locked—it swings outwards. But there is something there." Again he paused. "A sinister shape, a threatening figure—can you see it?"

More voices answered him.

"It's a scary-looking guy, in this uniform like a soldier's or something. He's got a gun."

"I see a dog. A huge black dog with glowing eyes."

"Mine's a dragon."

Claire saw the driveway stretching before her, and standing in the middle of it was a young lion with a shaggy, half-grown mane. *Of course—my guardian, my protector, my guide,* she thought. And she remembered what Leo had told her—that the guardian daimons kept constant watch over the minds of human beings, to protect the privacy of their wards and keep them safe from other daimons who would exploit them. She had to stop herself from smiling.

"What you all see in these visions," van Buren intoned, "is your supernatural enemy. The watcher on the threshold, the guardian of the gate. The one who bars your way to the spirit plane. Now imagine you are walking past that figure. Show no fear. It can only threaten; it cannot really harm you. Imagine yourself leaving that watcher behind, venturing forth on your own."

Claire imagined herself walking along the driveway. But the fingers of her right hand were twined in Leo's mane, and he walked at her side, a strong, protecting presence.

"In ancient times people performed rites like these, dream quests that led them to the spirit world. The spirits they encountered there, often in animal form, they took to be their guides and so they obeyed them. In the Dark Circle we know better. On the spirit plane the first being you encounter is your enemy, your jailer or warder. Where in the old days the quest was to reach this entity and seek its counsel, *our* goal is to reach past and beyond it—to free ourselves of the warder's domination and explore the higher realms unfettered." Somehow Claire felt his words were directed mainly at her, and she longed to stand up and contradict him. To tell the other kids that he was lying, that the spirit guardian was your friend and helper, a daimon who warded off others of its kind from your mind so you would be free to do as you wished in life, follow your own destiny without interference from rogue daimons.

"For rules exist to be broken. Greek mythology tells us of Prometheus, the god who stole fire out of heaven and gave it to mankind, in defiance of the other gods. I tell you this because, like Prometheus, I want you to learn and grow. To be free of the domination of these spirits and their rules that are designed only to benefit themselves and to keep you weak and ignorant."

Well, thought Claire, *that's really nice of you, Mr. van Buren. But nasty cynic that I am, I can't help wondering what's in it for you . . .*

"All right, you may open your eyes." Claire opened hers and kept her face blank as she sat looking ahead of her. Van Buren turned to her. "Cereus, you didn't say anything. Were you having trouble coming up with a mental image?"

"No. I just saw the gate in front of a friend's house. And my figure looked like some kind of thug," Claire lied.

"Good!" he said. His eyes turned towards Josie; she was sitting bolt upright on the sofa, looking smug. "And were you all able to get past your guardians and go on your way unhindered by them?" Heads nodded. Claire nodded too. "Excellent. You've made the first step on your journeys, then. Once you break free of the dominance of the warder, you can enter the spirit plane as often as you wish and go anywhere you want. Now for the second test. Nick, will you pick up a couple of the objects, please?" Nick went to the table and picked up the dagger and one of the jewel cases. "Nicholas will show each of you these relics and you will tell us what they mean to you. And I will come around with these." He took up the goblet and the little casket. "Let us know of any mental images or memories they may evoke as you look at them."

Nick walked to and fro, holding the two objects out to each person in turn. A couple of kids tried to fake reactions. One girl said that both objects made her feel funny, but she couldn't come up with anything specific. A boy said he thought he once owned the dagger. Nick's lip curled in contempt, but he said nothing. He came to Claire, but she had already recognized the case. She shook her head when he opened it to reveal Alice's pearl necklace. His uncle had surprised her with it the first time she came here, and come perilously close to provoking an emotional reaction from her. But there was no shock of recognition this time. "I've seen that necklace," she said in a bored voice. "Your uncle showed it to me. The dagger doesn't mean anything either."

When van Buren approached she looked at the goblet. It, like the dagger, stirred no memories. Then she glanced into the little open box in his other hand and felt a reeling sensation.

Inside it there lay a lock of hair—pale, fair hair, curled into a circle. It was obviously very old. *My hair—it's Alice's hair! I'm sure of it. But how—how did they find it? William must have cut a lock and kept it—*

"Anything, Cereus?" Mr. van Buren asked, watching her face.

She realized she'd been staring too long. A surge of panic seized her, just as when she had first seen the pearl necklace. Her eyes were misting over. She must not cry, not here, not now . . .

Looking up at van Buren, she shook her head. He moved on to the next person and Claire drew a deep breath, trying to calm herself. So they were looking for Alice. The goblet and dagger were mere controls in the experiment; the true revenant would pick the necklace and the hair. Nick was showing his two objects to Josie now. The girl looked long at the necklace.

Then she lifted it out of the box and said, "I know this! It belongs to me."

Nick looked at her, and for a moment his mask of insouciance slipped and he actually seemed taken aback. Van Buren too was staring at Josie, as if at a cat that had suddenly barked like a dog. Whatever was going on, it hadn't been rehearsed.

"What is it, Nighthawk?" inquired van Buren. "What are you saying? Are you really having a memory from a previous life?"

"I'm not sure."

He held out the goblet and the jewelled casket. She looked at them for a moment, her brow furrowed as if in deep thought. "I might've drunk from the cup," she said. "Or maybe not. But I definitely recognize the hair. It's mine too." Josie closed her eyes. "I'm seeing a place from a long time ago. It's weird—I feel like I must have lived there. A big old house in the country somewhere. In—Scotland! Yes, it's Scotland. I lived there, and my name was . . . Alice."

There was dead silence in the room. The others were staring, evidently wondering whether to believe her or not. *What in the world are you doing, Josie?* Claire wondered, feeling bewildered at this new turn of events.

Van Buren gazed down at the girl. "You've never mentioned any of this before," he said, and there was a new sound to his voice, a tension that had not been there previously.

"I just remembered it all now, when I saw my hair. My boyfriend must have cut that lock of hair when I died and kept it."

"Your boyfriend." Nick stepped forward, staring. "What was his name?"

Josie appeared to be concentrating. "It began with—*W,* I think. Yeah, *W.* I know—it was William! William Macfarlane. We lived in Scotland hundreds of years ago."

Both van Burens had lost their suave manner now. They exchanged quick glances, and Nick looked towards the dog on the zebra rug. It was sitting bolt upright now, staring at Josie. Claire thought she heard it give a soft, low growl.

"That's awesome," exclaimed Josie. Her face was flushed with excitement—or was it satisfaction? "Really amazing! It felt so real. I *was* that person, wasn't I? Long, long ago."

With a visible effort van Buren mastered himself. "So it would seem," he said, and turned back to the other coven members. "And now, it's getting late and I know that some of you have curfews. Perhaps we should wrap up this meeting early."

Chapter 13

"THAT WAS WEIRD," said Chel.

The girls were sitting in the cafeteria, talking about the events of the previous night.

"Yeah," Chelsea agreed, picking at her salad. "It was a mistake going back to that stupid Circle thing. They wouldn't even talk to me about Dave, after. They can't help me, or else they won't bother."

"I meant Josie," said Chel. "She acted so strange."

"You haven't seen her do anything like that before?" Claire asked, approaching their table with her bag lunch in hand.

"No. We all did the reincarnation thing in the beginning, but usually Nick hypnotized us. We did have that necklace shown to us, along with a whole bunch of other jewellery, but none of us remembered owning it before."

"Josie didn't claim to recognize it the first time?"

"No."

So the test was *to see if anyone picked the pearl necklace out from among all the other objects,* thought Claire. *Like recognizing someone in a police lineup. Josie didn't understand the importance of the necklace before. But now she gets it. She knows it has to be important, or the van Burens wouldn't keep trotting it out. And she's learned something about my former life since then. So tonight she knew she had to go for the things most likely to be owned by a woman—by Alice Ramsay. The dagger and the goblet were just the controls as I thought; she guessed she was supposed to react to the necklace and the lock of hair. Josie nearly goofed over the goblet, but she was careful not to commit herself too much.*

"And you never saw that other thing—the box with the lock of hair in it—before?" It was hard to get the words out in a neutral tone of voice. That forlorn testimony to the long-dead William's sorrow found too strong an echo in her. She grieved and yearned for him as never before.

"No—that was definitely new," said Mimi.

A recent addition to their collection, then? Claire wondered how the van Burens had come by the jewelled casket and its contents. She would probably never know. But there could be no doubt that it was intended to provoke a strong emotional response in the revenant Alice. Claire had mastered her feelings only with tremendous effort.

"Speak of the devil," said Chel.

Claire looked up and saw Josie approaching. There was no fear or resentment in her face now; she looked like the proverbial cat that had stolen the cream. "What was all that about last night?" Chel asked her. "We didn't understand it."

"The warlocks weren't just looking for any old reincarnation memories. They were searching for someone in particular," replied Josie, leaning on the table and smirking. "A very powerful, reincarnated witch. And they found her all right. She's *me*."

"So what does that mean?" Mimi asked.

"It means I'm different. Special." Josie was speaking to Mimi but looking at Claire. "I get a higher ranking in the Circle. And it means certain people had better be more careful around me."

"And certain other people are supposed to be grounded," Claire pointed out. "I saw you there last night, and I'm not the only witness."

"You really don't get it, do you?" Josie's smirk widened. "From now on I can do whatever I want." Claire turned away and headed towards another table. But Josie wasn't through yet. "And Nick is my guy. I told you all to stay away from him. That means you, Mimi—and you too, Claire."

"Me?" Claire faced her and stared.

"Thought you could fool me, didn't you—putting on that act, pretending you hate him."

"It isn't an act," corrected Claire. "I do hate him."

Josie's eyes narrowed. "I saw you last night. You couldn't take your eyes off him."

"I'm not chasing him, if that's what you think. I wouldn't take him at a discount."

Josie took a step forward, her eyes glinting now. "So what're you saying? Someone *I* like isn't good enough for *you*?"

"Josie, either you want me to want him or you don't want me to want him. Make up your mind."

"C'mon, you two, you know you're not supposed to be talking to each other. Why don't we talk about something else?" said Chel. "You know, Claire, I saw you take your glasses off last night. You look much better without them."

"Yeah." Chelsea gave Claire a long, critical look. "Have you ever had a makeover done? With the right clothes and makeup and stuff you could look pretty good."

"But the glasses should go," added Mimi. "Maybe you could get contacts. Or have laser surgery to fix your eyes."

Fix her eyes? Leave her with no way to detect daimonic illusions? "No!" Claire blurted in involuntary horror.

"Geez, it was just a suggestion," said Mimi, offended.

Josie sniggered, pointing at Claire's chest. "You can get surgery for *that* too, you know."

Claire pretended to consider. "Oh, gee, I dunno. Special surgery's expensive, isn't it? How much did you pay for your lobotomy?"

Josie glared and seemed about to respond. Then she appeared to change her mind. Smiling in a gloating fashion, she turned and walked away without another word. Claire felt a prickling sensation along her arms.

◊ ◊ ◊

"Leo, if you're not too ticked off to talk to me, I'd like to have a conference," said Claire.

She was sitting on her bed. The marmalade kitten was curled up at its foot, apparently fast asleep. There had been no word or sign from Leo for the past twenty-four hours. She had gone straight to bed last night, exhausted from the stress of the Circle meeting. A full day at school had left her feeling tired again. Her father wouldn't be home until late tonight, as he was helping to install a computer system at an out-of-town business. She was feeling very alone again, and it was with a sense of longing that she reached out to her familiar across the gulf of silence that had once more separated them.

After a few anxious moments he responded, his mind touching hers. The kitten stirred, then stretched with a gaping yawn that showed all its little pointed teeth. *"I am not, as you put it, ticked off. I have been very busy watching the enemy's house—all of last night and today as well."*

Sensing his worry, Claire felt contrite. If she had gotten herself into danger last night, he wouldn't have been able to do much for her. "You'll want to hear my report, then," she said, and proceeded to tell him of the strange events at the gathering. In retrospect, she found the Dark Coven experience more frightening than she had at the time. The elder van Buren had been so persuasive, so gentle in his manner; she recalled his benevolent smile as he called her by her new coven name. He'd intended to flatter her, and for the merest instant as his eyes dwelled on her, she *had* felt almost flattered. A dangerous man, Mr. van Buren; he had changed a great deal from his former incarnations. As Mamba and Morley he had only sneered and threatened. Now he had learned to be subtle, to manipulate. He had known exactly what bait to offer her—Claire, the class misfit. Power and prestige, the chance at last to stand out, to be the dominant member of a group. And he'd offered her knowledge, too. He had played on all her wants and insecurities and frustrations without ever referring directly to them—and how easy it would have been to respond, to be taken in . . .

She forced herself to focus. "Josie must have learned about Alice from Al Ramsay's notes. She sent her rat familiar to read them—remember when I found him inside the house, and the notes were lying all over the floor? There's a lot about Alice's life in them. I wonder how far she got? Did she read the part about me being reborn?"

"If she did," said Leo, *"she wasn't the only one. The daimon controlling the rat she was linked to was also reading the notes, and it would certainly report whatever it learned to Phobetor and van Buren."*

"But that would mean they know everything!" cried Claire, springing up in alarm.

"They haven't been acting as though they know everything. Those Dark Circle meetings are obviously a pretext, a front for searching out the revenant Alice, and they have been continuing with them since the incident with the rat. Right up until last night, when they produced a new relic of your past existence. And from what we both heard inside the house, the boy Nick plays a rather limited role; I doubt he really is a revenant. It sounded as though he's there mainly to attract young women to the Circle meetings. They're continuing to use him, so they still see a need for him. No, they don't know everything."

"Josie thinks of Nick as her personal property. She seems to feel she's got some kind of claim to him, especially after last night's little act."

"Yes. It would seem that she looks upon him as a sort of prize—the one who is revealed as the revenant gets Nick van Buren as a sort of royal consort. No doubt the Circle girls were encouraged to think that."

"If she only knew they want to find me for different reasons—not to put me on some kind of pedestal, but to fight me. They don't actually believe her, though—do they? I mean, they must know by now what Al Ramsay wrote and can tell she's just been cribbing from his notes."

"The rat daimon will have told them all, yes—unless . . . Claire, is there any chance that Josie could have read Ramsay's notes at some other time, without using the rat?"

"No—I'm pretty sure she couldn't have. She'd have had to break into the house, and Myra or I would have seen the signs. She only broke in the one time, when I was on the roof."

"But do you know what time she broke in? Did you hear the window smash?"

Claire tried to remember. "No—but it could have been when I was running upstairs to the widow's walk. I might not have heard it then."

"So there would have been time for her to read at least some of the notes, perhaps by holding them up to the window? Or she might have had a small flashlight or a candle in her jacket pocket."

"Omigosh—I never thought of that! Leo, that very night I was reading all the stuff Ramsay wrote about Alice being reborn. After the power went out I left those sheets lying on the desk in the study, right in plain sight. She probably searched the whole house for me, room by room, before going up to the attic . . . She *could* have stopped and read those notes!"

"So the question is, did she? And has she shared that information with the warlocks or not? If not, then she knows more than they do. And she knows enough of what they do know to be able to pretend she's the one they seek. Those extra little details—William's name, for instance, appears nowhere in the published accounts of Alice's life—would be very convincing."

"They couldn't believe her! She was so *fake*. I could tell she was lying, right away."

"You could tell that because you knew for a fact her statements were false. It might not be so obvious to the warlocks and their daimons."

"And anyway, if we've figured out when she had a chance to read the rest of Al's notes, they should also suspect where her extra knowledge came from."

"But they don't know what's in those notes. They don't know Ramsay mentioned William, for instance. They would have had to read all the journals themselves to be sure of that, and there is no evidence they ever have. So—they're unsure. Perhaps they will try another test on Josie. Or place her under hypnosis. It's very fortunate that Ramsay never mentioned your name in his notes. I doubt Josie suspects who the real Alice is."

"I hope you're right."

The kitten jumped down from the bed and began to pace like a tiny lion. *"I'll have to risk spying on their house once more to see if I can learn anything more definite. This is important. If they do come to believe Josie, she would be in considerable danger."*

"I know. What an idiot that girl is! All she cares about is being thought important and getting whatever she wants. Well, she may be getting more than she bargained for this time. But Leo, what will you do about a host?"

"You remember that room we saw in the van Buren house, full of caged animals? I think I might be able to connect with one of those animals and use it for a host. And if I helped to get one of the rats or mice out of its cage, I might be endangering the animal, but I would also be giving it a chance at life. They're intended as food for the bigger animals, after all. I can send the rodent creeping about the house to see if I can listen in on any conversations." The kitten's eyes turned up to

her. *"And no, you are not to participate this time. It's not worth the risk."*

"All right. Let me know as soon as you learn anything, will you?" said Claire.

After he had gone Claire fed the kitten and herself, then sat and watched TV for a while. Then she took out her homework even though it wasn't due until Friday. The assignment wasn't difficult, but she found herself reading the same questions over and over again without really understanding them. She was too restless and ill at ease to concentrate. Darkness fell outside the windows as she waited. The night too was unquiet; the spell of mild unseasonal weather had ended and a chill wind was moving the branches of the trees. Claire got up and turned the thermostat higher, then tried to get back to work.

Leonardo the kitten was sleeping again on her bed, utterly unconcerned. She checked on him several times to see if her familiar had by any chance returned. It gave her something to do. Abandoning her homework, she started to pace the floor as Leo had done. Seven o'clock—eight o'clock—nine. Still no word came to her. Nine-thirty—ten. Her father had told her he'd be back around eleven or eleven-thirty. She hoped Leo would be back well before then.

Where was he? She realized she was worried by his prolonged silence and told herself not to be ridiculous. Nothing could hurt a daimon. A creature with no body couldn't be injured or killed. All the same, she felt her heart beat faster as the hands of the kitchen clock inched forward. She reached out to him, but got no answer. He might, she thought, be too preoccupied to respond. His absence seemed to leave a gaping void within her. Already it was impossible to imagine her life without him . . .

"Stop it!" she said out loud. "Get a grip on yourself. He'll be in touch as soon as there's anything to say." She looked up at the clock again. Could it be only ten past ten? The minutes were passing like hours. She stood up and paced again.

And suddenly he was there, the sensation of another's thoughts touching hers, light as a moth's fluttering wing. Relief flooded her mind. But almost at once it turned to alarm.

"Claire, I know what they mean to do. I was there and heard it all. I helped a rat to gnaw its way out of its cage and then got it to free a mouse from the next cage—I wanted to use the smallest host available—and sent it down the stairs to look for the warlocks. Van Buren and the dog Rex were in the living room. They didn't see me, and I heard all van Buren had to say."

Images flashed through Claire's mind like falling fragments of glass, each reflecting a separate scene. Halls and rooms grown gigantic from the perspective of a creeping mouse, the figures of a man and dog looming taller than trees. And there were voices, too, roaring like thunder overhead.

"They mean to kill her. Josie. They're convinced that she is you. I didn't catch all that van Buren said, only that they will find an excuse to send her alone into the ravine tonight, and that the wolf-dogs will deal with her there . . ."

Chapter 14

CLAIRE RAN FOR HER ROOM. Her sneakers were lying on the floor where she had kicked them off. She scuffed into them and tried to tie the laces with trembling fingers. The kitten awoke and looked at her with inquiring eyes.

"What exactly are you doing?" Leo asked her.

"I'm going after her, of course." Claire grabbed a small flashlight off her bedside table—she had made a habit of keeping it there since the last power failure—and dashed out of the room again. The kitten sprang up off the bed and followed her.

"But how are you going to find her? The Willow Creek ravine is twenty kilometres long."

"She'll be down at this end of it, won't she? If she's leaving from the van Buren place."

"We don't know that she will be. She may be leaving from her own home and meeting them in the ravine. And I think it very unlikely that she would be attacked so far to the south. There are too many people about. Someone would hear her scream."

Claire stood still in the act of pulling her jacket on. It was true—down here at the southern end, near the mouth of the creek, there were all those houses facing onto the ravine. Farther down lay the Marina, and Lakeshore Park, and the Performing Arts Centre, where people might be coming out of the show about now. And the firehouse also backed onto the ravine, its crews ready to handle any kind of emergency. No—Leo was right, there would be too many potential witnesses even at this hour, too many people who could go to Josie's aid. But farther up the ravine deepened and widened, while the residential area gave way to commercial and industrial zones where no one would be after ten o'clock at night.

"They still have to be careful, you see," said Leo. *"Someone might see the dogs and realize what they are, and it's known that van Buren is a breeder. Suspicion might well fall on him. He's hoping that what happens to Josie will be blamed on wild animals, coyotes or wolves, so it will help if no one sees the attack take place."*

"We have to go north, then," said Claire. "But how can I get there? It would take forever on foot. Could I take a taxi?"

"There's no time to wait for one," said Leo. *"We may be too late as it is. Three of the wolf-dogs have already been loosed from their kennels."*

Claire stood for a moment, irresolute. Then she rushed for the kitchen telephone. "I'm phoning Myra." Her hand shook as she punched the buttons. There was nothing else to do; Myra would have to become involved. It might endanger her, but Josie was in even greater danger. She waited in anxiety for the phone to ring at the other end. It did—once, twice, three times . . . four, five. Claire fidgeted, but continued to wait. It was a big house, after all. Six, seven . . .

At the tenth ring she slammed the receiver down. "She's not home! What'll we do? I can't *run* there—and we'll need a car to get away. I don't want to try to outrun a pack of dogs!"

"Your father didn't take his car, did he?"

"No, he left straight from work, in the boss's car with a bunch of other people. But it's no use, Leo. I can't take Dad's car."

"You may have to. As you said, an escape vehicle is needed."

"Leo, you don't understand! I don't know how to drive. I've only had the most basic tips, and I have no licence."

"I can show you how," said Leo.

"*You* know how to drive?" She stared.

"When you and your father took the kitten to the veterinarian, I used Leonardo's eyes to watch him drive. I was curious to see how it's done."

"But—you only saw him do it once!"

"Once was enough. I told you, daimons have photographic memories. Claire, there's no time to argue."

Claire gaped at him for a moment. Then she whirled and headed for the door. "I can't believe I'm doing this," she muttered.

The kitten followed her. *"Take Leonardo along, Claire. I need him to see."*

"Okay." She snatched her father's extra key chain off its hook on the kitchen wall. Then with Leonardo at her heels she hastened out the door, locking it behind her. Her father's dark blue Honda was parked in the driveway; she unlocked the driver's side door and then slid into the seat. The kitten sprang up onto her lap.

She pulled the door shut, took a deep breath, and said, "Here goes." She started to put the key in the ignition.

"No, first hold down the flat pedal on the left. The one used for braking."

"Why?"

"I don't know, but it's what your father does. I suspect the car won't start otherwise. A precautionary measure."

"Oh, yes. I remember now." She pressed down on the brake pedal with her right foot. Then she inserted the key into the ignition and turned it. The engine roared.

"You'll need to have your lights on," Leo said. *"Your father drove in daylight, so I can't tell you how to do that."*

"It's okay, I know how—oh shoot!" The windshield wipers sprang to life, squeaking across the glass. She switched them off. "Turned the wrong thing," she said with a shaky laugh. "Here goes." The headlights flashed on, illuminating the front of the house. She groped for the gearshift and pressed the reverse button, as her father had shown her. "Now what? Leo, I can't remember!"

"Ease the pressure of your foot on the brake pedal."

"I don't use the accelerator? The right-hand pedal?"

"Not yet. You'll find the car will move, but slowly."

The car began to slide backwards out of the driveway. Claire looked swiftly from side to side, but there were no other cars in sight. *"It's all right, I'm looking too,"* Leo told her. The kitten had climbed onto the back of the seat; its head swivelled to and fro as Claire eased into the empty street, then turned the car until it was positioned in the right-hand lane. She braked and shifted to drive. *"Now, release the button and press on the accelerator– "* The car shot forward and Claire gave a startled cry. Frantically she stamped on the brake and it stopped again with a screech.

"–gently," Leo finished. The kitten was clinging to its perch with all its claws.

Her teeth were chattering. "Leo, I don't think I can do this."

"Yes, you can. I will guide you all the way. Just refrain from panicking, go as slowly as the law allows, and you'll be all right. Remember, a life is at stake here."

Claire leaned her forehead on the steering wheel. "The crazy thing is, I'd actually be safer if the van Burens went on believing Josie was Alice."

"I'm afraid so. You won't be helping yourself at all by helping her."

Claire groaned. "So—I'm off to risk my life helping a girl I don't like, who won't thank me, and I'll be worse off for doing it. Umm . . . Leo? Tell me again why I'm doing this?"

"You helped others before," Leo said. *"When you were Flower-in-a-drought, and Alice . . ."*

"Yes, I seem to recall galloping off to the aid of Helen Macfarlane—and look where *that* got me."

"I'm sorry, Claire, but as one of your species has observed, virtue is its own reward."

But she was already driving the car forward. At the corner she turned onto the cross street that connected Maple with Birch. "I think I'll be okay now," she said, her spirits lifting. "I do know the basics—they're pretty simple, like stopping at stop signs and red lights."

"Ah, yes—the red lights. I remember them."

"Remember? What do you mean?

"I have to remind myself which ones they are when I use this host. Cats can't see the colour red," explained Leo.

"Wonderful! I'm getting driving lessons from a colour-blind daimon!"

"Fortunately, as I said, daimons have photographic—watch the road!" The kitten sprang onto her shoulder as she braked again to avoid a turning car.

"Leo, that's not helping."

"If you're pulled over things will be decidedly awkward," he reminded her. *"And your chance at helping Josie will be gone."*

"Yeah—I can picture it," said Claire. The wheel felt slick under her sweating palms. "No driver's licence in my wallet, nothing. 'It's okay, officer. You see, I wasn't actually doing the driving. My kitty was giving me instructions.'"

"Look out for that car backing out of the driveway."

"I see it. 'Seriously, officer, it's not my kitty who's telling me how to drive, it's the invisible person who talks inside my head—'" Claire knew she was blathering. Between her worry about Josie and her fear of being apprehended by the police, every nerve in her body jangled. She felt an irrational certainty that anyone could tell she was driving illegally—that it must somehow show on her face for all to see. At the same time, she felt a rush of giddy excitement at driving—at long last—on the street. To be driving herself for once, not just sitting in the passenger seat. She knew this euphoria was dangerous and would cloud her judgment if she gave herself over to it completely. She kept her eyes fixed on the road. Luckily, traffic was lighter at this time of night, even on the normally busy Birch Street.

Birch followed the ravine until it met Bond, then dipped into the ravine, curving down at a steep incline along its eastern face and passing under a railway trestle before curving again to cross the creek in the form of a bridge. It had always made Claire nervous; she worried that cars making that long, swooping turn wouldn't be able to stop in time, particularly in winter when the street was slippery with ice. The whole arrangement made her think of a roller coaster. She had always been secretly relieved when the road returned to level ground.

Now she had to make that descent herself, and in the dark. And she could feel the gusts of wind striking the car as she turned onto Bond at the traffic light. She was grateful for Leo's calming presence; and with the lighter traffic she could at least make as slow a descent as she wished.

Down they went, while the forested eastern slope of the ravine rose on her left and the western slope loomed beyond. The railway trestle with its towering supports passed overhead, huge and black and ominous. The road itself was well lit, but beyond its edge the ravine was very dark. Claire shuddered at the thought of Josie walking alone through those shadowy groves, far from the sight and hearing of the few motorists on the bridge high above her.

The road mounted upwards again, meeting the western slope of the ravine and following it to the level ground at the top. Here Bond Street continued through a large commercial zone of strip malls and factory outlets, interspersed with a few modest high rises. But at the edge of the ravine lay a piece of undeveloped land, with a field of wild grasses and some trees. Claire turned at the traffic light and pulled into the parking lot next to it. Her hands were cramped and stiff from gripping the wheel.

"There," she said, pressing the brake pedal and shifting to park. She turned the key in the ignition and the engine fell silent, but she left the headlights on. "This is Willow Creek Park. There's a sort of rough trail over there behind the trees that goes down into the ravine." She felt in her pocket for the flashlight.

"Claire, you must stay here. It's too dangerous."

"But the search will go faster if there are two of us," she argued, though she was feeling uneasy herself about the dark rift below. She could hear the cold murmur of the water now that the engine was off.

"And what will you do if you're attacked by the wolf-dogs? You have no weapon."

Claire was silent for a moment. "Okay, I see your point. So what should I do?"

"Wait here. I've brought the barred owl to the ravine and will get him to fly around and look for Josie. When I locate her I'll let you know. Go to the top of the trail and turn on your flashlight. That and the car's headlights will show Josie where to run. The owl will drive her up the slope towards you, so the two of you can escape in the car."

"All right," said Claire. She wasn't happy about having to wait again, but she knew her familiar was right. The image of the attacking pack of wolf-dogs filled her with a remembered terror. Josie had once conspired with the rogue daimons to give Claire nightmares about being hunted by them. It was supremely ironic that Josie herself was now in danger from the real dog pack. But Claire had no wish for her to be harmed—or killed.

The kitten, finding himself without his invisible companion, settled down on the passenger seat and fell asleep. Outside, a small shape circled in the sky, and Claire heard an owl's hooting cry as it swooped down into the darkness below.

◆ ◆ ◆

She waited, once more, for what seemed an eternity. Behind her were the faint rumble of traffic and the far-off clatter of a freight train. Ahead were the night sounds rising out of the gaping gorge. The wind set the tree branches thrashing overhead. She tried to sift through all the sounds, listening for the baying of a dog pack in furious pursuit of its prey. Or would they attack in perfect silence, giving their quarry no warning at all? Her thoughts shied away from this horrible picture, and she tried instead to imagine the barred owl on its aerial patrol.

At last Leo broke his silence. *"There's still no sign of her. But the three dogs are there, waiting—as though they expect her to come."*

"Leo, are we even sure she's going to be there? Maybe her parents didn't let her go out after all." This seemed unlikely, given their track record, but Claire could only hope. "I know what. You go on searching, and I'll phone her house and see if she's there. If she is I'll try to warn her." That too seemed hopeless, but she had to make the effort, at least. "There's a phone booth up the road."

"Very well. You do that, and I'll stay in touch."

Claire got out, locked the car, and walked out of the parking lot and the street. She was nervous about being out on her own at such a late hour. Gangs of teenage boys and other more sinister types were known to hang around the intersection of Bond and Macdonald Drive at this time of night. She walked at a brisk pace, looking straight ahead and trying not to show her unease as she focused on the well-lit phone booth on the corner. There was a group of teens hanging out in front of a variety store across the road, but they only whistled at her and did not approach.

She slipped into the booth. There was a dog-eared phone directory hanging from a chain, and she hefted it and flipped through the pages. She didn't know Josie's number or address, but how many Sloans could there be?

There were nine, as it turned out, some spelled with an *e* at the end and some without. Claire couldn't remember how Josie's surname was spelled, which would have narrowed the search. Nor did she know Mr. Sloan's first name. Well, there was no avoiding it—she had to phone them all. She reached into her pocket for her wallet and opened the coin section. Yes, she had enough change. She set to work dialling the first number.

Sloan, Albert, didn't know of anyone named Josie. Sloan, B, was an elderly and somewhat confused lady who apparently lived alone. Feeling guilty, Claire apologized for disturbing her and hung up. She moved on down the list. Sloan, E, had retired for the night and gave Claire an earful for waking him up. He didn't sound at all like Josie's smooth-voiced father, and Claire hung up in haste. Sloan, Geoff, was a jolly, jokey type who didn't know any Josie but tried to keep Claire talking. She hung up on him too and phoned Sloan, Lawrence. Five more to go, she thought with a grimace.

"Hello?" said a woman's voice.

"Hello. Could I please speak to Josie?" asked Claire for the fifth time. Her voice sounded flat and robotic after all the repetitions of that sentence.

There was a pause. "Who's calling?"

"A . . . friend," Claire replied.

"Well, she can't come to the phone just now. She's doing her meditation exercise."

Claire's heart leaped. "Listen, are you sure I can't speak to her, just for a moment? It's kind of important."

"No, but I'll tell her you called. Can I have your name?"

In desperation Claire said, "Mrs. Sloan? This really is important. You can't let Josie go out tonight. You've got to watch her. She may try and sneak out, late. She'll be in danger if she does."

"Who is this?" Mrs. Sloan asked in a sharp tone. "What do you mean by ringing up at this hour?"

"Please, I'm just trying to warn—"

There was a click, followed by the dial tone.

Claire hung up the receiver and walked back to the car, oblivious now to the taunts of the boys across the road. She got into the car and locked herself in. "Leo?" she said. "Josie's still at home. Her parents say she is, anyway. She's supposedly in her bedroom meditating."

"Unless she slipped out without their noticing—through her bedroom window, perhaps."

Claire sighed and felt in her pocket for the car keys. "I've got to make sure. I've got her street address now, from the phone book. It's 183 Pine Crescent. I can go and bang on the door and make a fuss till they send for the police. Then we'll find out if Josie's inside the house or not. *Blast* that girl! I could kill her myself at the moment."

She drove out cautiously through the intersection, then turned south. Pine Crescent, according to the road map in the glove compartment, was in west Willowville. Maddeningly, every light turned red just as she reached it, all the way down Macdonald. At each traffic light she fumed and drummed her fingers on the steering wheel. At last Macdonald Drive met Lakeside and she was able to turn right. On this larger thoroughfare she could dare to pick up speed a little, though she was still under the legal maximum. The road to turn on to was Portland Avenue, three blocks west. She spotted it and made the right turn. Six blocks to the north now, and she'd be there. Spruce, Donnell, Wayland, Evergreen, Morris—there it was: Pine Crescent. She swung to the left and followed the moon-curve of the suburban street. 175, 177, 179, 181 . . .

A large modern house came into view. The lights were all on, and several cars stood in the driveway: there was an SUV and a shiny, gold-beige sedan.

And a low-slung black sports car that sent a jolt of recognition through her nervous system.

"Nick's here!" Claire pulled the car over to the curb and killed the engine. "Meditation my foot! He's probably upstairs in her room with her. Her parents would allow it—they're too-cool-for-words. Leo, do you think the warlocks changed their plan?"

"He wouldn't murder the girl in her own home, surely? He'd be the prime suspect, no matter how careful he was."

Claire jumped out of the car, leaving the kitten and closing the door on him. *"Claire, where are you going?"* asked Leo.

"I've got to do something!" She ran across the street, up the path to the front door and jabbed at the bell. After a moment the door opened. Mrs. Sloan, wearing a floaty floral dress and pearly earrings, stood staring at her.

"Don't I know you?" she asked, frowning a little. "Wait a moment—you're that girl! From the school, the one who made all that trouble for Josie—"

"Is Josie here?" Claire asked. A carpeted staircase behind Mrs. Sloan rose in an elegant curve to the second floor, and Claire glanced at it.

"Was that you who phoned us just now?" Mrs. Sloan asked, her frown deepening.

There was no use denying it. "Yes. No, please—" Mrs. Sloan moved to close the door. "I'm not trying to make trouble, honest. I really am worried about Josie. Is that guy Nick van Buren with her? I think he may be trying to talk her into doing something dangerous."

"Who's that at the door?" called a voice from the room to the right of the hallway, and Mr. Sloan appeared in his shirtsleeves. When he saw Claire he glowered. "Not you again!"

A door banged upstairs and Nick appeared on the landing in his trademark black jacket and jeans. "What's all the noise? I told you Josie needs to concentrate for this exercise—" He saw Claire and trailed off. "What are you doing here?" he demanded, just as he had at the door of the mansion.

"Well, what are *you* doing to Josie?" returned Claire. She faced Josie's parents. "Are you absolutely sure she's in her room?"

"Of course she's in her room," said Mr. Sloan. "Where else would she be? She's grounded, remember?"

"Are you the police now?" snapped Nick, coming down the stairs. "Checking on Josie? She's in her bedroom, and you can look if you don't believe me," he added to Mr. and Mrs. Sloan. "She's in a deep trance."

Claire stepped back. If Josie really was in her own room, then she was safe for the moment. "Please do check on her," she urged, "and make sure she doesn't get out later."

"I'm not her jailer," snapped Mr. Sloan. "And speaking of jail, if you don't leave our property right now I'll phone the police and have you charged with harassment." Claire jumped back as he slammed the door in her face.

She went back to the car and slumped in the driver's seat, staring out the windshield. In her mind ominous thoughts were beginning to take shape, like dark figures looming up through a mist.

"Claire? What's happening?" Leo asked her.

"Nick's got her doing meditation in there. He told her parents to check on her if they wanted to, so she's definitely still in the house. But why meditation exercises now . . . ?" Suddenly she sat bolt upright. "Leo! Josie's *body's* in there all right, but where's her mind?" She grabbed for the keys and slammed them into the ignition as she answered her own question: "In the ravine!"

Chapter 15

CLAIRE STARTED THE ENGINE and pulled the car away from the curb with a screech of tortured tires. She raced along the quiet crescent, heading for the exit onto Portland.

"Of course, they wouldn't dare hurt Josie while she was in her own home," she said. "But they can easily talk her into linking her mind to an animal of some sort. Then they get her to send the *animal* into the ravine—where the dogs are waiting. If her host animal is killed, she dies too."

"Yes–I believe you're right. That's why the pack is already there. The hunt is in progress. But they're not hunting the girl herself; they're hunting her host."

Claire drove to the foot of the street and swung to the left, heading back east along Lakeside. "It's the perfect crime. No marks on her body, no poison, no bullets—nothing! No one knows about daimonic nerve induction—except a few people like me, and who'd believe me? Not the police, that's for sure!"

"Where are you taking the car?" The kitten was sitting upright now, looking at her with inquiring eyes.

"Back to the ravine."

"There is nothing you can do there, Claire. Leave this to me. I'll return to the owl and see where the pack is going. When I last looked they were heading south along the east bank of the creek."

"There isn't a lot you can do either, Leo. You don't even know what kind of animal Josie's linked with. It could be anything at all."

"Not anything. It wouldn't be any kind of bird, for instance. It has to be something the dogs can pursue on foot. A raccoon or a rabbit, perhaps. Or a stray cat like Leonardo."

"So what are you going to do?" Claire drove past Macdonald Drive. She glanced at the glowing numbers of the digital clock on the dashboard. Five to eleven.

"It's hard to say. If the quarry is small enough—a squirrel for instance—I can get the owl to catch it and lift it into the air, away from the hunters. If it's larger, I might try flying low to distract the dogs and allow their prey to escape."

"It's too bad there are no bigger birds around that you could use."

"There was one—a large owl, a great horned owl I think. I saw it flying over the treetops just to the north of where the pack was. But I suspect it's already under enemy control. It would be useful for them to have an aerial spy to help them spot their prey."

"We should be doing the same thing. One of us in the air, the other on the ground. Leo, can any of your daimon friends help?"

"Perhaps—though they don't usually approve of such direct interventions. But it's too late to attempt to persuade them now. Time is of the essence."

"Then I'll do it." Claire turned the car up Birch Street.

"No. It's too dangerous."

"Josie's in danger too. If anything happens to her and I know I could have saved her—Leo, she's just a kid! Just let me get this car back where it belongs and I'll join you. Please!"

There was a pause before he replied. *"You always were impossible to argue with. All right, then—if I haven't located her host by the time you get back home, you can help."*

With that he withdrew again, and Claire knew his owl-host was flying through the trees on either side of the ravine, scanning for signs of movement below. The owl was well suited to the task, with its keen night hunter's eyes and soundless wings. Only now it wasn't seeking to take a life, but to save one.

She took the lane south of the small central park to get onto Maple, then headed for the house. If her father was home, there would be an incredible row. She could never hope to explain to him what she had been doing. To her vast relief, she saw that the house was still dark. She pulled into the driveway, switched off the ignition, and reached for Leonardo. He allowed her to gather him up in one arm, though he mewed softly in protest. She got out of the car, kicked the door shut and locked it, and dashed into the house.

Once safe inside, Claire set Leonardo down. Her legs felt shaky, and she headed straight for her bedroom and flung herself on the bed, not even bothering to turn on a light. She seemed to see against her shut eyelids roads stretching before her, rising, falling, winding, swerving, and her fingers curved as if she still clutched a steering wheel. It was all right, she told herself again and again—she was back safe, she had survived. The police hadn't pulled her over, and she and the car hadn't been smashed up in an accident.

And the car wouldn't be needed after all. They didn't have to transport Josie's physical body to safety, only her mind.

But the real danger had only begun. She might be lying on her own bed in her own home, in seeming safety. But what she was about to do was easily as risky as attempting to drive the car.

"I'm ready, Leo," she said. Out of the darkness his answer came to her, swift and urgent.

"Most of the potential hosts in this area are now asleep, but some nocturnal animals are available. The great horned owl I saw earlier is in use as a host. When I touched its mind, I felt an alien presence there, and I pulled away from it quickly—too quickly for a positive identification, but I suspect it's a daimon on the enemy's side. There's a raccoon not far from the pack's current position, but I prefer not to use such a relatively slow-moving animal. Farther south there's a fox in a den under the roots of an oak, on the east side of the ravine, and another is hunting on the west bank. There are a few coyotes much farther up, beyond the edge of town, about half a dozen spaced along the gorge and vacant fields on either side of it. But they're too far away to be of any use to us.

"Link to me now, Claire. I will connect your mind with that of my own host, the barred owl. It will be safer for you to be in the air. We'll monitor the activity of the dogs and try to intervene to save their quarry."

Claire felt his mind connect with hers and draw it away. She opened her eyes—or seemed to, for the view she saw was not her own room. There were trees all around her, huge trees with massive trunks rising to what seemed impossible heights. A faint grey light like that of early dawn was all around her. In the next instant she realized that the trees weren't huge; it was she who had apparently grown small. She was once more linked with the barred owl, and it was perching on a rotten log on the sloping floor of the ravine. The owl's light-sensitive eyes turned what would have been pitch-darkness to Claire into a dim twilight. The owl's head turned, and she saw the creek flowing at the bottom of the ravine—a vast canyon it looked to her now—and the tree-clad slope on the western side.

She put it into the owl's head that now was the time for hunting, for flying. The owl was hungry, and it obeyed the suggestion with little prompting. Gathering itself, it flung out its wings and leaped off the log, flapping upwards through the pale night. In and out of tree trunks and branches it wove, its huge eyes turned downwards as its head turned to and fro, searching for any sudden movement.

"I will leave you now, Claire," said Leo. *"Keep the owl in the air for as long as you can. When you see the dogs approach, get the owl to safety—have it perch in the trees somewhere, or their own owl will attack it. If you* should *come under attack, break the link at once."*

"Where will you be?"

"I'm going to persuade the red fox on the opposite bank to swim the creek. He's not under daimonic control; he's just out looking for food. I'm going to see if I can use him to flush out any small animals that might be hiding in the bushes or in the reed beds on this side. If one of them is in Josie's control, that will make her flee before the pack comes down this far."

"All right—let me know if you find anything." The owl continued to loop its way among the trees. It was certainly easier than driving a car; this vehicle knew what it was doing and could take care of itself, leaving her free to observe. The wind had died down a little and the trees were calm, only

their smallest twigs stirring. As the bird flew out of the trees over the bank of the creek she cautioned it to be on the lookout for the other, bigger owl Leo had seen. It altered its flight, climbing higher and then circling to take in the whole ravine and the night sky above. There was no sign of another bird anywhere. In the distance towered the high-rises of the west end, all but a very few of their windows darkened. But the glow of the city reached up to illuminate the low-hanging clouds, increasing visibility.

Feeling safer, the owl flew on—northwards as Claire urged it, wanting to see if there was any sign of van Buren's dogs. All it and she could see were the trees, some still thick with foliage, massing to either side of the creek. The grassy banks also seemed empty.

Then, far to the north, Claire saw a hovering speck. Another owl, circling, seeking prey—or something else. She hastened to warn her host, but it had already recognized the shape of a rival and foe and was gliding back down towards the safety of the trees.

Gone were the thick canopies of summer offering camouflage and shelter. At last the owl had to settle for a high branch in an aged maple, stripped by the wind of all but a few of its leaves, and there it perched with all its feathers fluffed out. Claire suggested the owl move a little closer to the trunk and so hopefully evade detection. The bird was too agitated at first to comply, but presently it let itself be coaxed into moving sideways along the branch until its brown-barred body was pressed close against the tree's trunk.

There was a sound of barking in the air. Claire and the owl were both startled, and the latter whirred up from its hiding place in alarm. More barks came from the direction of the creek, but Claire realized now they were too high-pitched for dogs. Even as she thought this a dark fleet-footed shape came running along the bank, followed closely by another.

Foxes! She remembered what Leo had said about the two red foxes in the ravine. *"Leo, is that you?"* she called out with her mind as the owl landed in another tree. One of them must be his host. How many foxes could there be in this area?

"Yes—mine is the male fox," he answered. His thought-words came to her in a torrent, full of concern. "*I managed to get him across the creek. The female is his sister—they are two of a litter that was raised here this spring. I used his sense of smell to search for animals and came across the other fox. I saw her heading north and followed her. She tried to bite me when I got close."*

"Sounds like Josie all right."

"She keeps wanting to go that way, no matter which direction I try to herd her in. Her den is several metres to the south of here. I'm trying to get her to go back there."

"Let me see what I can do." Claire talked the owl into leaving its branch, but when she tried to get him to fly at the vixen he balked, flying back up into yet another tree. *Too-big,* he was thinking as he looked down at the foxes. *Too-many. Not-prey.*

"Here—let me help. I'm used to coaxing that owl." She felt Leo's thoughts join with her own, working to convince the owl that it wasn't hunting, merely warning off the large animals that had intruded onto its territory. One low swoop would do, he told it. It wasn't necessary to actually touch the animals or go too near.

The owl accepted this and launched itself off its branch. Uttering a couple of angry hooting calls, it dived, talons extended, passing just a couple of feet above the foxes' heads.

The male, no longer guided by Leo, turned and bolted with a yelp of dismay. But the vixen did not flinch. She sprang up in the air, and Claire heard the click of her teeth as they snapped together. The owl swerved to avoid her and flew upwards again.

"That's it," said Claire to Leo. *"Either she's Josie or she's rabid."*

Leo agreed. *"Not normal behaviour at all. I think we have found her. Now if we can only get her to turn back to the den—"*

There was more barking, to the north of their position. But these weren't the shrill vocalizations of foxes—they were the deep bays of the hunting dogs. *"Quick!"* said Claire.

They made the owl plunge again. But this time the vixen ignored them. She began to run—not away from, but towards the dogs.

"They will have told her not to flee," said Leo. *"She thinks, no doubt, that van Buren's dogs will not harm her. After her!"*

The owl circled in the air, then followed the vixen's flight through the trees. Ahead of them, they saw the wolf-dogs come loping along the bank of the creek, the black dog in the lead. They caught the fox-scent and began to run about, noses to the ground, whining and yelping in excitement.

The vixen appeared to hesitate, standing with one forepaw crooked. Perhaps it was finally dawning on Josie that something was very wrong—or perhaps her host's fear of larger carnivores was overpowering her. At any rate, she wasn't moving forward any more. Leo spurred the owl to attack again, this time without a warning call that might betray their location.

The vixen spun around and darted uphill, her long, plumed tail flying. The owl followed, urging her on with repeated lunges. But that was too much; a shrill yelp burst from the fox's throat as she jinked to and fro, trying to evade the owl and see where the dogs were at the same time.

The dogs' heads all turned as one. With a snarl the black Rex charged towards the wooded slope, followed by the others. It was no use, Claire thought in despair as the panicked vixen ran on. She wasn't going to make it . . .

There was a rush of wings then and a huge owl dropped from the sky. It dove directly at the fleeing fox. *The enemy owl,* Claire thought in horror. *While the dogs distracted our attention it sneaked up from the air—* She waited, sick with fear, for the owl's great claws to close on its victim.

The owl swooped, pulled up, and flew on leaving the vixen untouched.

But now she was running in the right direction, back along the slope towards the den. Claire felt Leo's surprise, knew he was as stunned as she was. The great horned owl was not an enemy. Who it was, they could not begin to guess, but it was not an ally of Phobetor's after all. Barks and snarls of fury arose from the dogs.

"She's still not going to make it," said Leo.

The big owl was flying in the opposite direction now, attacking the dogs. But it could attack only one at a time. The black dog lowered his head and raced up the slope, ignoring the howls of his companions as the owl strafed each of them in turn.

"We'll never stop him," said Claire. Josie must be made to leave the fox.

"Josie," she thought. *"Break the link. Go back to your own body, your own home. Be safe."* And she thought with all her might of the other girl, picturing her in her mind, trying to think how Josie would think, to know what it was to be her. She imagined the girl safe in her room at home, but thinking herself

trapped in the body of a wild animal, doomed to die with it as it turned, at bay, to meet the dog's savage attack.

And then suddenly she was there—without warning: inside the fox's mind, inside Josie's mind. How the transition had happened she had no idea, but her view was no longer the owl's aerial view; she was on the ground now, looking down the slope as the vast shape of the dog raced up, huge as an elephant from her viewpoint, its bared teeth glinting in the wan light.

She felt the fox's terror, and Josie's too.

"Go, Josie!" she shouted silently, pushing with her mind at the other girl's. *"You must go back! You are in your room at home—in your room at home—"*

The dog seemed to be running in slow motion; she could see its hindquarters bunching for the final leap on its prey. But the abject terror that was Josie was now gone. Her consciousness had fled. There was only the fox and Claire, and they gathered themselves for a last, desperate defence, even as the dog sprang, even as the two owls dove together at his lunging form with claws outstretched in a desperate bid to stop him.

Something whined overhead like a darting wasp, tearing the air asunder. The dog twisted in mid-leap, yelping, limbs flailing; then as she stared it crashed to the ground, its body rolling over to collide with the vixen and knock her off her feet. And then it lay motionless, struck down as if by some invisible lightning bolt in the midst of its attack. The other dogs halted in the act of running up the slope, then jerked up their heads, staring at something high above them. They turned tail and fled, howling.

"Come, Claire," called Leo's voice. And for an instant she was back with him again, seeing what the barred owl saw: the slanting forest floor with the dog's dark body sprawled upon it, the vixen bounding away through the trees, the other owl flying

in wide circles beneath. Higher they flew, and higher, until the gorge fell away, and she saw standing among the trees at its top a short, plump figure, holding in its hands a rifle whose long barrel gleamed in the faint light.

And parked at the side of the road that followed the edge of the ravine was a car, a Volkswagen Beetle, whose light-coloured paint shone palely through the dark.

Chapter 16

CLAIRE WENT INTO HOMEROOM the next morning feeling tired and bleary-eyed from lack of sleep. She'd been tempted to skip school altogether, but with her father at home she couldn't sleep in. She couldn't even pretend to him that she was ill. Though she couldn't tell him everything—not yet—concealment was one thing, deliberate deception another. She wouldn't lie to him again for any reason, she had decided; and if that meant she must one day tell him the entire incredible truth, so be it. She would face that day when it came.

So she sat at the back of the classroom, her chin propped in one hand, her eyelids drooping, listening to both the morning announcements over the PA and the chatter of Mimi and the Chelseas, but paying no real heed to either. They were just morning noises, like the ringing bells and the banging of locker doors, just part of the familiar routine of the day. When she saw Josie enter the room—also looking pale and wan—her eyes opened a little wider. The other girl's eyes briefly touched

Claire's before flicking away again. But it was long enough to convey vital information. *She knows. She realizes I was the one who saved her . . .*

The announcements ended, and a general babble of voices joined those of Mimi and company as the students left their seats and began to stream towards the doorway. Josie, Claire noticed, remained behind with Mimi and the Chelseas. They were deep in conversation, and while they talked they shot several glances in Claire's direction.

As she walked past them on her way to the door, she heard Mimi say, "Oh, that's really tough. Well, maybe your parents will change their minds."

Josie looked at Claire again, meeting her eyes this time, and Claire saw in that direct gaze, not gratitude, or contrition, or shame—only a smouldering resentment. The girl turned and stalked off. *Well, I didn't really expect a thank-you,* Claire thought.

"Don't mind Josie," said Chel. "She's just in a lousy mood. She and Nick van Buren have split up or something; she won't say exactly what happened. And now her parents are sending her to a new school. She's totally ticked."

"New school?"

"Yeah, St. Mary's Academy for Girls. It's a boarding school run by nuns. Her parents decided she was hanging out with the wrong kind of people. They want her to be with nicer kids." She rolled her eyes.

"Josie's parents actually put their foot down about something?" said Claire, incredulous. "Did they make her ditch Nick too?"

"Maybe," Mimi chimed in as they left the room. "She didn't say. But it's mostly you Josie's mad at."

"Me? Why *me?*"

"She says her mom and dad decided to change her school mostly because you were being such a pain—well, that's what *she* says—so, like, it's kind of your fault she's leaving."

"Well, as long as I don't have to see her again that's fine with me," said Claire. "I feel sorry for St. Mary's, though. They have no idea what's in store for them."

She walked on down the hall by herself, wrapped in thought. Well, that was that; another enemy out of the way, at least for now. In time, Nick would probably find himself another Josie to use. But she would enjoy this respite, brief as it might be.

"Claire?" a voice called. "Hey, Claire!"

She looked up, startled, to see Brian Andrews and Earl Buckley standing near the main staircase. "Was that you I saw at the dance on Sunday?" Brian asked her. "With Mimi and her friends?"

"Um, yes. But we had to leave early."

"Yeah, I saw that. Too bad. You should've stuck around—it was fun." His bespectacled eyes dwelled on her just a little longer than was necessary before he looked away. He started to walk up the stairs, then paused and turned to look back at her. "You know, some of us are hanging out in the computer lab after school. A sort of club. You should join us sometime, Claire."

"Oh. Well, thanks. I might do that," she replied.

Claire stood gazing after him and Earl as they disappeared up the staircase. For the first time, no image of William Macfarlane had intruded as she looked at Brian. Had Leo been right, after all? She would likely never have another great romance like the one she had known four hundred years ago. But it might be rather pleasant, she reflected, to go out with someone just for fun, on a casual date—just to have the pleasure of someone else's company. To live Claire's life, and not spend it in mourning for Alice's long-gone one.

After school she caught the bus as usual and sat staring pensively out the window. The suburban streets swept past, then were left behind as Lakeside Boulevard came into view. And there was the old stone wall and cedar hedge of Willowmere. On an impulse she reached up and tugged the cord. The bus rolled to a halt as she got off, then rumbled on again. She crossed Lakeside and walked briskly along its southern sidewalk, her coat collar turned up against the wind. The weather had turned colder since Monday night, and the last clinging leaves of autumn had been shaken loose; though the winter solstice was still nearly two months away, there could be no denying that the seasons had changed. But the afternoon sun was still bright above the scudding clouds, and beneath it the lake was a vast dazzle of light.

Coming to the gate of Willowmere, she paused for a moment, staring up at the stone lions on its posts, the proud upright figures and stone frowns familiar and dear to her from all the memories of two lives. She pushed the iron gate open—it wasn't locked—and walked on up the drive. The trees here were bare too, and the flowers in the large sprawling beds had finally wilted, but the lawns were still velvet-smooth and green. Across the west lawn Myra's pet peacock Dudley strutted with his usual air of regal ownership.

The yellow Beetle was parked in its accustomed spot outside the stable-garage. Claire glanced at it as she passed. Her owl's eyes had not been able to distinguish the hue of its paint, nor make out the licence plate in the shadows, but there had been no mistaking the figure standing next to the car last night. She walked on towards the house.

Myra was standing on the grass near the front porch, tossing a ball for Angus. Claire halted again, watching and smiling at the picture they made: the plump little woman wore her favourite orange jacket, startlingly bright in the sun, and the collie's coat had the gleam of burnished gold. He had just caught the ball in his teeth and was running back towards his mistress, but catching sight of Claire, he turned in mid-stride and galloped up to her instead, wagging his tail. She bent to pat his head and he spat out the ball to give her hand an affectionate lick.

Myra also advanced towards her, beaming. "Claire, dear. How lovely to see you! But it's a bit chilly to stand around out here, isn't it? Why don't you come in for a while?"

The three of them headed for the house. Glancing back towards the wilder end of the gardens, Claire spotted the great horned owl perching in one of the maple trees. "Is that safe?" she asked, pointing. "What about Dudley? And are any of your cats outdoors?"

"They're perfectly safe. Matilda won't let the owl harm them."

"Matilda?"

"That's what I've decided to call my daimon." Myra paused for a moment, letting the sentence and its final word hang in the air between them; then she smiled at Claire again and continued. "She's just using the great horned owl for a temporary host. The one she uses most often is the grey parrot, Tillie. And Tillie was named after my great-aunt Matilda. My daimon says she doesn't really need a name, and up till now I haven't really needed one to call her by. We just call each other 'You.' But now that you and Leo will be joining us, I'll need some sort of handle for her—it would be too awkward to refer to her as 'my daimon' all the time. And Matilda suits her,

I think. She reminds me quite a lot of my great-aunt: sharp-eyed and sharp-witted."

Claire could find no words to say in response and merely nodded. It would take a while, she reflected, to get used to this new openness with Myra on the subject of daimons. But it was also a relief to have someone to discuss the whole business with. Someone human. She and Myra were silent as they entered the house and walked down the hall to the kitchen. Presently Claire spoke again. "How long have you known?" she asked.

"About the daimons? Many years now. That's why I looked so startled when I first heard you use the word; it's not a common one, and only my uncle ever used it for the beings in the alternate dimension. He told me about them long ago and about his strange calling. I had great difficulty believing it at first. But I knew Uncle Al would never lie to me. Finally I tried a summoning ritual out of one of his books, and my own familiar came to me and told me all about her plane and her kind."

"Yes—your uncle's notes mentioned that you'd started to accept his story. I just wasn't sure how much you knew, how close you'd come to the daimons and their world. I'm sorry about peeking at his notes, but it was Tillie—or rather Matilda—who first led me to them. On one of my earliest pet-sitting jobs here she made the parrot escape from the aviary and fly upstairs to the study, so I had to follow her to try to catch her; and she even got Tillie to perch on the papers, to draw my attention to them. I can see now she wanted me to read them, so I could learn who I really was. And that was what I meant with my question just now. How long have you known I was Alice?"

"Not very long," said Myra as she put the kettle on. "I started putting two and two together after I really got to know you. I didn't immediately connect you with the reborn Alice in my uncle's notes. But so many things fit together—your mother leaving and the loss of your pet cat, and of course your own fascination with Alice made me suspect who you were. On your very first visit you said you thought you'd seen her portrait before, even though you'd never been to the house. But as time passed and I connected all the clues, I grew convinced that you didn't know the truth yourself yet." She paused. "So, you see, I tried to shelter you from that knowledge because of course it would be upsetting, not to mention dangerous for you."

"And I've been trying to protect you, too! I was scared that if I told you, you would try to get involved—take some action against the warlocks and end up getting hurt by them. They'd already made three people ill with their mind tricks."

"Matilda saw your encounter with Josie on the roof. She was watching through the eyes of a host-bird not far away, and she was thinking about intervening on your behalf when your own daimon came to your aid. When she told me what she'd seen, I thought for sure you must be Alice. But when you didn't open up to me, I began to wonder if I was wrong. Surely Alice wouldn't be so evasive, so secretive? I even arranged for us to meet up by the supermarket while you were learning to drive with your father, just so I could offer you an invitation to come and visit. With him there you'd have trouble turning it down, I thought. But I could see you were resisting the idea, and that troubled me. Now, of course, I understand you were really trying to shield me."

Claire laughed. "We've both been sort of dancing around each other, avoiding dangerous topics, protecting each other from things we already knew!"

"Well, now it's all out in the open. But the danger's a little less for the moment. We've got a bit of breathing space."

"Thanks to you. How did you guess what was going on in the ravine last night?"

"Matilda gets the credit for that. I asked her to keep an eye out, especially when I was away. I was getting worried about our friends down the road. When I got back my familiar reported everything she'd seen. We knew you had a daimon on your side, but we didn't know whether it was Leo or not. When you went to the enemy's mansion we were both very concerned."

"I was just doing a little espionage."

"So I gather. But when Matilda told me about the strange goings-on last night I knew something was definitely up. First the dogs being sent to the ravine, then the junior van Buren setting out in his car, then you driving all over the place, when I knew for a fact you don't drive yet! I couldn't decide whether to go to your house when you returned or check out the activity in the ravine. I decided in favour of the ravine—and a good thing too, as it turned out."

"Yes, you saved my life. The black dog would have gotten me if you hadn't shot him. Was that rifle your uncle's, too?"

Myra motioned to her to sit down at the table. "Rifle?" she chuckled. "My dear Claire, I don't punish the innocent with the guilty! The dog can't help being used by a rogue daimon. I shot him with a tranquillizer dart."

Claire stared at her, then began to laugh. "Myra, you're incredible! Where in the world did you get a tranquillizer gun?"

She winked. "It's a long story. I thought it might come in useful when dealing with daimons. The bigger ones, anyway. This way I can stop them from doing harm without harming their hosts. Our enemies, of course, have no such compunction. When I arrived at the spot my daimon told me about and saw the van Burens' dogs pursuing that poor fox, I knew it was no ordinary hunt. I knew you were probably involved, given all that Matilda had observed that night. So we both took action right away. And it *was* you linked to the fox! Why didn't you break away?"

"There was no time," Claire replied, and as they sat drinking tea she told Myra the whole story of Josie and the night hunt.

"That poor, foolish girl." Myra shook her head. "Well, I hope she's learned a lesson, that's all. Though I doubt she'll ever find the grace to thank you."

"I don't care. I won't be seeing her again, anyway." Claire explained about St. Mary's Academy for Girls.

"Does the enemy still think she's you, though?" asked Myra. "Is she still in danger?"

"Not after last night, I think. She must've been linked to that fox through a daimon, and it would sense me turning up in the link and interfering."

"Ahh, yes, just as the real Alice would. You're right, they must surely have some idea of their enemy's true character and would know that Josie's rescuer was behaving more like Alice than Josie herself was. You endangered yourself, saving Josie's life. Had you just stood aside you'd be safe now, because they'd think when they got her that they'd got *you,* and they'd stop searching for Alice. Unless the whole thing was a ruse—using Josie's silly bid for attention to try to get the real revenant out into the open. I hope they don't know who you are now."

"So do I. Leo doesn't think they could identify me just by hearing my thoughts when I was linked with Josie. But they may guess. I think Josie did, and she isn't exactly Einstein."

"Well, there are two enemies you don't have to worry about any more."

"But I thought the dog was just tranquillized. And anyway Phobetor can easily get himself another host."

"I didn't mean the daimon. Of course there's little we can do about him. But I thought you'd heard about the older van Buren?"

Claire set her teacup down and stared. "No. What about him?"

"He's had some kind of stroke. When I drove back home last night I saw an ambulance outside his house. And one of the neighbours told me he's still in hospital and likely to need lots of rehab, so it must have been severe. It could just be coincidence, but I suspect he was linked to the dog Rex during the hunt. A man like that, a hunter, would want to be in on the kill, as they say. And when the dog was shot it must have given quite a shock to van Buren's own system—enough to set off a physical reaction that could lead to a stroke if he was susceptible to that kind of thing. He is not a young man. So—he's out of the game, at least for now. But of course there's still Phobetor, who can switch from body to body, and the young man, Nick. It looks as though he'll be your chief adversary now; he's obviously been groomed to take over his uncle's job."

"Yes. They run a company that's trying to alter people genetically, to make hosts on demand for the Legion—the daimons who want to control us all. They want to change our destiny."

"And do you think you can stop that?" asked Myra.

"I don't know. But I have to try. It's what I came back to do." Claire gave a sigh and pushed her empty cup away. "Oh, it's not over, that's for sure. But I refuse to worry about it just now. Myra, I'm so glad it's all out in the open between us."

"So am I, dear, so am I. I was feeling a bit lonely too, without my uncle to advise me. Well, we're in on this together now. It's such a shame Uncle Al is gone; he was much more learned than I and would have been a greater help to you. But

I'll do everything I can." She smiled. "I wonder how many of us shamans there are in the world? Perhaps we could get in touch with them all—have a convention or something." Claire smiled back, her tension easing. Myra leaned forward and laid her hand on Claire's.

"Welcome home, Alice dear," she said.

◇ ◇ ◇

Of course there would be more dangers to come, Claire reflected as she prepared for bed that night. Not thinking about them wouldn't make them go away. And she still hadn't made contact with her mother; and it troubled her that her father was still unaware of all that had happened to her. She had narrowly missed having a major confrontation over the car; if he had returned home half an hour earlier, she'd have had to provide some kind of explanation, and he would never have believed the truth. Someday, somehow, she would have to find a way to tell him. All these things were in her mind when she got into bed and turned out the light. Sleep eluded her. She lay for a while staring up at the ceiling and stroking Leonardo da Vinci, who was curled up purring in the crook of her right arm. "Are you there, Leo?" she whispered into the kitten's ear.

At once his voice came into her thoughts, gentle and affectionate. *"Always,"* he answered. *"Whenever you want me."*

"I'm glad," she said softly. That was one good thing about all of this: she would never be truly lonely again.

"Are you very tired?" he asked. *"Because if you're not, I and some of my daimon friends would like you to join us in a simulation. It's something new we've come up with. It will be quite safe, I promise."*

"Well . . . I guess I could come for just a few minutes," she replied. She was tired, but something in his mind-voice piqued her curiosity.

The dark bedroom faded from her sight. She knew she was really still in her bed, the kitten still nestled in her arm, but she no longer felt them; her mind was wandering free through the dream realm that was the daimons' universe. She found herself standing on a sloping, grassy lawn under a night sky. The full moon above was impossibly huge and white, and its light was so pure and strong that she could see every detail of her surroundings: cypress trees and hedges, the jewel-like flowers studding the grass, the ornamental marble fountain that played a few metres away. It was shaped like a dragon with twisting coils, spouting a plume of spray from its mouth.

In the distance reared a palace with fantastical pointed turrets, lamplight glowing warm and yellow from its many windows. A quick glance downwards showed her that her phantom body was dressed in a gauzy white gown sewn with pearls, a gown fit for a princess. *A Princess of Faerie,* she thought in amazed delight, recognizing her surroundings at last. It was the cover of the fantasy novel.

She heard soft footsteps on the grass behind her and turned to see Leo in his human shape, dressed in princely attire. He smiled as he approached her. "Virtue is its own reward, I said. But I thought you might enjoy this." He held out his velvet-clad arm. "There's a party in your honour up at the palace, if you'd care to join us. Myra and Matilda are there, and some of my friends. Even that old grump Vecchio said he would drop by. Shall we go?" Grinning, she slipped her arm through his; and together they strolled towards the fairy-tale palace and the sound of laughter and music that poured out from it into the night.

High in the moonlit sky above, a bird flew in wide, slow circles—no night bird but a swift and keen-eyed falcon, banking on one silvered wing as it bent its watchful gaze on the figures below.